One Perfect Touch
(Very Irresistible Bachelors, Book 3)

LAYLA HAGEN

Dear Reader,

If you want to receive news about my upcoming books and sales, you can sign up for my newsletter HERE: http://laylahagen.com/mailing-list-sign-up/

Chapter One

Rob

"Do you want me to go with you to see the house today? I can make time," my sister Anne said as we sat in a nook in our flagship restaurant in lower Manhattan, a neighborhood referred to as Tribeca.

I was in the process of moving to the city again and needed to find a place to live. My sister and her daughter lived in a suburb, and I was hoping to find a house close to them. After having been back in town for three weeks, I was tired of living in a hotel. Looking out the window at the mix of high-rise buildings and restored factories, I'd realized just how much I missed New York.

"No, Anne, I'm good on my own. You and Lindsay have things to do." I ruffled Lindsay's hair as she squealed in delight. I loved this little kid as if she were my own, and this last year had taken a toll on them both.

I managed the Dumont chain of restaurants, a business handed down through the family. Over the last ten years, we'd grown into a substantial empire. We had two headquarters: one in New York, one in LA. Anne's ex-husband had been the CEO of the East Coast restaurants, headquartered in New York. I'd been the CEO of the West Coast branch. After Anne's ex left not only his family but also the business, I replaced myself in LA and returned to New York. It was good to be back home.

This location was one of our finest; the inside mirrored that mix of architecture typical for Tribeca. It was a combination of glass, wood, and red brick, each used in a variety of ways. The tabletops were made out of glass, the window arches from red brick, and the lighting fixtures hanging from the ceiling were a mix of wood and black metal, giving the restaurant an industrial decor.

"Uncle Rob, is it true you're not going back to LA?" Lindsay asked. She was eight and much taller than most kids her age. She was like a mashup of my sister and me. Anne and I didn't look much alike. My hair was dark, my eyes green. Anne was blonde with blue eyes. Lindsay had green eyes and blonde hair. Fortunately, not many of her father's genes came into play. *That asshole.*

"I'm not, bops. I'm staying here, and I'm looking at houses close to you and your mom."

Lindsay smiled from ear to ear. She was my weakness. Since the day she was born, I'd had a soft spot for her, and it had only grown over the years. Even when I lived on a different coast, I'd made time for her. Whether on business trips to the city or weekly FaceTime chats, Lindsay knew she could always count on me.

She glanced at Anne. "Can I have fries and nuggets?"

Anne shook her head. "We're here to taste the new menu, remember?"

Lindsay pouted before focusing on me. "But I don't like the menus. They taste funny."

I chuckled but didn't disagree. Our five-course menus were definitely not for children—too many vegetables and spices that didn't appeal to their palates. It was one reason why we had a kids menu with the standard fare.

"Fine, you can have fries and nuggets," Anne said.

Lindsay squealed. Rising from our table, she went to the edge of the private nook, waving at the waiters excitedly. Someone was impatient for her nuggets.

With Lindsay out of earshot, Anne leaned in, whispering, "Rob, are you sure you want to move to the suburbs? You love Manhattan. You used to live in a penthouse on Park Avenue. You don't have to do it for us." Now that she and Lindsay were on their own, she thought I was trying to take care of them, which I was... but I wasn't admitting it.

"I told you, that's *not* why I'm doing it." I put my best give-me-a-break face on, hoping it looked sincere.

"Uh-huh. Just like you're not moving back to New York for us?"

"The LA business is running smoothly. It was time to come back home. As to why I'm moving to the suburbs, it's not just to be closer to you two. I've grown accustomed to having a yard for the last four years. I want that here too, and that's hard to find in the city." I winked, hoping to put her at ease.

Although my arguments were solid, the truth was that I *was* coming back because Anne had just finalized her divorce two weeks ago, and she and Lindsay were going through a rough time. I wanted to be closer to them to be available to help out in any way I could. I could have just hired someone else here to replace her ex and stayed in LA. It would have been easier, but I never chose the easy way.

Our parents had moved to the south of France after retiring, and we didn't have any other family in the area. So yes, I *was* moving to the suburbs primarily for them. I wanted us to be able to get together spontaneously for meals, and it was easier if we lived in the same suburb. The yard was just a bonus; I could take it or leave it.

"You've been looking for a place forever," Anne continued as a server approached Lindsay. "I just don't want you to do something you'll regret in the long run."

"What can I say? I'm picky." Up to this point, I hadn't found anything I wanted, and besides, I'd been busy. I'd started looking for a place two months ago, when I was still in LA. The transition was taking more time than I'd hoped, and finding a place to live was not high on the list of priorities right now. I'd like to get settled, but there were pressing issues with the business that needed attention too.

"That you are. With houses *and* women. You never seem to find the one."

I wasn't looking for *the one*. Life was perfect just the way it was. But I did need a house.

"How are you holding up?" I asked. I just hated to see her going through all this because of that asshole she married.

Anne sighed, looking away. I knew she didn't like my asking, but I cared about her and Lindsay. "Fine. Just fine."

My niece returned to the table the next second, proud for having placed her order. I couldn't question Anne anymore. To my frustration, I never managed to get another answer out of her. I could tell she wasn't okay though. I usually paid zero attention to details, but even I couldn't miss that she'd lost a lot of weight and had dark circles under her eyes. She lived her life by the motto *When you're going through hell, just keep going.* It was kind of our family's MO as well.

My sister was the forgiving type, whereas I wanted to make that cheating bastard pay for hurting her. I was only staying out of it because Anne wanted her daughter to have a good relationship with her father.

But I wasn't the forgiving type. It was one of the reasons I had the reputation of being difficult to work with in business circles. As far as I was concerned, that had helped me more than hurt, because I always got what I wanted. Her ex hauling ass and leaving it all without a backward glance didn't make a good impression on anyone, least of all our financial partners and our employees. It was important to reassure everyone that things were under control.

I was running only the restaurant part of the Dumont empire—a total of one hundred twenty units spread across the country, as well as fifty in Europe. Anne was running the chain of ninety gourmet supermarkets. Although operating under the same brand, they were two separate companies. Anne and I didn't see each other often for business purposes, because each was run differently with little crossover.

Anne sighed in relief when our first course arrived.

"Let's focus on all these goodies," she went on quickly, changing the subject. "They are truly delicious."

We were the third generation of Dumonts in charge of fine dining. Every time we changed something on the menu, Anne and I did a tasting—it was just how we did things.

Lindsay dug into her plate of fries and nuggets, grimacing when she took note of our asparagus with lemon sauce and fish.

Her enthusiasm was through the roof when it was time to taste the dessert though.

Right now, we were replacing some key ingredients in our trademark Dumont cake: cream cheese with ricotta, honey with maple syrup.

"I'd say this is just what the dessert needed," Anne said, taking a bite of the cake. "And our maple syrup suppliers will be happy we're finally using their product in a flagship dish."

"It's delicious," Lindsay said, eyeing my plate. I hadn't finished my dessert, and my niece seemed overjoyed by it, especially because I pretended not to see that she kept forking the leftovers onto her plate. Anne just smiled, shaking her head.

"I like the changes too."

After a bit more conversation, Anne checked her watch.

"Lindsay and I have to go. She has ballet, and I'm meeting some new suppliers. When is the showing again?" she asked, grabbing her bag from the desk.

I checked the calendar on my phone.

"I'm meeting Skye Winchester at seven o'clock tonight."

"Is she a real estate agent?"

"Not sure. I saw the ad online, and it looked interesting. And it was in your neighborhood".

"Okay. Tell me if you change your mind and want me to join you."

"I'm good," I said. Honestly, this house probably wouldn't work either, and I didn't want to waste Anne's time. But it had more potential than others I'd seen, based on the online video that was available, so I wanted to check it out.

After they left, I finished things up and made

my way to the company's headquarters for a meeting I'd scheduled with my team. The building was in the East Village, next to Tompkins Square Park. After a quick subway ride from Canal Street to Astor Place, I walked the rest of the way, just another few short blocks. As usual, it was full of tourists gaping about and locals shopping. With the Fourth of July weekend behind us, it was business as usual in the city. Having been born and raised here, I'd always wanted to come back. I'd only moved to LA the past four years because the West Coast had needed closer supervision. Since my family was located in New York, the East Coast branch had always outperformed the West Coast one. Now the reverse was true. My ex-brother-in-law hadn't been just a shitty husband but also only a moderately competent CEO—but we'd wanted to keep things in the family, for him to feel included.

Dumont Foods was known worldwide. Besides the supermarkets and the restaurants, we also had a massive online platform that had taken on a life of its own. Customers could do everything from finding recipes to ordering gourmet products. The facility that handled the shipping and orders was in LA, and the team that was now managing it all was doing great work. I loved the business. It was in my blood.

My earliest memories were with my parents, playing in the kitchen in one of the restaurants. They had always carted us to work with them, and as kids we felt privileged to go along. My sister and I were both loyal to the family business.

Our education had been in the culinary arts and business. In this industry it was important to have knowledge of both. Anne was one year older, and we'd always done things together, except for that one year after college when I went to study in France, at a culinary school in a town where my father's side of the family came from. She'd gone to a local school in New York, where she also met her then future—now ex—husband. I'd liked him too, I had to admit it. Nothing about him said *cheating bastard*. But hindsight is twenty-twenty, and Anne and I were going to pick up the pieces together, as usual. I was as close to her at thirty-three as I'd been as a kid.

Memories of my parents popped up when I entered the building. I chuckled, thinking about those times, but then schooled my features, preparing to meet the team. With my employees, I was a business-all-the-time sort of guy, and everyone knew it and respected it.

I'd invited chefs, sous-chefs, and the entire management team to this meeting. There were ten restaurants in New York, and I wanted all the staff to be aware of some changes I wanted to implement.

Everyone was already gathered on the floor of the meeting room, and they stood straighter the second I stepped out of the elevator. I was a hard worker. That was how I gained their respect years ago, working side by side with my father at twenty-six. Since I'd been gone for a while, the team wasn't used to my constant presence anymore.

"Let's start," I said with a smile and nod. Most of the team was now seated on chairs. "Hi, everyone! Thank you for being here. Anne and I just completed the tasting, and we loved the changes. Great job!"

The menu would be changed regardless of whether Anne and I liked them, since it was about the customers' desires, not ours, but it was tradition for us to taste it, and I liked to compliment my team. A few nodded, some shrugged. I tapped the laptop my assistant had set up earlier for me, projecting the content on the screen directly on the wall behind me.

"As you know, I'm taking over from my brother-in-law. I've been in LA for the past few years, where our restaurants are more profitable than on the East Coast. The goal is to raise profitability of this branch too. I'm going to go through the plan I devised, and I'm looking forward to your contributions. It's July now. By Christmas I want the East Coast to match the West Coast profitability."

I surveyed the room carefully, taking in their reactions. I could practically hear them thinking, *Yeah, he's just as difficult as we remember.* Or for those who hadn't worked with me before, *He's just as difficult as we heard.*

I was hungry for success, to make my own mark on the Dumont empire. My standards were high, but I also gave 100 percent to everything I did, and I required perseverance from those who worked for me. I could be a hard-ass... but really, I was just hard to please.

Chapter Two
Skye

"Okay, everything looks ready," I murmured, checking the time on my phone. Ten minutes until the clients would arrive and I looked a mess, but that couldn't be helped.

The future owner would choose the house because they liked it, not me.

I'd barely made it on time from Lower Manhattan to give the place one last sweep. I lived next door, and when my neighbors had moved out, they asked me to handle the selling process. Their youngest daughter got very sick, so they quit their jobs here and moved to Houston, where they were from, so their families could help out. I missed my neighbors, and I hoped they'd be able to recover quickly, building a good life in Houston. The mother had already found a job there, but they were struggling financially. Wanting to help them, I'd said yes. In college, I'd worked part-time at a real estate agency, so I knew the nuts and bolts, and a friend of the family was a lawyer, so he was going to take care of the legalities. My job was to show people the house. It sounded easy, but between running the lingerie store and the commute, I'd been in over my head for the past week.

So I'd decided this time I'd schedule everyone at once with the hope that one of the buyers would work out. There were two families with kids, one guy, and an elderly couple.

I was keeping my fingers crossed for one of the couples with kids. I liked having young children next door.

Five minutes to go.

I looked at myself in the bathroom mirror, combing through my hair with my fingers. My shoulder-length brown hair was in complete disarray. I had a blunt cut, with bangs that almost fell into my eyes. I loved them—they usually looked sophisticated, but now they were a complete mess and a bit curled. My black eyeliner was a little smudged under my blue eyes. I looked unprofessional, which wasn't like me at all, but I had no time to run over to my place and reapply makeup. I did refresh myself at the sink, though—I drew the line at sweaty armpits.

At seven o'clock on the dot, the bell rang. Both families arrived at the same time, without their children. The elderly couple arrived a few minutes later.

"If you want, you can look around on your own, and then I can find you and answer your questions. I'm just waiting for one more. Or you can just wait with me and I'll give you a tour."

"We'll wait," one of them said. The rest nodded.

I was keeping my fingers crossed for the guy not to show up. I already had a good feeling about one of the couples, and fewer people at the viewing meant fewer questions.

"Okay. We can begin the tour," I said five minutes later. "It looks like—"

The sound of the bell interrupted me.

"Ah, one second. The last client must have arrived."

I opened the door and came face-to-face with the most gorgeous man I'd seen in a long time.

"Hello. I'm Robert Dumont. I have an appointment to see the house."

"Yes, we were just about to start." I was mesmerized by his eyes. They were so vibrant that I couldn't look away.

Taking a step back, I made space for him to walk inside. His hair was wavy, somewhere between dark brown and black in color. And those eyes, dark green with full lashes that framed them, were incredible. He was beyond handsome. Now I wished I'd redone my makeup. I caught myself smoothing my hands over my lilac dress, then finally crossed them behind my back. The man had me on edge already.

Robert had to be at least six foot two and had the physique of a pro athlete. I just couldn't stop looking at him. He was wearing jeans and a black shirt, and the top button was open, showing just a bit of skin. My cheeks were warm, and my brain was on pause. *Wow, way to win this crowd over, Skye.*

"Shall we join everyone?" I asked. As we approached the others, I realized it wasn't just me though. There was a shift in the group as all three women instantly looked at him. Two were blushing. The men threw him unhappy glances.

"Okay, everyone. Let's start. I'll walk you through each room, and then you have fifteen minutes to explore the house on your own. You received all the information I have via email, but of course, if you have any additional questions, I'll do my best to answer them. Anything I can't answer, I will forward to the owners and get back to you tomorrow."

I made eye contact with everyone, trying to ignore the way my stomach tumbled when I locked eyes with Robert. How could he be this good-looking? New York was full of attractive men, but Robert Dumont was in a league of his own.

Turning on my heels, I led the group through the house. It was a lovely home. The family had lived here for three years before their financial situation went from super good to super bad. There was no furniture now, but I remembered it the way it had been, decorated with a lot of love and care. Each bedroom had had a different wall color, and even in the living room, the wall next to the kitchen island had been painted terracotta. Now everything was white, which experts said increased the chances of selling a property.

There was a fireplace in the living room with a marble mantelpiece where one could put picture frames. The kitchen itself was the only room that looked as before—a Scandinavian mix of white and wood with a granite countertop.

The living room and kitchen were open-plan, and at the end of the hallway was a spacious guest bedroom.

The upper floor had the master bedroom and en-suite bathroom with ample closet space. The attic was huge and could be used as an office or yet another bedroom. From time to time, I looked at the visitors, trying to gauge their reactions as we walked through the home.

Eh… I couldn't lie to myself. I was glancing at Robert far more often than at everyone else.

"Okay, that's it. Does anyone want to see the garage?"

There was a chorus of no, but the elderly couple nodded.

"Okay, come with me. Everyone else, you're welcome to look around now. I'll just show the garage quickly, and then you can find me downstairs if you have any questions."

The garage visit didn't take very long. Unfortunately, I could tell the elderly couple wasn't sold on the house.

"This isn't what we're looking for, I'm afraid," the woman said. "But thank you for having us. There's no point going back inside with you, but I wish you luck with the others."

"Thank you for coming by. Have a great evening."

Feeling a little disappointed, I headed back inside. There was no one in the living room, but I took it as a good sign that everyone was still looking around. It meant they were interested. One of them would buy it, I was sure of it.

I wanted to call Tess, my sister. We owned a lingerie shop in the city, and evenings were busy. I felt bad for leaving her to mind the store on her own, but I could only schedule everyone together in the evening.

I'd barely reached for my phone when I heard someone step inside the living room. I knew before turning around that it was Robert. I couldn't even tell how I knew, but the second our gazes crossed, my pulse quickened. I licked my lips, pushing a strand of hair behind my ear.

"Everything okay?" I asked.

"Yes. I have a few questions."

"Of course."

"Is it available right away?"

"Yes." Wow. He was seriously considering it? My heart was racing.

"Okay. There's no furniture in here right now, but is there anything in storage?"

"The family took the furniture with them. I'm afraid we can't help you with that."

He frowned, rubbing his jaw. I could imagine he was the type of guy who preferred everything to be ready.

"Right. I'll figure something out. Lastly, is your commission included in the costs on the website, or do they come on top? It wasn't clear on the listing."

Ha! He thought I was a realtor.

"Oh, I'm not getting a commission. I just wanted to help out the family. I'm not a real realtor… but I'll help you facilitate everything."

He cocked a brow, making me realize how odd that sounded.

"Their youngest daughter is sick, and they had to relocate to Houston. Finances are tight, and they didn't want to lose money by giving a realtor a commission. I'm in charge of showing people the house, and they have a lawyer for all legalities," I added even though he hadn't asked for specifics. But everything from his body language to his tone of voice told me he was used to having all the details, used to being in charge. And damn, I liked that a little too much. I was hoping he wouldn't use the information to lowball them, but in case he did, they could always deny his offer.

"In case any issues arise after the sale and I need to contact the previous owners, how do I go about it?"

"Through the lawyer or through me."

"And how do I contact you?"

"Messaging, calling, or emailing will do. Or throwing stones at my window." I smiled, and a strange hiccup sort of laugh escaped my throat. *How can this be happening?* "I'd be your neighbor. I live next door."

"Excellent bonus point. You should've started

with that."

Holy shit. I almost swooned right there. My throat instantly dried up as Robert's gaze perused my body, slowly and deliberately. I suddenly felt so hot that I wished I could down a glass of ice water right now... or even better, throw a bucket of ice all over my body.

The other couples descended in the next second, bombarding me with questions. It was mostly stuff already written in the listing, but I didn't mind repeating it. I felt Robert's gaze on me, determined and smoldering. He was quiet, but his presence still dominated the space. He was confident, sexy, as if he owned the universe.

I wondered why he wanted to live here. He looked like he belonged in a penthouse in Manhattan. The owners of the house insisted any interested parties should send me an application before so no one wasted my time. His position and last address had been in it, so I knew he was a hotshot CEO who was moving here from LA. Quite honestly, I couldn't imagine having this sexy god as my neighbor.

"Right, I think we've covered everything," I said after the last question. "Do let me know within seventy-two hours if you're interested."

"Can we take another look around?" a man asked. "We'll just show ourselves out afterward."

I was so happy, I could dance. They were going to take it, I was sure of it.

"Of course."

"I'll take another look too," Robert said, gaze

fixed on me.

Damn. There was that flash of heat again.

The second couple left as Robert and the pair who wanted to take another peek went upstairs.

This time, I did manage to call Tess.

"Hey, everything all right?" I asked.

"Yes, it was a successful evening. Twenty percent more sales than yesterday."

"Awesome."

"How did the house showing go?"

"I'm still here, waiting for three clients to finish a second tour."

"Families?"

"One is a couple with two kids, the other is a guy."

"Dumont?" she asked. She'd gone through the potential buyers' information with me.

"That's the one."

"What's he like?"

"Ah, I'm trying to think what the best way to describe him is. Smoking hot or fucking gorgeous. He has green eyes and lots of muscle. I'm surprised I didn't catch fire just looking at him."

"Wow. How many muscles are you able to see exactly?"

"None. But the contour of his ass looks sexy as hell even in jeans. I definitely saw some pecs under his shirt."

A light sound alerted me that I wasn't alone anymore. Shit. I turned around slowly, bracing myself. Robert stood at the bottom of the stairs, smiling.

"Tess, I've got to go," I murmured. Oh God, he could *not* have heard that.

"What? But you were just getting to the good part. And—"

I disconnected the call, clutching the phone tight.

Crap! He did hear me; I was sure of it. My cheeks were on fire.

"Any questions?" I asked.

His smile grew more pronounced. Masculinity just rolled off him, wrapping around me as he came even closer.

"One or two, but I think you and I are better off if I keep them to myself."

Chapter Three
Rob

I couldn't get Skye Winchester out of my head. The woman was amazingly hot, and I knew she felt the same attraction. It had all been there in her body language and the things she'd said on the phone to whomever she'd been talking to. Her wild hair and curvy body were branded in my mind.

After the showing, I went back to Manhattan. For now, I lived in a hotel by Central Park. I was currently on a run through the park, and I had to admit, I'd forgotten how humid New York was in summer, even at night. Most people liked running early in the morning, but I preferred the evening. I liked clearing my head before going to sleep.

But tonight, running seemed to have the opposite effect. The faster I ran, the more Skye came into focus. She'd been so passionate in the presentation of the house, even though she wasn't actually making any money out of it. She just wanted to help out her neighbors. I couldn't remember the last time I'd met someone who did things without expecting anything in return—from me or anyone.

I chuckled, remembering her delicious blush, the way she fidgeted when she realized I'd overheard her. I'd been close to kissing that woman, even though I'd barely met her.

I pushed myself to run faster, breathing in the hot air. The thumping in my ears blocked out any sound. Far from clearing my mind, I couldn't stop imagining how Skye would react if I kissed or touched her. I wasn't one to give up, but it was time to admit there was no forgetting about Skye tonight.

I slowed my pace when my phone started vibrating. Anne was calling.

"Hey! I'm running," I panted into the phone.

"Wow. Even after the long day? I need to borrow some of that determination of yours. Except, wait. I hate running. Oh, never mind. Heard you scared the whole team today?"

I grinned. "A few of them looked as if they were about to shit their pants. They'll get used to it."

"I bet they will. How did you like the house? Is it what you want?"

"The house is solid. Big, but you know me. I like my space."

"So you're taking it?"

"Not sure."

Anne groaned. "Why not?"

I chuckled, barely believing what I was about to say. "I'm attracted to the woman who did the showing. She lives right next door."

"Rob... you'll never find a place at this rate."

Well, shit. I didn't want to disappoint my sister. I was determined to help her through this tough time. Every day I was prolonging this search was one more day I wasn't there for her. This was the closest place to Anne I could find.

"I'm still considering the house," I told her, hoping to encourage her and ease her mind.

"Good. But leave the poor woman alone."

"Yes, ma'am."

"I mean it."

"Didn't think you were joking," I assured her. I wasn't exactly known for having long-lasting relationships. For the past few years, I hadn't even considered it. I'd moved from New York to Paris for culinary school, then back to New York, then to LA. My last steady girlfriend had been in high school. I'd moved too often, given too much of myself to the business to seriously think about relationships. I didn't see that changing in the near future considering where I was at this point in my life. I needed to get things here in New York back on track and take care of Lindsay and Anne.

"You never know. Just don't break her heart."

"Ouch."

"Ah, sorry... just oversensitive with everything happening with Walter."

The tone of her voice killed me.

That scum and I were nothing alike, but I knew she was in pain. The divorce had been hard on her.

I didn't do relationships, but I was upfront about that. I didn't mislead my dates or mistreat them. I didn't marry someone and then cheat behind her back for ten years. I balled my free hand into a fist. Every time I thought about that scumbag, I wanted to hit something.

"What I meant was that things can get messy, and you don't want that kind of relationship down the road, especially when it comes to neighbors."

That was true, especially since I planned to buy and not rent.

I'd always preferred that. I even owned a house in LA, though it had been clear from the beginning that I was only going to be there temporarily. I just didn't feel like a place was truly mine unless I owned it.

"Anne, I'll get a place soon, I promise. Can you put Lindsay on?"

"Sure."

A few seconds later, my niece giggled in the phone. "Hi, Uncle Rob."

"Hey, bops. How are you?"

Before reaching the edge of the park, I slowed my pace even more, not wanting the sound of the traffic to drown out the conversation.

"When are you moving close to us?" she asked.

"Soon," I promised.

"Can you take me out for ice cream, like Daddy did?"

"Sure thing."

"*Yes.* Do you know why Daddy doesn't call? Mommy says it's because he's busy."

I ran a hand through my hair, gritting my teeth. I'd promised Anne I'd never bad-mouth

Walter to Lindsay, and I wouldn't. But if that asshole wasn't even calling, it was high time I had a chat with him.

"Your mom is right."

"Okay. When you move, can you teach me how to make fries?"

"We can certainly try." I was grinning now, making a mental note to tease Anne later about this. Anne and I were in a friendly competition, wondering which part of the business Lindsay would like when she grew up: the restaurants or the supermarkets. So far, the restaurants were winning by a decent margin. Since I'd be living close to them, I foresaw plenty of opportunities to teach Lindsay some tricks in the kitchen.

Anne had never liked cooking—at least not as much as I did, hence why she preferred the supermarket end of the business.

The competition was all just a friendly pastime, because Lindsay might choose to do something else entirely, and that was fine. We didn't want to put any expectations on her, just as our parents hadn't laid any on us. We'd chosen to work in the family business because we'd liked it.

"I love you, Uncle Rob."

"I love you too."

I wasn't used to hearing her say it. She'd only started doing that recently, and I had a hunch why. She missed her father. I couldn't replace him, obviously, but I wanted to be there for her in any capacity possible. Anne and I had had a happy childhood, and I wanted the same for Lindsay.

After hanging up, I guzzled down water, taking in deep breaths, deciding I wanted to go for another few miles. I'd forgotten that Central Park was the official gathering place in Manhattan. I spotted couples going for a walk and fellow joggers on the pathways snaking under the thick foliage of the trees. Somewhere nearby, someone was listening to loud music.

I was slowly putting the day behind me, even though I was still pondering whether I should soften my leadership style. But it was just my way, which resembled Dad's.

He'd always said I was a born leader. I'd itched to change things even when he was still the CEO. I'd been young and determined and wanted to make him proud. I still wanted that. He and Mom were having the time of their lives in France, and they rarely asked about business, but they were bursting with joy every time Anne and I brought them up to date regarding our numbers. My being a hard-ass (yeah, I could admit that to myself) had gotten me results. It made no sense to change it.

I looked at pictures of the house again. I could practically visualize Skye in every single photo. I shook my head, laughing at myself.

I did like the house. It wasn't exactly what I'd envisioned, but something about it just spoke to me. I could see myself there, and I couldn't explain it, which was odd for me. I was rational, always weighed pros and cons. I didn't follow whims or instincts.

I was torn. I hadn't made up my mind about the house, but I was sure about two things.

One: I wasn't going to let down my sister and niece.

Two: I wanted Skye Winchester.

Chapter Four
Skye

I didn't remember making such a fool of myself since my high school days. I'd been embarrassed the entire evening. Thankfully, the couple had joined us right away, before things could get even more awkward, but I hadn't been able to meet Robert's eyes again. Honestly, I was still embarrassed the next morning. I replayed the evening in my mind as I entered Soho. This was my favorite part of the city. Soho was unlike any other section in New York. On Broadway there were big-brand stores, coffee shops, art galleries, and restaurants, not to mention street sales associates and even impromptu flea markets.

I liked the stores that were on the smaller, less popular side streets, like ours—Soho Lingerie. There one could find true gems and unique shops catering to every taste imaginable. I stopped by Joe's, where I bought my coffee every morning. I'd sworn by Starbucks for most of my adult life but had decided to support local entrepreneurs once we moved here.

"A latte, please," I told Joe. "And a cappuccino."

"That's for you too, or for Tess?" Joe asked.

I grinned. My caffeine addiction was so well-known that even Joe was policing my intake.

"For Tess, of course."

"Coming right up."

Knowing Tess, she'd arrived two hours ago and was already in need of a second dose of caffeine. The smell and taste of coffee always took me back to the time I'd worked in a small lab, fresh out of college. That was when I'd gotten addicted to coffee. I'd majored in biotech, and I'd loved working in the lab. Two years later, a fashion company reached out to the lab, asking for the development of a special type of fabric. I'd worked on-site for three years, and then had stayed on as director of R&D. None of that really prepared me for running a business, but I'd taken the plunge anyway. Even though I was a little out of my comfort zone, I loved what we were doing: creating lingerie for women of all shapes and sizes. I'd always been curvy and far too busty from a young age, so this was personal to me. I wanted every woman to feel comfortable in her body, to feel proud of herself. It was my mission.

I also loved that I didn't have a boss. I liked working hard, just didn't like to do it on someone else's terms. I liked having a say in my own schedule. Granted, for the past year, that had meant working nonstop, but I was optimistic that things would settle down... eventually.

Most of all, I loved working with my sister. Tess and I balanced each other. We had complementary skills, and that came in handy.

"Morning, sis," I greeted, stepping inside Soho Lingerie. We'd decided on the name easily enough—they made great key words for search engines, and when we eventually expanded (we had big dreams) it would serve us well. Soho was known all over the globe.

Tess looked up from the counter, where she was hunched over her laptop. "Oooh, you come bringing coffee. I love you more every day, I swear."

I handed her the cappuccino, admiring my sister's fashion sense. Currently wearing a knee-length white lace dress with long sleeves, she also had a red belt around her waist. Tess rocked whatever she wore, no exception. She had her own style. Her hair was light brown with blonde strands—sometimes she added pink or green highlights in for fun, especially since her hair was getting so long, almost reaching her waist now.

I peered over her shoulder. "What are you doing?"

"Answering customer complaints."

"We should really hire someone to help us with the online shop."

Tess pressed her lips together. "We've got this."

Yeah... except we didn't though. We had a backlog of emails, orders... everything. We'd had the online shop for four years, and we'd run that while holding full-time jobs. I only remembered that time in a blur, as if it happened to someone else. We'd quit our jobs just before opening the brick-and-mortar store. I loved interacting with customers, finding the perfect lingerie for them.

I loved every nook and cranny of our store. We'd handpicked everything. The customer couches were dark green velvet. We had two of them, one in the front and one in the back, separating the changing rooms. The brass light fixtures and light pink walls were just beautiful. We'd replaced the original flooring, which had been a gorgeous wood, but it had darkened the place too much. We'd gone with a light oak, and it made the shop look bigger.

As much as I loved our store though, I couldn't deny it—we were running on a hamster wheel.

We had two sales associates, Jane and Olive, but still handled too much ourselves. We also had a secret weapon: our family.

We were tight-knit... and there were a lot of us. Tess was the oldest of the group. Then came our cousin Hunter, just one year behind. He'd lived with us as a teenager, so sometimes we even forgot he wasn't actually our brother. I was two years younger than Tess. Our brother Ryker was two years younger than me, and Cole came directly after him. Mom had confessed once after a fabulous meal where we'd had far too much to eat *and* drink that he was the surprise baby. At thirty-two, I still considered my siblings my best friends.

Anyway, Cole, Ryker, Hunter, plus Mom and her husband were pitching in to manage the store on Sundays. Honestly though, that wasn't okay.

Everyone had crazy busy schedules without spending their time here. Cole and Hunter were running a real estate empire. Ryker was a Wall Street guru. Mom was a school principal, and her husband was in charge of setting up concert stages. They could all use their time off for a break.

I knew they wouldn't stop dropping by until Tess and I hired someone though. It was just the way our family worked—every time someone was in over their heads, the others came to the rescue.

My family had always been close, especially after our dad left us. Once upon a time, we'd been the picture-perfect family. Then our financial situation imploded, and to make matters worse, Dad left Mom for another woman. It had been such a difficult time that I mostly tried to block it from my memory. We'd been living in Boston in a large house. Mom had been a homemaker, so we were suddenly in a terrible position. Luckily, she got a job at a school here in New York. Mom started as a teacher and worked her way up to principal.

She was tough as nails and raised her own four kids and our cousin by herself. She was my role model. She'd taught us the value of hard work and independence and sticking together. We'd taken that to heart and added a few indispensable attributes to our family dynamic… namely teasing each other about absolutely everything.

Even though the rest of the gang worked in various fields, we had one project in common, the Ballroom Galas. From September to June, we organized galas raising money for charity. Working on that meant we met up regularly. Now the events were on summer hiatus, but we still found plenty of excuses to get together. By the time we met next, I hoped we'd have made some progress in finding someone to cover for us on Sundays.

Right now, I didn't even have time to think about it, because the store was bustling with customers as soon as we opened.

We only took a real break shortly before lunch, both sitting on the couch next to the counter.

"Sooo... want to tell me a bit more about last night? You were saying something about a hunk before you rudely hung up on me and then didn't call me back," Tess said, batting her eyelashes.

I laughed. "Well, I told you the essential information over the phone."

"But I live for details. Is he tall, short? Blue, green, brown eyes? How long is his hair?"

"Geez, woman. Slow down. Breathe."

Tess pressed her lips together, a sure sign that she was barely holding back what she really wanted to say. She kept batting her eyelashes like she had something in her eye.

"First of all, he actually overheard me saying that stuff."

Tess's eyes bulged. Giggling, she covered her mouth with a hand. "Oh, Skye."

"Hey, not funny. I was trying to make a good impression."

"I bet he was impressed."

I blushed just remembering that daring smile on his handsome face.

"You think he'll take the house?" Tess went on.

"I don't think so." I was keeping my fingers crossed for one of the families to move in. A too-hot-to-handle neighbor was more than I could deal with right now.

"Aww, girl, he's really something, isn't he? You're blushing."

I pressed my palms on my cheeks. They were burning.

"I need to get it together."

"Nah, just go with it. Daydreaming about hot guys is relaxing. For me, at least."

Tess wiggled her eyebrows before bursting out laughing. It was so contagious that I started laughing too. *This* was what I loved most about running the store with Tess. We shared tidbits of our day-to-day lives, giving each other advice.

An image of Robert popped into my mind. Yumm... all those muscles, those perfect cheekbones. I felt my shoulders slump, but my limbs seemed lighter as I practically swooned just thinking of him. I grinned at my sister. "You're right. This is a much better relaxation technique than visualizing waterfalls or whatever."

I'd never been able to get the hang of meditation. *Ever.*

"I know, right?"

Our much-needed break came to an end as the door opened and a customer walked in. Ah, Ramona, one of my favorite clients.

"Ramona, hi. What can I do for you?" I asked.

"Well, that bra you talked me into buying last time is the best thing since sliced bread. It's comfy and super sexy. I don't know how you girls do it, but I want three more."

"Coming right up. How about panties to match?"

"Sure. Why not?"

Ramona had been shy on her last visit to the store, conscious about her curves, but now she was radiant, adding a lace nightgown to her purchases. I lived for this: watching women become confident with their bodies because we created the lingerie to fit their needs.

After she left, I noticed I had an email from the homeowners, asking me how the showing went. Then I saw another email, from Robert. I was usually bad with names, but I knew *exactly* who Robert was: six feet of hotness that spelled all kinds of trouble.

Ms. Winchester,
I'm interested in the house. Let me know about a convenient time to call to discuss the remaining details.

Robert Dumont

Holy shit. I was getting a too-hot-to-handle

neighbor after all.

Chapter Five
Skye

I'd barely gathered my wits enough to email him back when he called me. Stepping to a corner of the store, I answered.

"Skye Winchester," I said.

"Ms. Winchester, this is Robert Dumont."

Oh. My. God. His *voice* was panty-melting.

"I figured from the number. What can I do for you?"

"I want to make an offer on the house, but I want to discuss some details. Can you put me in contact with the sellers' lawyer?"

"Sure thing. But I can also try to answer some questions if you like."

"Okay. I've had a real estate agent look at the listing and I have some notes. I've printed them out, and I can meet with you to go through them."

"You can also just email everything."

"I prefer to do certain things in person."

His voice was so captivating, low and rich, that my imagination just ran wild. Laughing, I ran a hand through my hair. If my mind wandered like this when I was on the phone with him, how could I do better face-to-face? Or if he moved next door to me?

I licked my lips, shaking my head. One thing at a time.

"Okay. I'll be at work until nine. I suppose we can meet after that."

"Where exactly is your workplace?"

"Soho Lingerie—a store in Soho."

"I can drop by in half an hour. My office isn't that far. If you have time."

That take-charge tone sent shivers down my body. Awareness curled through me. Why did I like it so much?

"I'll make time. I'll text you the address after hanging up."

"I look forward to seeing you."

Was his voice even richer, or was I just making it up? Imagined or not, my whole body lit up in anticipation. Somehow, I couldn't picture him in here, surrounded by lingerie.

After texting him the address, I darted to the bathroom to check my appearance.

As a self-declared lab rat, I had never considered myself particularly fashionable, even though I worked *in* fashion. I liked makeup but never put too much thought into it. So why was I in the tiny bathroom at the back of the shop, trying to decide if I looked better with my hair down or up and if I should use eye shadow?

"Okay, hair down," I murmured to myself, arranging my bangs before heading back to the front of the store. Tess was smiling from ear to ear.

"You look fabulous, just in case you want to

know," she said. I was certain my phone call had been overheard.

"Thanks for not teasing the hell out of me."

She winked. "The day is still young."

"Ah, of course."

Checking my watch, I realized the half hour had already flown by. I planned to take Robert to the back, in the small makeshift office. Really, it was just a desk in our storage room. It didn't get any natural light or decent cell reception, but it worked for now.

I glanced around proudly. Our store was inviting but not sexy. We'd designed it this way so customers wouldn't mind dropping by even if their kids were with them. That was usually the case, especially on Saturdays.

I exhaled sharply when Robert walked through the door. The man was just breathtaking. He wore a custom-made navy suit and a white shirt. I assumed it was custom not only because it fit him so perfectly but also because his initials were sewn in at the breast pocket. I also noticed he was holding a stack of papers in one hand.

"Mr. Dumont, hi. This is my sister, Tess."

Tess was unnaturally still, right up until she stretched out a hand, shaking Robert's.

"Let's go to the back. We have a small office there. Tess, let me know if you need help."

"Sure." I almost giggled as my sister seemed speechless.

I led the way, acutely aware of him. His presence seemed to fill the whole space while he looked around curiously.

"Sorry about the mess. This is actually our storage room," I said once we were inside the office. It was dark and slightly claustrophobic in here, given the sheer number of boxes on the shelves and littering the floor.

"You own the store?"

I nodded proudly. "Tess and I set it up. Started with an online store, then opened this." Glancing at the papers he held, I asked, "Is that the list of questions?"

The stack of papers seemed far too thick for it to be just questions.

"Yes, as well as the contract. I had it reviewed by lawyers."

To simplify the process, the owners had allowed the applicants who came to see the house to also download the contract from the online platform where the house was listed.

I cocked a brow. "I assume all was standard, or did you find any issues?"

"No issues, but I like to cover my bases."

That take-charge tone, damn. I was betting he was nobody's fool, ever. He was used to being in control, and I admired that... liked it even. His gaze was trained on me, making me hyperaware of my own body. I barely kept from squirming and was determined to make eye contact the whole time.

Easier said than done. I could practically feel my heartbeat pulsating throughout my whole body.

He placed the stack of papers on the desk.

"Do you have a pen? I want to make a few notes on the contract."

"Sure." I took one from the first drawer, pushing it toward him. Our fingers touched briefly. I sucked in a breath. I gave up, darting my gaze away, only training it back on him once he was hunched over the papers, making notes on them. I never knew shoulders could be sexy, but Robert's definitely were: muscles that were perfectly defined but lean.

"So, my lawyers say the asking price is about 2 percent too high... but I'm willing to overpay in light of the family's situation."

"Much appreciated." In fact, he had no idea how much. The owners would be over the moon, but so was I... because I'd just discovered that this man with six feet of pure muscle had his heart in the right place.

Hmmm... why did I care, though? Well, it was good to have nice neighbors, right? I kept telling myself that was the only reason.

"I do, however, want them to hire independent companies to check the wiring and plumbing. After they confirm it's good to go, we'll schedule the closing. I don't want any nasty surprises after I move in, and I don't have time to handle this myself."

Fair enough. When he straightened up, his lips curled into a smile along with a twinkle of amusement in his eyes. I looked away quickly, but he caught me checking him out.

"Okay. I'll pass the information on. I'm sure

they'll accept, because they want to sell as soon as possible. When do you plan to move in?" I asked.

"As soon as we have a deal."

"Okay. Then I'll have their lawyer contact you, and you can finalize everything with him." I played with a strand of hair between my fingers, acutely aware of the energy between us thickening.

"Ms. Winchester, I think we need to clear the air."

"Oh?"

"What was it you said... you don't know what describes me best: smoking hot or fucking gorgeous."

His gaze trapped me in my spot. My whole body was instantly on alert. Heat coiled through me slowly.

"If I return the compliment you made me, would that even the playing field?" he continued.

Wow. He doesn't pull any punches, does he? I smiled but remained silent. What could I say?

"Skye, I need to look for some merchandise," Tess called from the corridor, effectively saving my ass.

"Sure," I replied, grateful for the interruption.

My sister walked in, heading straight to the shelves with merchandise.

"I'll see myself out," Robert said. He paused a beat at the door, winking at me. "About what I asked... let me know."

In a fraction of a second, heat replaced the amusement in his eyes. The air between us charged.

My throat went dry, and so did my lips.

Holy shit, I could barely handle this. How could we possibly be neighbors?

Chapter Six
Rob

The paperwork was completed quickly. Honestly, I was astounded at the speed, but it was much appreciated. I liked it when people were fast, efficient, and didn't waste my time. On Saturday afternoon, I was ready to move in.

Since there was no furniture except the kitchen, my assistant arranged for my LA stuff to be brought here. A team packed everything in one day, and the moving company brought it across the country in three. They'd delivered everything yesterday. Things were going according to plan.

I'd just brought a suitcase with me from the hotel. When I got out of the Uber, I took a good look at the house, with its limestone façade and green roof, satisfied with the purchase. In a flash, I realized what had drawn me to it, despite it not ticking off all the architectural boxes I'd wanted. It reminded me of my grandfather's house in France. Anne and I had spent a few weeks there every summer as kids. They were the highlight of our year, and we only grudgingly returned to New York in the fall.

Taking out my phone, I snapped a picture, sending it to my grandfather.

Rob: Kind of reminds me of your old house in France.

Grandpa: Ha! That old thing was falling apart.

That was true, especially since it had been his childhood home. It had been old as shit when Anne and I were there and had looked like it. But we'd loved going to France every summer nonetheless. Our grandfather was in France now too, with my parents. They had a different house, large and modern with all the comforts, but I still missed Grandpa's old one.

At least now I understood what had drawn me to this house... aside from a certain sexy-as-hell neighbor. I surveyed the surrounding area for Skye, since she had the keys.

I spotted her two minutes later, just outside her house, crouched next to a bunch of roses. Her place was a smaller version of mine, and I liked that our houses were so close. There were no more than forty feet between the outer walls. I could see myself coming up with reasons to knock at her door.

She was wearing a simple red dress that barely covered her ass, especially because now she was lowered on her haunches. I could just imagine how she'd look with that dress hiked up to her waist. How she'd react if I peeled it off her.

Fucking hell, what was I doing?

I was in no position to start up a relationship. With the business, Lindsay and Anne, and deciding how to handle the scum she used to call her husband,

I had no time for the dating scene. And Skye was someone you'd date. I barely knew her, but she deserved more than a fling. I was supposed to behave, but all I wanted was to cross the distance and kiss the hell out of her. When it came to this woman in particular, I just didn't seem to have any control over myself.

Walking up to her, I said, "Hello, neighbor."

She straightened, eyes wide. She licked her lips, smiling nervously. I liked surprising her. She wasn't able to compose herself, and I saw her unrestrained reaction to me.

"Hi! I was just checking the sprinkler system. I checked yours earlier too. Everything seems to be working."

"Why are you doing this yourself? Didn't the plumbing company take care of it?"

I didn't mean to sound ungrateful, but I didn't want to see her take on even more than she already had.

"No, they don't do that. Gardeners take care of the outdoor area, but the previous owners are trying to cut costs as much as possible. It really is a tough time for the family. I don't mind helping them out. I worked in a real estate company back in college, so I know a few things."

I was caught off guard again. Her concern for others was not necessarily an unexpected trait, but I personally valued it. Why did it surprise me though? When had I become so cynical that I expected people to only be looking out for themselves? The truth was,

I hadn't come across someone who just did things for others without any expectation in a long time. It didn't help my determination to stay away from her.

"I can pay someone to check all this out, Skye. It's my responsibility anyway."

I usually liked delegating any organizational tasks, but Skye already seemed to have enough on her plate. Judging by her dress and the flats, she'd hurried here from the lingerie store to do this check and give me the keys.

On the other hand, if it meant I had an excuse to get her to come here....

"All good." Her smile was infectious.

"You came directly from the store?" I asked.

"Yeah. Saturday is a busy day, but we have a sales associate helping us out."

"So, you and Tess are there seven days a week?" I understood hard work, and my upcoming weeks would be just as packed, but I also knew you had to take time for yourself.

"Six. Our family is helping out on Sundays."

"Your family?" Now that was interesting. I liked the fact that she was close to her family.

She nodded. "I have two brothers, plus our mom. But we're looking into just handing the reins over to one of our sales associates on Sunday, so we can truly take time off."

"And you mentioned before that the two of you are also managing your online store?"

"Yes." Skye looked so proud when she answered. A hardworking woman was intriguing to me, on top of all of her other assets. That determination to keep my distance was just not working.

The more I was around her, the more I wanted to know this woman.

I whistled appreciatively, impressed by the sisters' work ethic. "I'm guessing you don't have many dull moments."

She laughed. "You could say that. I don't have much free time either. Or when I do, I'm so unaccustomed to it I never know what to do half the time."

"Lucky you have a neighbor who can help out with that."

"Oh, really?" The questioning look on her face was adorable.

"I'm the king of making the most out of free time."

"Modest much?"

"Not one ounce of modesty in my bones, I promise you that." I took one step closer. Skye licked her lips. I wanted to trap her against the side of the house and just not let go. It was impossible not to flirt with her, especially when she reacted like this to me. The sexual turn this conversation had taken was palpable. She cast her gaze away, blushing just the way she did that first night when I overheard her phone conversation. Which reminded me...

"You still didn't give me an answer," I said. "To my question about returning the compliment. You said I was *smoking hot* or *fucking gorgeous*. If I return it, will that clear the air between us?"

Her blush intensified. "I thought the question was rhetorical."

"It wasn't." I let my gaze wander down her body slowly. "I can add some more. Stunning, sexy, beautiful."

I heard her inhale sharply. The tension between us was strong. I couldn't explain this impulse to get to know her: the store, her family, her life in general. I wanted to know everything.

Yes, she was a beautiful woman, and I wanted her in my bed, but that wasn't all.

"Robert...." She'd only called me Mr. Dumont before.

"Rob. I only go by Robert in my work life."

"Robert," she insisted.

Her voice was a bit shaky. Instead of flirting back, she pressed her lips together, smiling but averting her gaze. She was fighting to keep herself in check, but her body language was intoxicating. She had goose bumps on her arms, and her breath was becoming more labored.

"Skye...."

I'd always lived by the credo *I see something I want, I do everything in my power to have it.*

And I was going to have Skye.

***

Skye

I was undeniably attracted to this man and

didn't have a prayer of hiding it. His direct way was taking me by so much surprise that I didn't have time to compose myself.

My sexy-as-hell neighbor was doing his best to flirt the panties off me... and he was succeeding.

"Here are the keys, before I forget them."

Before I forgot my head altogether, that was. I'd tucked them in one of the pockets of my dress. Taking them out, I handed them to him. The second our fingers brushed, my whole body just hummed. Holy hell!

He chuckled, taking a step back before looking over his shoulder as someone called his name. I followed his gaze. A knockout blonde and a young girl who seemed to be the spitting image of both Robert and the woman stood on the pavement in front of the house.

"Home, sweet home," the woman said, grinning. The girl ran straight toward Robert, hugging his middle.

Robert moved toward the blonde. I followed suit, even as a weight landed in my chest.

"Skye Winchester," I said, holding out my hand to the woman.

"Hi! Great to meet you. Thank you for finally convincing this stubborn mule to decide on a house. He kept us all on our toes."

After dropping her hand, the woman affectionately pinched Robert's arm.

"Nice to meet you too. Well, I'm done here, so I'll leave you all to get settled in," I said before walking toward my house. I inhaled deeply several times, trying to make sense of this. Once I was inside my house, I paced around, unable to sit or even stand still.

I couldn't believe it. He was actually flirting with me seconds ago before his wife and daughter walked up. At least, I thought that was his daughter and wife? It wasn't totally impossible, even though the status on his application said single and that it would be a one-person household. So maybe not his wife but a very steady girlfriend. It had to be; the uncanny resemblance between him and the young girl was evident.

I'd flirted with him, and he'd flirted right back!

I pressed a palm to my chest, trying to calm down and be rational. Was I being naive again?

It had happened once before, before we opened the store, when I was still working full-time. This guy who'd recently started there had flirted with me like there was no tomorrow. I'd then found out from a coworker that he had a girlfriend. I still remembered the humiliation and that deep ache at knowing I'd just been a joke to him. Not to mention the guilt. It was nagging at me now too. I would never, ever intentionally—*knowingly*—date someone who was involved in a relationship.

How was I supposed to face Robert now? Or his… *partner*? Actually, I didn't have to face them at all. My involvement was over. Except for that tiny little detail that he lived next door.

Well, I'd handle it somehow.

I had shit luck when it came to dating. The last guy I went out with, Dean, broke up with me after Tess and I had had a horrendous week. The investor we were talking to had dropped us. Since we'd already budgeted the money, it forced us to go back to the drawing board. It had been intense, and I'd felt completely defeated. Instead of comforting me, Dean said life was too short for him to waste time with someone who moped around all the time. *Jackass.*

Yeah... I hadn't been on a date since. Honestly, I didn't mind. With everything going on with the business and helping my neighbors with their house, I'd been crazy busy. I'd been varying between being single and dating for a few years anyway and hadn't been in a *real* relationship since college.

I wasn't exactly a romantic, but was it too much to ask to meet a guy who was decent and loyal? Someone who didn't make me feel small and meaningless?

I shook my head, focusing on all the great things I had. My life was full as it was, with my family, the business, and the Ballroom Galas. I liked having complete freedom. I was so comfortable now with doing what I wanted to do, when I wanted to do it, that I wasn't totally sure I'd like to be in a full-on relationship anyway.

After we lost our investor, Tess and I decided to grow the business at our own pace. With an investor, we could pour more money in product development, even open more stores, but for now, we were grateful that our store was bringing in solid sales and profits, enough for us to live comfortably on.

To take my mind off everything that had just happened, I called Mom while sitting on my indoor swing. It was one of those modern ones with a half-moon metal railing and a rattan cocoon hanging off it. They were meant for outside, but I'd brought it in once during a storm, and it had looked so stylish and cozy that I left it here.

It went well with my white furniture and pale pink couch. My bedroom was upstairs, in white and pink tones too. Several friends had mentioned that I had a "girly house," but well, I was a single woman renting the place of my dreams.

This house was very small compared to the others on the street, which was lucky for me, because the owner had had trouble renting it out. Most people who moved to the suburbs had kids and needed more space, so he'd lowered the rent enough that I'd thought it was a mistake when I first saw the listing.

My mom didn't answer, but the second I disconnected, I saw a notification from the WhatsApp group I had with my family (well… except Mom, because some things were not for parental eyes to see).

Ryker: Anyone else dying for the weekend to start?

Cole: Hell yes. How are my favorite ladies doing?

I loved how the roles in our family had reversed. Tess and I used to fuss over our younger brothers, even after they finished college, so they wouldn't burn out with all they were doing. Now *they* were the ones fussing over *us*, checking in on us regularly, making us take breaks.

Tess: I'm now indulging in an ice cream.

Skye: I'm already home.

Ryker sent a few pictures of a gorgeous view of a lake surrounded by green. I knew what that was before he explained: he'd gotten engaged recently, and he and his fiancée were planning a wedding in December. The venue was at a restaurant located on a lake outside New York.

Skye: Ooooh, that is beautiful.

Ryker: Wedding location looking good. Now I just need to convince the wedding planner to side with me on a few issues. Muahahah.

Cole: Is she hot? I can put my charming skills to use... all to help you, obviously.

Ryker: Cole... do NOT hit on our wedding planner. The last thing we need is for her to bolt.

Cole: Is it just me, or is Ryker becoming more intense by the week?

Tess and I responded at the same time: **It's not just you.**

Cole: I think we need a strategy to help

him... relax.

Ryker: Still here, folks.

I grinned widely. The fact that Ryker was now engaged was such a surprise to Cole that he kept teasing him about it. He hadn't seen it coming, and honestly, neither had I. My brothers had declared a long time ago they'd be bachelors for life—just like our cousin Hunter... who was now married. Yeah, things were changing fast in our family. Tess and I took turns teasing each of our brothers, depending on what the situation required. Right now, I was definitely siding with Cole, but only because Ryker did seem to need the teasing to relax a little.

I bit my lip, looking at that gorgeous picture. Ryker definitely had enough going on, organizing the wedding on top of everything. It was paramount for Tess and me to find someone to man the store on Sundays.

I laughed, sitting in my swing again when Cole wrote Tess and me in a different group message.

Cole: Best strategy to tease Ryker?

Tess: I have something in mind. Maybe we can tell him that we'll have strippers at the bachelorette party.

I burst out laughing. Ryker was very possessive when it came to his fiancée, Heather.

Skye: Are you crazy?

Cole: We should at least consider the possibility.

This was just what I needed. A Winchester conspiracy/strategy to sink my teeth into and forget about everything else.

Chapter Seven
Rob

"You've got yourself a great place," Anne said.

She'd inspected the house in far more detail than even I had. I'd promised Lindsay we'd get ice cream, and we'd just gotten back now, eating it directly out of the carton with plastic spoons. We were sitting on the couch demolishing our dessert as Anne gave me her opinion on everything.

"Thanks. It was the closest I found to you," I commented between bites.

"You're a good brother," Anne said.

That was debatable. I should have realized something was off with Walter way before he left her and Lindsay—at least known more, done more to protect her better. But I couldn't change any of that now. What I was going to do was concentrate all my efforts on doing my very best for her going forward.

"When are you unpacking the rest of the boxes?"

"I'm going to start later tonight." Not that I wanted to, but it needed to get done at some point. When I'd moved to LA, I had stuff sitting around in boxes for weeks. I hadn't wanted the movers to open the boxes because I didn't like strangers touching my things.

Anne put her hands on her hips, surveying the room.

"Well, Lindsay, what do you say? Should we stay a little longer so I can help Uncle Rob? He might live out of boxes for a month otherwise."

And that wasn't too far off from the truth.

"Yes!" Lindsay exclaimed. Done with her ice cream, she was playing with a set of small figurines.

Rising to her feet, Anne inspected the stack of boxes. "Let's start with your kitchen boxes."

I'd forgotten that my sister was far more organized than I was.

"By the way, I think I sort of know your neighbor," Anne said.

"How?"

"I knew the name Winchester rang a bell. From the Winchesters behind the Ballroom Galas. I googled her, and she's one those Winchesters."

I knew Anne received invitations for each one of the events. They were quite the charity and did excellent work.

"Did you go to any?" I asked.

"No, but I send a check with my RSVP every time. They're good people, the Winchesters. At least, that's what I hear. They put all that money they raise to great use."

"That's good to know. When's the next event?"

Anne grinned. "Why, eager to see your

neighbor in an evening gown?"

"Very cute, sis. No—well, maybe, but I'd like to make a donation."

And yeah, I'd like to see Skye wearing one of those extravagant dresses… and then have the privilege of taking it off.

"Well, not until September. They're taking a break in the summer."

We talked about some other things but mainly focused on the boxes after that.

"I was thinking of going for a week to visit Mom, Dad, and Pops. Lindsay is psyched. What do you think, want to come? The south of France would do you good."

I shook my head. "Just took over here, and I don't think it would be a good idea to take time off already. I'm just getting into it. And I think the employees are just getting used to me."

"I guess you're right."

"By the way, doesn't this place remind you of the old house Grandpa had in France?"

"Hmm… the limestone looks familiar. God, remember how much fun we had? And that swing in the backyard, I loved it so much."

"We had a lot of fun."

Anne tilted her head, a smile playing on her lips. "I wonder what the team would say if they knew you're such a sentimental guy. It would undermine your reputation of being a hard-ass, right?"

"I think my reputation's safe," I replied, stone-faced.

She laughed. "Oh, Rob. Well, your style works for you, so there is nothing else to say."

***

The next morning, I saw Skye sorting through her mail on her way back to her house while I was having breakfast. I walked out right away, joining her.

"Hi," I said.

"Good morning."

Something was off. Her tone was cold.

"Skye, what's wrong?"

"Did your guests have a good time?"

"Yeah." Why would she be pissed about that?

"Liked the house?" There was fire in her eyes, despite the glacial tone. Was she gearing up for a fight? How odd.

"My sister's happy I live closer to her now. They helped me open some boxes too, after we took Lindsay out and got some ice cream."

Skye straightened up, looking directly at me now and not her mail. "Oh. That was your sister?"

"Yes. Wait a second. Who did you think she was?"

Skye shook her head. "Never mind."

I did mind. I moved closer, until she could no longer ignore me.

"Skye, who did you think they were?"

"I don't know. The girl looked like both of you, so…"

"So you thought I was just flirting with my

neighbor before my wife and kid arrived?" That had to be what she thought. I was pissed, but the urge to protect her overwhelmed me more. In my experience, when people expected the worst, it was because they'd encountered the worst. "For the record, they are my sister and niece."

"I'm sorry, I just… I felt so bad last evening, you know. Thinking that I was…. I'd never do that. Get in the midst of a family."

Despite all the pep talks I'd given myself, I wanted this woman, plain and simple. I needed her. I decided right then and there that I was going to get to know Skye better. She looked like just the thought of getting involved with another woman's man made her feel sick. I regretted the misunderstanding, but I also liked that it had given me this insight into her personality.

"As I said, never mind," she mumbled.

I could let it drop, but I wouldn't let this opportunity slide by me.

"The way I see it, you owe me dinner," I said, stepping a bit closer. I barely kept from reaching out. I needed to touch her.

She laughed. "What?"

"You thought the worst about me. Dinner will fix it."

"How?" She looked half confused, half amused about my statement.

"You'll see. And because I don't want to invite myself over, and I'm not sure how good your cooking skills are, I'll make us dinner."

"My cooking skills are just fine, thank you very much."

"Good to know. We can have the second dinner at your place if the first doesn't fix things." I kept my eyes trained on her, right until she averted her gaze. That need to reach out and make physical contact almost overpowered me, but I was still hanging in there. Barely. I couldn't even explain it.

"What things?"

"You'll see."

She laughed again, crossing her arms over her chest. "What was that about not inviting yourself over?"

"That was before you told me you're a good cook."

She was wearing a sleeveless white dress. I couldn't hold back any longer and touched her shoulder, drawing the backs of my fingers down to her elbow. She shuddered but instinctively leaned in to me. She was close to agreeing, but something held her back. She was fighting this with all she had.

"I don't know. I'll be in Manhattan until late this evening," she murmured.

"I thought your family looked after the store on Sundays?"

"They do, but I'm meeting a supplier. It was the only day we both had time."

"I'm adaptable. I'm going into the city too for a few meetings. We can eat later. You won't deny your neighbor a 'welcome to the neighborhood' dinner, will you?"

"Fine, dinner it is." She nodded, licking her lips. That gesture spurred a primal need inside me. I just wanted to throw her over my shoulder and take her inside. Instead, I took a step back.

Being in close quarters with her and not kissing her was going to be impossible.

Chapter Eight
Skye

I had no idea where the day had gone. It felt as if I'd barely come into the city, and then I was out again, on my way home.

My brother Cole called as I waited for the train. He was at the store today, together with Mom and Ryker's fiancée, Heather. We'd agreed that the boys would always do tasks that required them to be in the back, because some customers might be intimidated by guys in a lingerie shop.

"Hello, brother," I greeted. "How's it going?"

"So far, so good. I'm staying in the back, as promised, but damn, I like your customers. They're hot."

I laughed. "How do you know they're hot if you're staying in the back?"

"I might break the rules from time to time and go in the front. How was your meeting?"

"It went well. They've got great fabrics, and I've negotiated a great price. You were right, leading with competitor prices was smart."

"Glad it worked out."

I loved that he checked on me, that we bounced ideas around. My brother was very good in negotiations and overall a brilliant businessman. Before we'd opened the store, Tess and I had spent a lot of evenings at Hunter and Cole's office. We'd wanted a place to work from in our spare time that wasn't our couch, and the boys had offered. They'd also hung around with us, offering advice on our business plan, which we'd appreciated.

"Do you need anything?" he asked.

"No."

"Are you sure?"

"Yes, I'm good. Heading home, where I think I'm in for a delicious dinner."

"What do you mean, you think?"

"Well, I—" Holy shit. I almost told him about the hot neighbor. I was in no way ready to talk about him, but if I didn't come up with an answer fast, my brother would sniff out that I was holding back.

"I just have to see," I said vaguely.

"Want me to take you to dinner?" he offered. Awww, my brother was adorable.

"Thanks, but I'm good. What, no date tonight?"

"Not yet, but the evening's not over yet. Could ask out one of your customers."

"Cole!" I admonished in a teasing tone.

"Have to go. Heather needs me in the front. Anyway, just wanted to check on you."

"Thanks, brother. For the call and taking care of the store."

"No problem."

After hanging up, I drummed my fingers on

the phone, sighing. My family was amazing for helping, but hopefully they wouldn't have to do it much longer. Tess and I were close to convincing Jane to take charge of things on Sunday.

My stomach rumbled, and my thoughts circled to Rob again. In an instant, I became all jittery and nervous. I was afraid to admit to myself how much I looked forward to our evening together.

To give myself something to do, I pulled out my phone, looking at the bookmarked sites. There was a scientific article about the best type of plastic to use in combination with fabric that was acceptable even for sensitive skin. I'd wanted to sink my teeth into it for a while, and the topic itself was not a quick read. I loved reading scientific articles on just about everything. My love for them started in college when I wrote a paper on biodegradable plastics and I needed to read up on all of the articles pertaining to the subject.

But I couldn't concentrate on that either. Damn. My thoughts kept bringing Rob to the forefront. I had no idea how I'd even agreed to dinner with him tonight. All I remembered was that I'd braced myself against his charm the second he'd walked up to me. After he'd cleared up the sister and niece topic, I lost the battle. In my defense, he'd worn a mouthwatering outfit: a two-button suit. I couldn't help wondering what kind of meeting on Sunday required that attire, but oh well, I was grateful for it. Rob looked delicious in it.

I'd planned to stop by my place quickly and

freshen up, maybe even change out of my white dress, but I didn't get a chance. Rob opened his front door as I approached the house.

"Hello, neighbor."

"Hi," I said back.

"Hope you're hungry."

"Starving."

He'd taken his suit jacket off but was still wearing the shirt and pants. I made a concerted effort not to look down his body... right until I realized he had no such qualms. His gaze rested on my shoulders before wandering farther down, stopping at my hips, and then traveling back up. My nerve endings lit up. Goodness, we weren't even in the same room and I was on fire. I'd never been so insanely attracted to anyone.

He smiled as he opened his front door. Ushering me in, he put a hand at the small of my back. A bolt of heat jolted me straighter. On instinct, I glanced to him, only to discover he was watching me intently. He curled his mouth into a smile.

He knew exactly how he was affecting me. Everything in his body language, from the way he leaned in slightly to the way he kept his hand on my back, made it clear that he lured me in here with a purpose... and it was not exactly dinner between neighbors.

"Wow, you've unpacked fast."

His living room and kitchen looked lived in already. There was a shelf behind the couch, and it appeared to be filled mostly with business books and thrillers. There was yet another bookshelf between the kitchen island and the window, this one filled with travel books and the occasional whiskey bottle.

"My sister was a big help."

"Did she also decorate it? I remember you were stressed about the lack of furniture."

He shook his head. "No, this is my stuff from LA."

I liked his style. The couch and dining chairs were a matching blue color, and there was a black-and-white carpet on the floor. On the mantelpiece were pictures of him, his sister and niece, as well as some other people I didn't know. I assumed family and friends. I loved that he liked surrounding himself with their photos.

"What are we eating?" I asked.

"Tuna steaks with sesame, soy, and honey, prawns masala, or vegetable curry. Your choice."

"All three sound delicious. I don't know how to decide."

"Pick one for tonight, and we'll find occasions for the rest."

Ah, so whatever plans he had, they included luring me back again. I smirked, taking a step to the right. Maybe I could think clearer if I wasn't so close to him.

"Let's not get ahead of ourselves. First I have to make sure you're actually a good cook."

Amusement flickered in his eyes. Honestly, I realized he was a great cook just from the dishes he listed. They weren't for the faint of heart.

"Let's make a deal. If you like our dinner, you promise to stop by again," he said.

Damn. How had I managed to talk myself into a corner?

"Dinner first. I vote for prawns."

"Whatever the lady wishes."

His tone was triumphant, which meant he thought he'd already won. Half an hour later, I knew why. His food was absolutely delicious. We'd set the table in the living room, and he paired the prawns with an excellent white wine. Damn. I couldn't resist a man who could cook.

"I know you own restaurants, but I assumed you studied business management. Did you also go to culinary school?"

"Yes. After college, I did one year of culinary school in France. Plus, I started as a kitchenhand when I was sixteen. My parents insisted I work my way up in the company."

"Wow."

He chuckled, sitting back in his chair, surveying me over his glass. I squirmed in my seat, fiddling with a strand of hair. The two glasses of wine I'd had certainly weren't helping me resist his charm.

"I wasn't thrilled. Rebelled every chance I had. But now I'm very grateful they insisted. Knowing how a kitchen works, what it takes to make customers happy is invaluable when drawing up strategies. I know which cost-cutting measures make sense, when to push for innovation or give the staff room to breathe."

"Not to mention you have amazing cooking skills," I added on a wink.

"That too. I take it you're impressed enough to stop by again?" He fixed his gaze on me.

"Hmm…." I tilted my head playfully, crossing and uncrossing my feet under the table. He moved his legs, touching mine while also leaning forward slightly. My heartbeat was out of control, especially when he lowered his gaze to my mouth.

"That's still up in the air. Depends on how entertaining you are."

"I have to prove myself?"

"Something like that." Oh Lord, what was I getting myself into?

"Challenge accepted."

His gaze traveled downward, resting on my breasts. My breath caught.

"Tell me about you, Skye."

"What do you want to know?"

"Everything." His tone was so demanding that it felt as if he wanted to know all my secrets and desires.

"Hmmm, might be more than you can handle."

"Try me." If possible, his tone became even more demanding. "Tell me about your store. How did you decide to open it?"

"A combination of things. I've always had trouble finding the right bra. I had breasts really early, and it was hard finding something that wasn't too sexy for a thirteen-year-old. Even in college, I kept modifying bras to fit me. It was a fun thing to do but also necessary. I studied biochem and then accidentally started working in fashion. One thing led to another, and Tess and I opened our online store. It went okay, but with lingerie... it's best if you try it on. I love being in the store to help customers find the perfect items for them, and to help them feel confident in their bodies. We have so many clients coming in ashamed of their figures—no matter if they're too curvy or too lean—but with the right items, their confidence just goes up. It's my favorite part, besides working with my sister. I've always loved sexy lingerie, always wear it, so—"

I pressed my lips together, wondering if I'd shared too much. Sometime during my monologue, I'd started my third glass of wine. I glanced at Rob. Holy hell, there was so much heat in his gaze. My whole body reacted to him: my nipples tightened, and my belly flipped twice.

"Anyway, so Tess and I work with factories that also have small design teams. We create the initial product, experiment on ourselves and see how it looks and feels. Then we finalize it with said design teams and commission a small batch to gauge the feedback from our customers. If they love it, we order a large quantity, and if it continues to sell over time, we keep it as a permanent item in our merchandise line."

"Very smart." His voice was a little rough, and the heat in his eyes was not lessening in intensity.

I needed to shift the focus to him. "What

made you decide to come back to New York?"

His gaze clouded. He set his glass on the table, crossing his fingers in front of him. "It's complicated. My sister just divorced, and her ex-husband was leading the operations of the East Coast restaurants. He's gone now. I replaced myself in LA and took over the reins here."

"It would've been easier to replace him though, right?"

"Yes, but I also wanted to be here for my sister and my niece. They're going through a tough time."

He cared enough about his family to make such a drastic change? I was simply melting. I was in over my head. Whatever he had in mind for tonight, I wasn't going to be able to resist him. I was sure of it.

My body had been on edge the entire evening. And now, when he trapped me with that determined gaze, I didn't know what to do with this heat billowing inside me.

"That's very thoughtful of you. It's important to stick together when the going gets rough," I said.

"Exactly."

"Your sister runs Dumont Gourmet, right? I looked you up and also found her."

"Yes."

"I love the products there."

"I'll tell her. Anyway, I want to be here for them in any capacity possible. Before, I just saw them on vacations, but now... I want to be a bigger part of their lives. My niece is already— What's with that smile?"

I caught myself smiling from ear to ear. "I just really like that you're a great brother and uncle."

"That's all?"

"What did you think I was thinking?"

"You really want to know?" There was a playful glint in his eyes again. Wait, no—it turned from playful to smoldering in a fraction of a second. Oh, goodness. I'd come here tonight hoping to establish a neighborly relationship with him and smooth over my blunder. Okay, so maybe those weren't the *only* reasons, but I hadn't expected to be completely smitten with him. Why was I being inappropriate? Then again, my appropriateness compass wasn't working quite properly after all that wine.

I blushed, focusing on my glass again. "Maybe not."

"Good. I'll keep that info for the next dinner."

"You're not letting that go, huh?"

"Absolutely not."

***

Rob

Once her plate was empty, she rose from the table with it.

"I'll deal with this later. Sit down with me." I

didn't want to waste one minute focusing on anything but her.

"I like doing it," she murmured. I watched her intently, rising too, joining her at the counter with the rest of the dishes. It took no time to clean up.

Skye checked her watch when she returned to the empty table. She didn't sit down, just leaned against it, sighing. "It's so late. I'm going to go. This dinner was really delicious. Thanks."

"Happy you enjoyed it."

"Is it your secret weapon to charm women?"

"So you're charmed?"

She chuckled, blushing, but didn't respond. I moved closer until our hips were touching, leaning in.

"My answer is no. I haven't done this in years," I said.

"Why not?"

"You're different from anyone I've met, Skye. You do things without expecting anything in return, like going to all this hassle for your neighbors. And you're so sexy that it drives me crazy. I want you. From the moment I saw you, I wanted you. And now? I can barely think straight."

"Rob...," she whispered.

"I'm Rob now? Not Robert. Good to know."

Blinking a few times, she rubbed at her eyes. "Oh, why did I have so much wine?"

She'd had a little too much, and I wasn't going to take advantage of it. I had to clasp my hands behind my back to make sure I wouldn't be tempted to touch her. But damn it, it was the hardest thing. All I wanted was to be closer, erase any distance between us.

"Come on, I'll walk you to your door."

"Afraid I won't find the way?" she teased.

"Something like that."

"I'm not that drunk."

"I just want to spend a few more minutes with you, Skye."

I tilted forward a few more inches, until I smelled her faint perfume. Damn, I was playing with fire.

Clearing her throat, she took a step back, pointing at me. "Just walk me to *your* door."

"Why, afraid you'll invite me in if I come to yours?"

"Maybe," she whispered. Fuck, her lips and smile looked absolutely delicious. The knowledge that she wanted me just as badly was driving me insane.

"You bite your lip every time I look at your mouth. Think I didn't notice?" I feathered my fingers over her cheek, then slowly over her lower lip. I was seconds away from kissing her.

She parted her lips on an exhale. My eyes flared, and I captured her mouth. She fisted my shirt, taking it out of my pants before slipping her hand underneath it, over my abdomen. I needed more than this kiss. I needed to touch her. She moved her hand farther up my chest before descending back down, right until she reached the metal clasp of my belt.

"Skye, fuck," I exclaimed on a groan, cupping her ass. Her short dress shifted, and I touched her bare ass cheeks. The next second she pressed her thighs together. She'd drenched her panties, I was sure of it.

She arched her hips into me, biting my lower lip lightly before kissing me again. She was pressed against me: her breasts, her hips. I moved my hands over her buttocks to her hips, then back down to her ass cheeks, dangerously close to the strap in between them. A light tremor coursed through her. I was so turned on that I could barely breathe.

Groaning, I tore my mouth from hers. "You're driving me crazy."

Her eyes were hooded, but when I pulled back a few inches, she exhaled sharply, glancing at the door. It was my cue that she wasn't ready for more tonight. Her body might have been, but she wasn't.

"After you," I said, tilting my head toward the door.

I walked slightly behind her but reached ahead of her and opened the door. I made to go out with her, but Skye pointed at me again.

"No. You stay here."

"Or what?" I teased.

She licked her lips. Fucking hell, was she trying to kill me? I clutched the handle tightly. It was either that or kiss her against the doorframe.

"I don't know. Just seems the smart thing to do."

"Fine, but first, I want you to promise we'll do this again soon."

"Maybe."

I laughed when she closed the door quickly, as if it was the only thing she could think of to cut through the thick sexual tension between us.

Hell, tonight had taken me by surprise in every way possible. I'd been attracted to Skye from the first time I saw her, but then again, a man would have to have ice running through his veins not to be attracted to her. She was beautiful and sensual, but tonight, that attraction had magnified by a factor of one million. When I'd spoken about Anne and Lindsay, she'd understood exactly what I was saying. Back in LA, some acquaintances told me point-blank that I was crazy to change things so drastically just because my sister was going through a divorce. But Skye... Skye was one of a kind.

She'd only said *maybe* to a repeat of tonight. But I was excellent at turning maybe into yes.

Chapter Nine
Skye

Over the next few days, I learned that having a hot-as-sin neighbor came with a few perks... especially because he went out for a run every evening at the same time. He wore shorts and a T-shirt that were unfortunately not very tight, but there was plenty to admire, such as his sculpted calves and arms.

On the third evening, he proved that he hadn't gotten those mouthwatering biceps by running: he did fifty push-ups right in his backyard. Yum....

How was a girl supposed to *not* have sexy dreams after such a performance every evening?

Truthfully, watching him through my kitchen window had been my only "interaction" with Rob since our dinner. He left early in the morning, and I returned late in the evening. Besides, his sister and niece stopped by for dinner almost every night.

Meanwhile, Tess and I had made tremendous progress in our search for someone to manage the store every Sunday.

After reviewing countless applicants and not finding anyone we could agree upon, we convinced

Jane to reconsider taking charge on Sundays. She'd been unsure if she could handle it, but she finally agreed. We'd also hired a student to help her out—since Jane knew the business inside and out, it didn't really matter if the person helping her had experience, and students were our cheapest option.

"To us learning to delegate and not be such control freaks," I said, clinking my cup of coffee to Tess's on Thursday morning.

She chuckled. "Speak for yourself, sis. I'm still working on the control part."

"It's going to be fine. Jane knows her stuff, and the new sales associate will just follow her instructions. Can't wait to give everyone the good news."

"Oh, yes. They'll be thrilled. I think I'm going to arrive a little later for our family meeting. George said he'd meet me half an hour later." George was the CFO of one of the factories we worked with.

"Okay."

We were meeting the whole gang today for one of our working lunches. Technically, there was no reason for them now. We'd set them up so we could work on organizing the galas, and those were not starting again until September. But then again, we used these meetings mostly to update each other on our lives.

I headed to Hunter and Cole's office later in the day. When I entered the conference room, my brothers, Hunter, and his wife, Josie, were already there. She wasn't just Hunter's wife—she'd been our friend forever, and I loved it that she joined our lunches whenever she had time. With chocolate brown hair she'd cut into a bob and a little black suit, she looked every inch the lawyer she was. Her blue eyes lit up as she waved at me.

I looked around the room once, content that no one appeared troubled or exhausted. Although the roles might have reversed now and the boys were more into our business, that didn't mean I could just drop my old habits. They'd been honed over more than a decade. Hunter, Cole, and Ryker were all over six feet and well built. The boys had also inherited the blue-eyed gene in our family, but other than that, they looked nothing alike. Hunter had light brown hair and high cheekbones, Ryker had dark blond hair that looked perpetually messed up, like he was preparing himself for a rock concert, and Cole... Cole was something else. His jet-black hair brought out his eyes in an amazing way. He didn't quite give off the bad-boy vibe Ryker did, but it was just as deeply ingrained in his DNA.

When Josie met us the first time, she nicknamed Ryker the Flirt and Cole the Charmer, and she'd been spot on. She'd also nicknamed Tess the Hurricane, which had been fitting because my sister was a force of nature. I'd been the only one left without a nickname (until recently, when Ryker said I was a dragon. I absolutely loved that... he might have become my favorite brother ever since).

"Hi, everyone. Tess will be a little late," I said. "What are we eating today?"

"Pizza," Josie said. "It's on the way."

Hunter squeezed his wife's hand, kissing her forehead. I sighed. He always looked at Josie as if she walked on water. I might not be a romantic, but I couldn't deny that watching them did something to me.

"Tess and I have some news, but I'll wait for her so we can share it together."

I rubbed my stomach, my mouth already watering at the thought of pizza.

My sister arrived at the same time as the food.

"Ooooh, I have excellent timing. Which one's mine?" Tess asked, surveying the stack of cartons.

"The one with your name on it," Hunter said. We'd been doing this long enough that we already knew each other's favorites.

The meeting room exploded with the smell of melted cheese, olives, salami, and anchovies.

All eyes were on Tess and me while we devoured our respective pizzas.

"What's up?" Tess asked.

"Oh, I told them we have news. So... we've finally convinced Jane to take over on Sundays, and we hired her a part-timer."

"Which means none of you has to sacrifice your Sundays anymore," Tess added. "We're very grateful for all your help."

My phone vibrated while my sister talked.

Rob: Hello, neighbor. Want to catch up this evening?

Skye: Not sure when I'll be home.

Rob: Past three days you've always been home already during my run.

Holy shit, he'd noticed me watching him? I decided to play dumb.

Skye: Oh, really?

Rob: Skye... I saw you through the window.

Skye: Couldn't just ignore what was right in front of me.

Rob: Which part did you like more, the run or the push-ups? I can take my T-shirt off, just for you.

My face felt so hot that I was certain everyone at the table could tell something was off. Glancing around, I noticed Tess was grinning at me, but everyone else was too busy devouring the pizza.

Hmm... I wasn't one to overshare, but I stood by the family's no-secrets policy. Tess had insisted on it after Dad left, saying that keeping things in wasn't healthy. We used to just sit together in circles and pour our thoughts out when Mom wasn't looking. She'd been so down anyway that it would have broken her heart. But the strategy worked, and after a sibling session, we all usually came up with ideas to cheer Mom up. I didn't miss those times, but we did grow very close because of it. Some might say our relationship was weird, but I liked that everyone had their nose in my business. My siblings and their better halves gave some good advice. Usually I only mentioned guys when I'd been on a few dates, but I decided to try another strategy this time. Perhaps if I spoke about this, I could get some perspective.

"So, my neighbors moved away," I said.

"That's right," Cole said. "You said you were helping them sell the house. How is that going?"

I took a deep breath. "Well, this gorgeous guy just moved in. I was already there for dinner once and it was delicious. We also kissed, and it was smokin'. Anyway, if anyone has advice on dealing with a too-hot-to-handle neighbor, I'm all ears."

I'd said all this very fast and was greeted with such an unnatural silence that I wondered if they understood me.

"He's the guy who just texted you?" Josie asked. As usual, she caught on the fastest. The lawyer of the group, always looking for clues.

Tess laughed. The boys were just stunned.

"Yes, how did you know?"

"I don't know. Body language. Also, you're blushing. And all that from some texts."

"I also can vouch for the fact that she's been daydreaming about said hot neighbor a few times at work," Tess said.

Cole whistled. "You know what, sis? Good for you."

My eyes bulged. "Wasn't expecting this reaction." My brothers usually were skeptical of any guy I mentioned.

Cole, Ryker, and Tess exchanged glances. Josie pressed her lips together.

"What's going on?" I asked.

"You were so down after you broke up with that last guy you dated that we're happy you're moving on," Cole said. "Just putting it out there, but I'm still volunteering to punch the moron."

I hadn't realized they'd all worried so much about me. I was slowly putting two and two together though. There was a lot of sibling support over the last weeks... like when Tess, who would sleep at the store if she could, had started suggesting we take the evenings off to go to museums or for walks in Central Park. Josie and Heather had organized girly evenings. Ryker and Cole had pampered me even more than usual.

It had all been a group effort to cheer me up.

I hadn't been in a funk because I was single but because the guy had made me feel like I was worth nothing, and it was a shitty feeling. Like goo I couldn't scrub off. And oh crap, now they were all hopeful I was moving on. I hadn't meant to get their hopes up. I mean... at least they weren't worrying about me, so that was a good thing.

"Let's recap," Josie said. "He's hot, a great cook, and, by the intensity of your blush, an excellent flirt. I'm giving you one week before you agree to whatever is making you blush."

"Nah, two weeks," Tess said. "Give Skye some credit. She's a tough nut to crack."

"Thank you for the vote of confidence, sis."

I turned to my brothers. Ryker was deep in thought, judging by his frown.

Cole whistled. "I usually agree with Tess, but

I'm with Josie on this one."

Ryker held his hands up. "I don't want to wake the Dragon, so I'm just going to withhold my opinion."

"We can do that?" Hunter said. "That's so smart! I'm with Ryker."

Tess burst out laughing. Cole was grinning from ear to ear.

"You're no help. At all," I concluded, but I was grinning just as widely as Cole. And when my phone lit up again with a message from Rob, I knew I was a lost cause.

Rob: Going for a run at the same time tonight. Want to come with me?

Chapter Ten
Skye

"I do feel like this is bringing out my boobs better," I told Tess. After lunch, we were both having one of our "research and development hours." Jane was dealing with customers, and we were in our dark room in the back. "I'll wear it for the rest of the day, check how comfortable it is."

"It is sexy as hell," Tess said, surveying me. We'd finished sewing this one yesterday. We had a small sewing machine and a ton of fabrics in the back, and twice a week, we blocked four hours in the afternoon for experimenting. Sometimes we stayed in the store so we could actually have some natural light, but if it was too full, we made do in the small room.

"I know, right?" It made my already huge boobs appear even larger. I'd been so ashamed by them when I was a teenager, so conscious of the looks they attracted. But now I was proud of them and of my body. It wasn't perfect, but I loved my curves. "We just need to make the straps a little wider—or use another fabric. It's cutting into my skin."

"I'm on it," Tess exclaimed. Rummaging

through the box where we kept leftover textiles, she picked two pieces of black stretchy fabric, carefully wrapping them around each strap. Instead of making them bulky, it added a layer of sexiness.

"Wow, now it's even more sophisticated than before. I'll just sew them real quick so they don't fall off," I said.

"I'll do that," Tess said. I took off the bra, and she quickly made the changes at the sewing machine. Then I put it back on, and we both admired the result in the mirror.

"That's better," I said.

"Let me just sew a bit of lace to the upper part of the cup. I think it'll look great—balance out the sturdier straps. Don't need the sewing machine for this. Just stand still."

I eyed the needle she picked. "Don't poke me."

"When have I ever poked you? Wait… don't answer that."

"Uh-huh." It had taken her a few months to get the hang of sewing a garment *on* me without making me feel like a pincushion.

"You're not exactly still. What's the matter? Thoughts of a sexy neighbor making you jittery?"

"Or the fear that my skin will get the pointy end of the needle."

Tess stepped back, pointing a finger and the needle at me. "Don't feed me tales."

I grinned apologetically. "A mix of both?"

Tess kept staring.

"Fine, I was thinking about Rob."

She smiled triumphantly, resuming the sewing. "There, that wasn't so hard, was it? You didn't give me any details about that dinner and kiss. Time you rectify that, don't you think?"

She kept glancing up at me, and I knew the second she split her focus between sewing *and* fishing for spicy details, my skin was in danger.

"Fine, I'll spill the beans. But give that needle here. I'll do it myself and keep my boobs safe from you."

Goodness, my stomach did two flips just because I was remembering that evening. My palms turned sweaty at the realization that I was heading home in a few hours.

"Perfect. So I just get to stand here, not work, and listen to you? *That* is what I call a relaxing afternoon."

***

I'd been home for two minutes when there was a knock at my door. I checked my watch, grinning. Yup, Rob's running time.

Breathe in, breathe out, Skye.

I made a concerted effort not to check him out, but I was failing. I just couldn't help drinking him in. I had only admired him from a distance. Up close, the effect was magnified. My pulse pounded in my ears. My mouth was dry.

"Good evening, Skye."

That voice....

"Hi!"

"You didn't answer. Want to come on a run with me?"

I'd completely forgotten to reply. I shook my head, whistling. "Pilates girl here. Plus, I exercise in the morning. Specialists recommend that."

"I find it relaxing in the evening."

"I actually just read a study on the best time to exercise." Taking out my phone, I clicked the library icon, pulling up said study. Rob was looking more incredulous with every passing second.

"A study?"

"I like reading or doing studies so much that I almost went for a PhD," I explained. I turned the phone around, showing him the lines I'd highlighted.

Rob chuckled.

"What?" I asked.

"Nothing. I just like finding out more about you. Like the fact that you're a brainiac. But I can't factor in running in the morning. I usually get a call about some fire I need to put out just when I get out of bed. It relaxes me to do it in the evening. Releasing endorphins and all that."

"Not the way to win over this girl."

"What is the way, Skye?" He tilted closer to me. His eyes were smoldering. And just like that, I was on fire again. I swallowed, glancing away.

Ah, I could think of one or two ways. His hands could do wonders for my back, I was sure.

Those full lips too. A current of heat ran through me. I could practically feel his mouth on my bare skin. How was this even possible?

Shrugging, I cleared my throat. "I'm just gonna drink a glass of wine and watch Netflix."

"Is that an invitation?"

I laughed. "You are unbelievable."

"Never claimed otherwise."

"I've pegged you for the type who doesn't drink this late. For sure not after a run, to take care of those muscles."

"You noticed them?"

"Hard not to," I admitted. Crap, I'd actually said it out loud? "Don't let me keep you from your routine."

"I'm tempted to ditch it tonight." There was a playful glint in his eyes, but something told me he wasn't joking.

"For wine and Netflix? That's a slippery slope, neighbor. Before you know it, ditching your evening run becomes habit."

"Not for wine and Netflix. For the company." That glint in his eyes was becoming more and more pronounced. I squirmed, feeling my entire body sizzle, yearning for a kiss or a touch.

"I want you, Skye."

His words had been playing in my mind on a loop for days—not just the words but every detail surrounding them, including the intensity in his eyes and body language.

He'd kicked the ball into my court, but I still

had no idea what to do with it. A one-night stand with my neighbor wasn't the smartest thing, and yet....

I shook my head, snapping myself out of my thoughts.

"No, no. Don't make me feel guilty for that. Come on, off you go."

His smile widened, but he nodded, backing away. My pulse was still racing when I closed the door and leaned against it. Amazing how much sense of safety a piece of wood gave me.

I almost expected him to knock at my door one hour later after his run, but he didn't.

To my astonishment, I was disappointed. Wow, this man was making me discover new things about myself.

I checked my phone before I went into my shower—no message. My stomach bottomed out.

I laughed at myself, taking off my clothes. The bra straps had left red marks on my shoulders, which meant they needed even more padding. I spoiled myself with a scrub and a hair mask. I was midway through rinsing when I heard my phone buzz with an incoming message.

My heart rate intensified the same second. I knew instinctively that it was from Rob. But what if it wasn't? I had to know.

With my hair still full of gooey cream, I darted out of the shower and almost fell on my ass. I grabbed the towel rack for support, drying my hands before tapping my phone.

Rob: Just read that study. Very impressive.

Skye: It's thorough, right?

Rob: Yeah. It's just missing one thing.

Skye: What?

Rob: Instructions on how to have proper motivation to work out in the morning.

Skye: It wasn't part of the research question though.

Rob: Plus, it comes down to personal choice.

Skye: True.

Rob: You can help.

I blinked at the screen, not really getting it.

Skye: What do you mean?

Rob: Train with me in the mornings.

Wow. Grinning, I leaned over the sink as I typed back. The mask was starting to drip, but I just couldn't put the phone down long enough to rinse.

Skye: Thought you didn't have time in the morning.

Rob: I'd make time for you.

I licked my lips, shaking my head. This man….

Skye: Think you could turn into a Pilates fan?

Rob: We could compromise. Half an hour jogging, half an hour of Pilates. You give in, I give in.

Skye: Sounds like making a deal with the devil.

I waited with bated breath for his reply.

Rob: It would be.

Skye: I'll think about it.

I was grinning from ear to ear. How was I even considering it?

Rob: Tell me one more thing about you. Something I can't guess.

Skye: But if I tell you, you'll miss out on the fun of finding out yourself.

Rob: There's so much to discover about you, so I'm sure we'll have plenty of fun. I plan to be very thorough.

He wanted to discover me? That sounded.... Holy shit, I couldn't even explain it, but it brought on a goofy smile. The mask started dripping in earnest. After placing my phone on the counter under the mirror, I hopped back in the shower quickly, rinsing the rest of the mask. My whole body was vibrating with excitement. I usually liked to linger under the spray of the water, but now I was ready in record time, wrapping my hair in a towel and putting on a robe.

Another message awaited me.

Rob: Tell me something you haven't told anyone.

Wow.

Skye: Aiming so high already?

Rob: Always.

Hmmm... what should I tell him? I made a mental list of possibilities, then chuckled at myself. I was taking this way too seriously.

Skye: I love to break rules occasionally.

He called me the next second. I went into my bedroom, sitting in the reading armchair next to the bed.

"I'll need more details," Rob said. "Pegged you as someone who sticks to rules."

"I do." I could barely keep from laughing. "I think they are there for a reason. But when I do break them, it's such a rush...."

He didn't say anything for a few seconds, but I thought he sounded as if he was stifling a groan. My body perked up at the possibility. I was getting feisty tonight.

"Give me an example."

"So, my family organizes these events—"

"The Ballroom Galas, I know. Anne told me."

"Okay. Well, one of the activities we do is that in order to dance with someone, you have to buy a ticket. There is a raffle, and the winner gets the dance. My brother Ryker invited his now-fiancée to one of the galas, and he wanted to make sure he got all her dances. He asked me to rig the raffle, and I said no—"

"Ouch, not even for your brother?"

"Wait, I'm not done."

"I'm listening."

"Anyway, so he decides to buy all the tickets for every dance, and he succeeds... except for one dance when another guy also bought a ticket. And what do you know, that other guy actually won. But I just didn't have it in me to do that to Ryker, so I declared my brother as the winner."

"I'm impressed."

I laughed. "No one knows though."

"And I won't tell."

"It's my favorite memory from any event."

"You're full of surprises." A beat later, he added, "So, tomorrow morning...."

"Haven't decided yet if I'll strike that deal."

"I see. So you're not sure if you want to help me develop a healthier lifestyle?"

"I like the angle you're taking."

"I know how to play my cards, Skye."

I had no doubt about that. Just hearing my name from his mouth was doing inexplicable things to me.

"I need to hang up," I said, checking the towel on my head. It was soaked. "Still need to dry my hair."

"Good night, Skye."

"Good night."

I usually fell asleep the second I climbed into bed, but that evening, I tossed and turned for what felt like hours. I was happy being single... but then Rob's face popped up in my mind.

I hid my face in the pillow, fiddling with my toes on the comforter. I was *not* going to think about Rob. That was a surefire way to stay up half the night... which was exactly what happened, of course.

The next morning, I woke up a bit later than usual, groggy as hell. Served me right for staying up so late.

I messaged Tess to let her know I'd be in around ten, then took my Pilates mat into the backyard. I instinctively glanced at Rob's place. I couldn't tell if he was still at home, because he always parked his car in the garage. He was usually gone at this time anyway.

I loved working out in nature in summer, feeling the warm sun on my skin, soaking up vitamin D. I was locked up so many hours a day inside the store that I would love nothing better than to spend all my free time outdoors.

I'd memorized the routine, and weirdly enough, watching the trainer explain the movements on the screen didn't motivate me at all. It just made me more aware of the burn in my muscles. So I put in my AirPods, started my Netflix app, and watched one of my shows. I was one of those who liked to rewatch old favorites ad nauseam, so even if I was in a position that didn't allow me to see the screen, I still knew what was going on just by listening. I called this multitasking. Exercising and watching TV. It was the most relaxing time of the day.

Midway through my routine, a shadow appeared on the grass. I was on all fours... well, not exactly. One hand and leg were stretched out.

"Morning," Rob said.

I lost my balance the next second, plunking my palm on the ground, then my toes. They made a cracking sound, and pain seared through me.

"Owwww," I exclaimed, turning around. I sat

on my ass, cradling my left foot. The toes seemed to have taken the brunt of the impact.

Rob lowered himself on his haunches until he was almost level with me.

"Skye! You okay?"

"I think so." I still cradled my foot, feeling my toes with my fingers.

Rob put a hand on my shoulder. "Are you sure?"

"Yes. My toes are okay. Not broken or anything." When I put my foot back on the ground though, I realized they were too sore for me to be able to walk normally. "I don't think I can continue my workout."

"Come on, I'll help you get inside the house."

I rose to my feet, awkwardly balancing my weight on one full sole and only using the heel of the other foot. Rob put an arm around my waist, pulling me in to him. Feeling his hard body against mine was overwhelming my senses. His cologne was delicious. Had he changed it? It was citrusy, with a light hint of mint.

Well, this was an interesting way to take my mind off the pain.

I hopped awkwardly on one and a half feet, grateful for his support. Inside the house, I sat on the couch, resting my bad foot on the ottoman, flexing my toes.

"It's getting better," I said.

"Want to ice them?"

"No, I think they'll be back to normal in a few

minutes."

He sat on the ottoman, close to me. I sucked in a breath when he placed his hand on my foot. I was wearing socks, but even through the thick cotton, his touch impacted me. A sigh escaped me. God, I hoped it sounded like a whimper of pain. I barely kept my composure. This man's touch was pure fire.

He moved his fingers from my foot up my ankle, skimming them almost up to my knee. When he looked up, he was smirking. Damn, I hadn't fooled him.

"I made an impression, didn't I?"

"What do you mean?"

That smirk turned into a grin.

"You scared me," I answered without giving him a chance to elaborate.

"If that's what you want to call it."

"That's what it was," I insisted.

It wasn't, of course. I knew it. He knew it.

"Why were you still home?" I asked, hoping that would distract him. "Didn't you say you always leave early?"

"Worked from home this morning, then saw you out there. I couldn't just ignore what was right in front of me."

Ah, I loved it when he threw my own words back at me. I couldn't challenge that, could I?

I blushed, moving my foot just a little out of his reach. If he didn't stop touching me, something was going to give—more specifically... me.

"Were you productive?"

"Not really. I was looking for a present for Lindsay."

"Did you find anything?"

He frowned. "No."

"Why don't you ask your sister?"

"She said to just surprise her. Any ideas?"

Aww, it was downright adorable how concerned he was about a present!

"There are kids' sections in a few department stores. I'm sure the salesperson can advise you. Soho also has some cute shops with handmade presents, but you have to know where to look for them. She might like that—having a one-of-a-kind item. I can go with you, if you want."

His mouth opened slightly as his eyes searched me. I'd caught him off guard.

"Sure. When do you want to go?"

"It'll be a late start for me at the store today, so I'll be the one closing. Can we go tomorrow?"

"Okay. I'll be going, then. How do you want me to make it up to you?"

"Huh?"

"The way I see it, this is my fault." He pointed to my foot. "You said I scared you. Unless you want to take that back."

"No, it's true," I teased.

"So I have to make it up to you."

"You don't have to."

"I insist. Any preferences?"

I laughed nervously. This felt a little surreal.

Rob Dumont was definitely unlike anyone I'd met.

"I don't know."

He winked. "Even better. It'll be my choice."

Something told me that was a dangerous thing to do, but honestly, I couldn't even think of one thing.

"Have a great day, Rob."

Nodding, he walked backward to the door. That intensity in his eyes made my breath catch. And I'd just agreed to spend tomorrow afternoon with him.

Chapter Eleven
Skye

My foot recovered slowly. I had to be careful not to put too much pressure on my toes for the rest of the day, but by the next day, I was good as new. Except that I became a tad nervous as the afternoon went by. I was meeting Rob in front of the store called Handmade in one hour, and I kept checking my appearance—first my dress, then my makeup, then my hair.

"Why are you so jumpy?" Tess asked.

"No reason."

"Would that *no reason* benefit from a sexy bra and panties?"

Oh, my sister knew me so well. I wiggled my hips and my eyebrows.

"Wearing some of my sexiest stuff already," I informed her.

Her eyes bulged. "Okay, then. I don't need to know more."

Ha! Right. As if she could help herself. I gave her two minutes before she asked what my plans were for tonight. She lasted all of one minute.

"Are you going on a date?" She kept her voice nonchalant. I could tease her, but then just remembered that she'd spent the last few months worrying over me even more than usual, so I didn't have it in me to do that.

"No, just helping Rob choose a present for his niece."

"And that required code red?"

Tess and I had developed our own sexiness code for lingerie.

Green was period lingerie. Yellow included everything from meh to sports bras. Red was fire: push-up bras, lace, silk... or all three.

"You know me, I'm all for red." It was the truth. I wore super sexy lingerie on a regular basis because it gave me confidence.

"I know, but there's something different about you." She pointed at me.

I felt different, so I couldn't contradict her. I was just as in the dark as my sister about what caused it though.

One hour later, as I headed out of the store, I was filled with an infectious energy. Usually at the end of the day, I was spent. Not tonight though. I eyed the ice cream shop across from us. My mouth was watering. I still had twenty minutes until I was supposed to meet Rob. That was just enough time to enjoy a cone with two scoops. (Yeah... I bought ice cream often enough that I knew exactly how long it took me to eat a cone.)

Maybe allowing myself to indulge in one temptation would make it easier to resist the other.

After buying a cone with mango and caramel,

I ventured down one of the side streets, peering inside the window displays. In the morning and during the workday, I was always on the run, too busy to actually take the time to see what was new around us. I enjoyed the evening stroll, especially seeing all the shops off the beaten path.

Henry, the most daring designer I'd seen in New York, was now selling shoes for the first time. Magda, the art deco painter, had added some esoteric-looking items to her stock, like moon globes and bracelets with various healing properties. It was a bit out there but also worked somehow. As far as I was concerned, Soho was magic. It was my favorite part of the city. Sure, I might be biased… but just a little.

"Good evening."

I startled, turning around to face Rob.

"Hi! You're early," I said.

"I know."

I'd just finished my ice cream. Clasping a hand around the strap of my bag, I tossed the napkin I'd held the cone with into a nearby trash can. My fingers were a little shaky.

Instantly, I realized why I was so exuberant and full of energy. The reason had a first and a last name: Rob Dumont.

"How is your foot?" he asked.

"Good as new."

I swallowed, wondering if he was only thinking about my well-being or if he also remembered that crackling electricity between us.

When he captured my gaze, I had my answer. He looked at me as if he knew I was wearing code red lingerie. My skin sizzled.

On an intensity level from one to ten, the fire in this man's eyes was somewhere around twenty. One thing was universally true: no matter if we were in my house, the backyard, his house, or the middle of the street, he could make my knees weak just by *smiling* at me.

"Glad to hear it. Want to lead the way?"

"Sure."

We walked side by side, and I couldn't believe how powerfully I felt his presence. Not the heat of his body—his *presence*. He dominated the space completely without even trying.

"Tell me about your niece. What does she like?"

"Honestly, I don't know."

"What does she usually play with?"

"Toys."

I laughed. "You're no help."

"I just want to buy her something to cheer her up. She's been a bit down lately, what with her dad *forgetting* to call."

"That sucks."

"Yeah. Had a little chat over the phone with him. Told him that he'd better remember, or I'd pay him a visit in person and wouldn't play nice anymore."

Oh, this man. How could I not like him? I had a weakness for people with empathy, people who weren't afraid to fight for the people they loved. That was how the Winchesters operated too—we all were there 110 percent for one another.

"I don't think I've been on this street before. I usually keep to the main one." He was looking around with curiosity.

"You can find real gems around here, trust me. I've been exploring every nook and cranny since opening our store."

"I admire you for your tenaciousness in going after what you want."

"Wow, thanks."

"It can't be easy."

I shrugged. "It's not. Has pros and cons, like everything else. I quite like working at my own pace and not having a boss, but it is nerve-racking to shoulder so much responsibility. Before, if I didn't like my job, I could just quit and search for something else… but you can't quit your own business. I mean, you know how it feels."

"I inherited a solid, successful business, so it's not the same."

"You grew it exponentially though."

He chuckled. "You read about me?"

"Of course. Had to know if you were a good fit for the house."

"What's the verdict? Am I a good fit?"

"For the house?"

"What else?" He leaned in closer. The almost touch was excruciating, but when his hand brushed mine, I realized the touch itself was even more so.

"Of course you are."

"I see." He scrutinized me intently. Being around him made me feel relaxed and on edge at the same time. "So... I have big plans for us tonight."

"Oh?"

"I need to make up for scaring you."

"And that's going to take a whole evening?"

"Even longer."

Good Lord, I'd only been in his presence for ten minutes and my hormones were already in disarray. My whole body responded to his flirty tone and suggestive glances. My nipples puckered, pressing against my bra. My lower belly was on fire. And I was supposed to spend the whole evening with him?

Bring it on.

***

Rob

Spending time with Skye was unlike anything I'd experienced before. I still couldn't get over the fact that she'd offered to come shopping with me, that she'd put thought into what Lindsay might like.

"What will we be doing?" she asked.

"You'll see. I owe you for scaring you."

She blushed deliciously, and this time, I didn't hold back. I touched her cheek, loving how soft her skin was, how her pupils dilated slightly.

"If you owe me, I should be the one who

ONE PERFECT TOUCH

chooses the activity, don't you think?"

I skimmed my hand up to her ear. She shivered lightly. I almost captured her mouth, right there in the street. It took all my self-control to drop my hand and point to the store.

"You've already put yourself in my hands. No going back from that," I said.

"There's no winning with you."

"Yeah, there is, but of another kind." I held her gaze firmly. She exhaled sharply, turning around and pushing the door to the shop open.

It was a crammed little space—more like a hole-in-the-wall, nothing like the department stores I was used to. My first instinct was to tell Skye to go right back out and head to Bergdorf's, but something made me keep silent and just watch her. She smiled at the salesperson.

"Hey, Tris. Sorry I haven't had time for a visit lately, but I brought with me a potential new client. We're looking for something unique for an eight-year-old girl."

Tris nodded, immediately heading to a shelf full of stones and beads. I still wasn't convinced I'd find something for my niece here. Skye picked up on my skepticism.

"I know it's a little unusual, but just give it a chance," she whispered, looking up at me hopefully, and I didn't have it in me to crush that hope.

In fact, I was looking forward to whatever Skye wanted to do next. I had an inkling that she could wrap me around her little finger if she wanted

109

to. I didn't want anyone having so much power over me.

"Let's move to the back," Tris said. "I have more stuff there."

No sooner did we pass through a curtain into an even smaller room than the bell in the front rang.

"Go attend to the new customer," Skye said. "I've got this."

With a grateful nod, Tris disappeared to the front.

"Oh, this place just makes me feel like a kid myself." Skye rubbed her palms together, heading to some shelves that held yet more crystals and beads. "Look at all this pretty stuff. Tell me about Lindsay. Does she like fantasy books?"

"Yes, yes, she does."

"Princesses?"

"How am I supposed to know that?"

"Okay, I'll work with the fantasy angle." Skye laughed, inspecting the merchandise closely.

"Want to check out the shelves with me?" she asked after a few minutes.

"No, thanks. I'd rather check you out."

A current of awareness shot through me. Skye straightened up, as if she'd felt it too. I moved closer, inexplicably drawn to her. I couldn't say why it was harder to keep my distance here than outside. Her scent was delicious. Apple? Peach? I couldn't really tell. It didn't matter. I just couldn't get enough of it. I couldn't get enough of her, period.

"Ah, what about this?" Skye pointed with her

thumb over her shoulder to a necklace with a pink stone. The details didn't register, but I was sure I hadn't seen anything like it before. She turned around, and her eyes widened. Clearly she hadn't realized how close I was.

"It's sophisticated and one of a kind. And...." Her voice trailed off. "You don't like it, huh? Okay, so let's go, then. To a department store, or even just another store. What do you want to do?"

"Fuck, Skye. I don't care. All I know is I want you."

She let out a small whimper, licking her lips. I didn't hold back. I couldn't. Cupping her cheek, I tilted her head up and then pressed my mouth to hers. She tasted delicious, like caramel and mango. I explored her, licking her lower lip, sucking on her tongue, groaning when she did the same to me. I felt that lick right along my cock and pressed myself against her. I wanted her to know just how hard I was. She moaned right in my mouth. It reverberated through me. I moved a hand to her waist before lowering it down her thigh. I wanted to touch her everywhere—mostly, I craved skin-on-skin contact.

I'd never lost myself in a woman this way. I forgot where we were, what we were doing. Nothing mattered. Absolutely nothing. Just bringing her pleasure. Fuck, how I wanted to bring her pleasure. I slipped a hand under her dress, along her inner thigh, until I reached her panties. Nothing but a scrap of silk. Parting her legs, I rubbed one finger down the middle. She trembled lightly, moaning against my mouth again. No, I couldn't do this here. Slowly, it came back to me that we were in a store.

I dropped my hand and tried to pull back before nearly losing composure yet again when Skye buried one hand in my hair and placed the other on my arm, pulling me right back to her.

"Skye," I murmured against her lips. "Open your eyes."

She did so, slowly at first and then blinking them wide open.

"Oh, wow."

She let go of my arm before looking down at her dress, as if expecting to find it on the floor. When she blinked back up, she touched her lips with two fingers. I groaned, almost kissing her again. Seeming to realize what that did to me, she dropped her hand.

Tris came in before I could say anything. "Did you guys find anything you like?" she asked.

"Definitely," I answered, still looking straight at Skye.

Chapter Twelve
Skye

My skin was still sizzling as we walked out of Tris's shop. Rob stuffed the neatly packaged necklace in the pocket of his suit jacket. I couldn't believe I'd lost my head like that... but honestly, it hadn't been just my head. I'd been completely lost to this man. The way he'd kissed me had just been surreal.

"Tell me you're ready to call this a day," he said in a low, dangerous voice once we reached my shop. Oh, I didn't want to disappoint him.

"No, I can't—I'm closing the store today. Tess has an appointment, so she can't do it."

He tilted his head. "What if the shopping trip took longer?"

I grinned at him. "I trusted my skills to find the right present."

"I'll grab an ice cream until you close up. We can ride home together."

"Oh? So whatever you're planning to make up to me... it'll take place at home?"

"That's right."

"I see." I could barely deal with this intensity radiating from him.

"I'm not nearly done spending time with you

tonight, Skye."

I loved hearing him say my name in that delicious voice. My skin tingled in anticipation. Something lit up inside me. Instinct warned me that this man could be my undoing.

I was completely lost in him, trapped in his sinful gaze. He drew his fingers from my jaw down to my neck. His touch, combined with that sinful gaze, melted my willpower.

"I recommend mango and caramel. They're delicious." My voice was full of sass.

He smiled, leaning in a little.

"I know. That's what you tasted like, and I fucking loved it."

His words ignited my body. Holy shit, I'd barely calmed down from the kiss, but now every nerve ending was on alert again. The heat between my thighs was out of this world.

His fingers lingered on my earlobe, tugging at it a little. He touched me with so much familiarity.

"I have to go," I whispered, though all I wanted to do was just stay here.

He dropped his hand, taking a step back.

I headed inside the store, sighing.

"Wait. I want to make a mental picture of you smiling like this," Tess exclaimed. She held her hands in front of her, mimicking a camera. "Also, please remember every detail of whatever brought you to this state of euphoria. I want to hear all about it... just not now, because these online orders won't pack by themselves."

"Oh, Tess." I shook my head but was grinning. I did the same to her every time she had some new guy in her life. I froze a little.

"Don't," Tess exclaimed when I joined her behind the counter.

"Don't what?"

She cupped my cheeks, tugging at them the way she did when we were kids.

"Be scared of this. I can see it on you."

I pouted.

"Okay, so I do need some details. Just a little something to fuel me with energy for the rest of the day. Sexy neighbor can't keep his eyes off you."

"Or hands," I confirmed. "Or mouth."

Tess let go off me, exclaiming in delight. "Yes! I thought you gave off the just-kissed vibes but didn't want to get ahead of myself. As I said, memorize every detail."

We went over the online orders, only taking a break when a customer came in. Despite the store, the biggest chunk of our sales happened online, which made me question if the brick-and-mortar investment would pay off. Time would tell, I supposed.

At eight o'clock, Tess had to leave for an appointment.

"Are you sure you can handle the evening traffic yourself?" she asked.

"Yesss! You've postponed your pedicure long enough. Just go."

Our late-night shopping hours were a success,

but they were also crowded. But my workaholic sister would probably sleep here if I didn't make her go home or do what she needed to do.

After she left, half a dozen clients strode in. I could barely tell my ass from my elbow. At nine o'clock, I turned the sign to Closed. There were still a few customers inside, and I wouldn't usher them out, of course, but I didn't want any new ones coming in.

I was at the counter, folding merchandise into gift boxes for my last clients, when my phone vibrated.

Rob: You're amazing.

I looked through the window display, smiling when I realized he was watching me.

Skye: How was the ice cream?

Rob: Delicious. But it tasted better on you.

One message. That was all it took for me to be hot and bothered again.

I didn't get a chance to write him back, because my customers were waiting for their receipts. After they left, I stood by the door, holding my fingers out for Rob to see, mouthing, "Ten minutes."

My phone vibrated on the counter the next second. I practically ran to it.

Rob: Five.

Skye: ????

Rob: I was patient enough while you had customers. I'll come after you. You and I, we're good in back rooms.

That we were, but still, I had to label some

boxes for shipping, and I did not want this sexy man distracting me.

Skye: Ten minutes.

Grinning, I put my phone down. My message had two purposes. One: establish that I really needed more time to complete the task. Two: rile him up. I was sure this would make him stride in earlier.

I heard the phone vibrate again but didn't want to give in to the temptation of reading it. I would never finish my task if I didn't focus. I lost the battle with myself twenty seconds later, picking up the phone.

My mood plummeted immediately. The message wasn't from Rob but Dean, my shitty ex.

Dean: Can you lend me some money?

Skye: No.

Dean: Come on, I spent a crap-ton taking you out to dinner, and you're loaded.

I blinked.

Skye: So let me get this straight... you gave me shit about my mood cramping your style when I had issues but think it's okay to ask me for money?

Dean: Is that a yes or no?

Skye: Read above. NO. FUCK NO.

I tossed the phone in my bag, but not before blocking his number. I had no clue why I hadn't done that before. I still had a few labels to stick on the boxes and was hoping my anger would melt away by the time I was done. Instead, it just intensified.

When Rob stepped inside the store, I was so

worked up that I couldn't even muster a smile. I'd finished the boxes and was sitting on the counter, clasping my bag.

"Is something wrong?" he immediately asked.

"Yes. How can you tell?"

"You're different."

I decided to fess up, because I didn't want him to think it had anything to do with him.

"A shitty guy I used to date just messaged to ask me for money." My voice was hard.

"I hope you told him to go to hell," Rob responded with such intensity, I had to look at him to see if he was okay.

"Of course I did. In fucking capital letters. Blocked his number too, but I'm still very annoyed. He just ditched me when things got rough, and now…. Sorry, you don't want to know that."

"Yes I do." He walked up to me. "Tell me. I want to know. To understand."

His voice was softer now, concerned… for me. Except for family, I wasn't sure I'd ever had that before.

"So he and I went out quite often a few months ago. Anyway, then Tess and I had some troubles. We'd been close to signing a deal with an investor who pulled out at the last minute. I can't tell you how much trouble that caused. We'd already spoken to suppliers for additional orders. We lost face and their trust. I wasn't exactly cheerful."

"Understandably."

"Anyway, Dean decided that I was too moody

and depressed, and he hadn't signed up for that."

Rob's eyes turned hard. I was irritable, and I preferred being by myself when I was like this.

"We can postpone whatever you had planned for tonight if you prefer." I hopped off the counter, shutting off the main lights, avoiding looking at him.

"Why would I want that?"

"I'm not cheerful, as you can see. I'm short of punching something. Not the best dinner companion."

In a few short seconds, Rob was behind me.

"I don't care. I want you with me tonight."

His directness and charm sliced through my anger like a machete. I turned around slowly, facing him. A few lights from the back were casting just enough light that I could still make out his features.

"Oh?"

"I have some methods to wind down after a tough day, push it out of your mind."

"It's not running, is it?" I teased.

He brought his mouth to my ear. "No, it's even better."

A shiver ran through me.

"I promise you won't even remember why you were mad in the first place."

"That cannot possibly be true," I countered.

"I'll prove it."

He took my hand in his. The skin on skin singed me. My breath caught. My whole body was anticipating the next second. Would he kiss me? He leaned in to me but veered right. The light end-of-day whiskers brushed my cheek.

"If you prefer, we can postpone everything," Rob said.

"What do you want?"

"For you to go home with me tonight." His tone was seductive with a hint of bossy. Yum.

"For dinner?" I whispered. I wasn't sure what I wanted him to say.

"Not *just* dinner." He pulled back a notch, staring me straight in the eyes. "I've got some skills to prove to you."

"Fine. In the spirit of neighborly relationships, you can test your methods on me."

"You'll love them."

"Hey, don't go raising expectations."

"I promise I can fulfill every single one of them."

I had no doubt. I tried very hard not to imagine every other expectation he could fulfill.

"Let's go, then," I said. Grabbing the keys and my handbag, I led the way out of the store. Rob was on my heels, almost literally. I could feel the heat of his body behind me as I locked the door.

It was a beautiful evening for a stroll. I looked around with a huge smile, enjoying that Rob was here with me.

"You really love it here."

"I do. But I just love the city in general more than any place I've visited."

"Do you travel a lot?"

"I used to. Back in college, I traveled the US

with some backpacker friends during vacations. Once I was more senior at my workplace, I was paid very well, and Tess and I went to Europe twice and went on a lot of tours. Once we started from Ireland, went to the UK and then France. The second time we started with Italy and then flew to Spain. I loved it."

"I can see that. You're lighting up."

"I'd actually thought about working abroad for a while, but Tess and I decided we wanted to give this business a try. So we saved and worked insane hours."

"Tell me about the investor you almost signed with."

I waved my hand. "It just didn't work out. He said he'd found a more profitable option."

"Are you searching for another one?"

"No, Tess and I decided that for now, we'll focus on what we have."

"Why did you want one in the first place?"

"More cash never hurts, and our initial plan was to expand rapidly, open a few more stores. But right now, our numbers tell us that we should focus our efforts on the online store. It's where 70 percent of our profit comes from. Another physical store would just be a drain."

"Personally, I think that working with investors is overrated. One gets caught up in the rush of expansion and investment, but the risk increases too, and the overall structure becomes tied to investors. It can tumble down like a house of cards."

"Exactly. We got a taste of that when we had

to call the suppliers and tell them we wouldn't be sending more business their way after all. We're happy with our decision for now. We'll see if things change in the future."

When we descended the stairs to the subway, Rob put his hand on my lower back. I loved it.

It was very hot in the station and then extremely cold in the car itself. The AC was freezing. I shuddered, and Rob gallantly took off his suit jacket, draping it around my shoulders. I grinned at him. "Thanks."

"You're welcome."

He still had one hand on my back. The other was on the railing, which put his mouthwatering bicep at my eye level. Oh, what a view. I typically read on the train—I had a Kindle app on my phone loaded with my favorite books—but there was no way I was missing out on the view this evening.

Every time our gazes crossed, I felt as if we were back in Tris's shop. Especially because the more time passed, the closer he leaned in and the harder he pressed his hand on my lower back.

"Should've taken an Uber. Then I would've had you all to myself," he said in a low voice. Something in his tone made me think he was considering getting off at the next station and climbing into a car for the rest of the way. A shiver ran through me at the thought.

"You're forgetting the driver," I whispered.

"Details. I can't wait to taste you again, touch that sexy-as-hell lingerie you're wearing."

My eyes widened. My cheeks were on fire.

"You thought I didn't notice?" he went on in that same low voice. "Just remembering how you felt... fuck."

Okay, that last word had almost sounded like a groan. This flirtiness was escalating quickly, and we were in a public place. I thought it was best to take a step back, put a few inches of distance between us. I grabbed a ceiling strap for support. I hadn't been holding on to anything before, thinking that if I lost my balance I could just... grab Rob.

For the rest of the journey, he followed my lead, not even attempting to close the space between us. When the train came to a stop at our station, he trapped me with his gaze again, and one thing was for sure: tonight wasn't going to end just with kissing.

Chapter Thirteen
Skye

Outside the subway station, I gave him back the jacket regretfully. I quite liked having it on my shoulders, being surrounded by that delicious manly smell. I took in a deep breath. The energy of the suburbs was so different to that of the city. Everything moved slower; people were calmer. Most were commuters, like me. My friends hadn't understood why I moved to a suburb, considering how much I loved Manhattan.

Not only did I want a bigger space than I could afford in Manhattan, but after spending the whole day in the hustle and bustle of the center, I liked slowing down in the evening.

I loved opening my window wide in the summer and hearing the birds, the sound of children playing outside and the trains passing in the distance.

Right now though, I wasn't paying too much attention to anything. I was too consumed by the gorgeous man walking right next to me.

"So," I said once I was in front of my house. "I want to freshen up really quickly, and then you can show me all those *methods* of yours."

Rob grinned. "Looking forward to it. Just

don't take too long, or I might come banging down your door."

"I need half an hour."

He cocked a brow. "To freshen up? It's already ten."

"Fine, twenty."

I was giddy as I practically ran to my house. *Please, please, please, karma, don't let things blow up in my face, because I don't want to dread coming home every day.*

I thought I'd calm down once I arrived inside, but instead, the opposite happened.

My nerves were even more frayed than before. I took a quick shower, then wrapped a silk robe around me and retrieved a set of lingerie from my dresser when I heard the bell ring.

Oh?

There was no delivery at this time. Who could it be? I hurried downstairs with the lingerie set, which I quickly threw on the couch before fastening the robe tighter. I looked through the peephole.

Holy shit, it's Rob! Have my twenty minutes passed? I glanced at the digital clock on my TV. Shit yeah, I was ten minutes late.

I was so not ready. My hair was wild, and my living room was a mess. But I couldn't keep him waiting, so I opened the door.

"Fuck!" he exclaimed. One word was all it took for me to go from nervous to turned on.

My body instantly reacted to him, and my nipples turned hard. Rob dropped his gaze to my chest. His pupils dilated a notch. The look on his face was one of pure hunger. I stepped back in a silent invitation. He came in, closing the door behind him. My heart was thundering against my rib cage. I was barely fighting off the urge to press my palm to my chest.

"I'm sorry I'm late." My voice was a little shaky, but Rob was watching me with such an intensity that I couldn't even breathe. "Want something to drink?"

"I just came to take you to my house."

"I know, but I'm not dressed yet. I could fix a drink for you while you wait."

"Sure. You have whiskey?"

"Yes."

"I'll have some on the rocks."

I fixed him one at the island in my kitchen. "Here it is. I'll just take everything upstairs and come down when I'm ready."

I pointed toward the couch, and he followed my hand with his gaze. He froze when he saw the lingerie set.

"You're naked under that?" He pointed to my robe.

I nodded.

"Fucking hell."

The next second, he closed the distance between us, kissing me fiercely.

***

Rob

All day, I'd been waiting for this moment, imagining it. Claiming her mouth, taking my time to taste and explore her. I wrapped a hand in her hair. It was a little damp, but still felt like silk in my fist. The scent of strawberry was strong. It was driving me crazy with lust. My instincts were battling my mind, and the my mind was losing. I'd wanted to take care of her, spend the evening talking, and then… then do this. But I couldn't let go. I couldn't bring myself to even take one step back, let alone leave the house. The knowledge that she was naked under that scrap of silk was tormenting me. I touched her neck with one hand, splaying my fingers wide, touching as much as possible, feeling her pulse, enjoying how wild it was. When I dropped my hand even lower, resting it on her chest, she tugged at my tie.

I drew back, watching her. Humming lightly, she opened her eyes.

"Take it off," I said.

Her eyes widened, but she immediately loosened the knot, pulling the tie over my head.

"Now my shirt."

I looked at her, straight into her eyes as she worked my buttons, taking off the shirt. Her fingers trembled, and her breath was shaky. I slipped my fingers under the hem of her robe, just a fraction of an inch. Skye gasped. I liked watching her succumb to the tiniest sensation so completely. I moved my fingers, cupping her breast, teasing the nipple between my thumb and forefinger. Skye She curled the hand she'd rested on my shoulder. Her nails scraped my skin. I wanted to do this all night: touch every part of her, drink in every reaction, no matter how small. But then she moved her hand down my chest, going straight for my belt buckle. Once again, my rational side lost it. She took off the belt, dropping it to the floor. The sound of metal on wood echoed in the living room.

I tugged at the knot of her robe until it opened enough that it still covered her breasts, but not her pussy. She clenched her legs, as if just now realizing how exposed she was.

I went around her until I was at her back. Grabbing the robe at her shoulders, I pulled it down, letting it pool at her feet. She was unbelievably sexy. On instinct, I grabbed an ice cube from my untouched glass and turned her around. She didn't notice the ice cube, but when I placed it between her breasts, she gasped, propping her hands on the counter behind her. I drew the cube lower between her breasts before circling one nipple. Her hips bucked forward, and I leaned in, needing a taste. I drew my tongue in a figure eight around her breasts before descending even lower. My mouth came first, then the ice cube... until she had goose bumps everywhere.

"Rob." Her voice was a bare whisper. I felt her contract the muscles in her belly when I reached her navel and smiled against her skin. I glided the ice cube right over her clit before pressing the flat of my tongue against it. Skye nearly toppled over me. I held her hips with both hands, pressing her against the cabinet. I wanted to hoist her on the stone counter and push her on her back with legs spread wide open for me, but she'd be uncomfortable.

No, this was good. This was perfect. I looked around, eyeing a stool she probably used to reach upper cabinets and pulling it toward us. I tapped it, and she perched one leg on it. I liked spreading her like this, opening her up for me. I drew my thumbs on the inside of her thighs, right up to her pussy before leaning in and pushing my tongue inside her, tasting her, driving her crazy. Her moans were maddening, so responsive. I pushed my own pants down, fisting my cock. *Oh, fuck, fuck. Fuck.* I focused on her clit again, alternating between nipping it with my lips and teasing it with my tongue until she came, crying out my name. I fisted my cock harder, still tasting her, right until she calmed down. Knowing I wouldn't last one moment longer if I continued touching myself, I held her with both hands, kissing down her thighs. Her breath was even shakier than before. I skimmed my mouth up her body, rising up, kicking off my pants and boxers, kissing each shoulder before stopping at her neck, nipping the sensitive skin there.

"I need…." I lost my train of thought when she wrapped her hand around my cock, pressing the heel of her palm on the head.

"What do you need?" she asked.

"This. You. Where's your bedroom?"

"Upstairs," she said with a wry grin.

I returned it. "After you."

She turned around, walking toward a narrow door near the couch. I caught up with her in no time.

"That sway in your hips wasn't there when I came in," I whispered in her ear, fondling her ass.

She wiggled it against my cock, and I nearly turned her around and propped her against the wall right there.

"No, but your... what was the word? Ah yes, your methods are amazing."

She wiggled her ass some more.

Gripping her hips, I steadied her.

"Woman. Upstairs. Now. Walk."

She glanced at me over her shoulder.

"Why? Too tempting?"

"Keep at it and I'll fuck you against this door. The wall. Whatever."

She bit her lip.

I stepped closer. "Later. Now, get me to a bed."

"Yes, sir." She went up the stairs, and I waited until she was two steps ahead before following. This had two purposes. One: I had a great view of her ass. Two: she couldn't wiggle it against me, testing my self-control.

The second we were inside her bedroom, she walked to the vanity.

"I have condoms," she muttered, opening a drawer.

She'd barely taken the package out when I pulled her against me, kissing her hard, losing the little self-restraint I'd shown downstairs. I'd made her come once, but that wasn't nearly enough. I walked her backward to the bed, ripping open the condom package without looking at it. I didn't want to be inside her just yet. I wanted to indulge in foreplay a little longer, but it was better to be prepared, just in case I lost it. That seemed very likely, especially when she sat on the bed, watching me hungrily. I handed her the condom, fisting her hair when she rolled it down my erection.

"You're doing great, Skye, just like that."

I climbed on her, kissing every part I could reach, then turned her on her belly because I wanted to explore her some more. Her skin was smooth and warm and begged to be licked and nipped. I moved my lips over each ass cheek, then turned her around again. I entered her, nearly losing my mind. Never in my life had anything felt so intense.

My vision was a blur. I pushed in and out, losing myself in Skye, in the way she just surrendered to me, the immense pleasure that just gripped me.

Tension concentrated behind my navel, spreading fast, gripping all my muscles until every single one was burning.

"Fuuuuck. Baby, fuck."

I thrust even faster, then slowed down, touching her clit, needing her to come again before I did. When she clenched tight around me, placing her heels under my ass, urging me deeper, I just couldn't hold back any longer. I exploded, grabbing the sheets, the pillow, anything in my reach, satisfied only when I heard Skye climax again.

Chapter Fourteen
Skye

"Do you want a robe, or are you good with a towel?" I asked.

"Towel's good."

We'd showered quickly, and I'd fastened my bathrobe as usual before realizing I hadn't laid out a towel for Rob. I whisked one quickly from the rack and regretfully watched as he wrapped it around his lower body, covering himself up.

"I can leave it off, if you prefer," he said with a wink.

I shrugged one shoulder. "I get to choose? Then I vote no towel."

He tilted his head, laughing... but also dropped the towel the next second. Now *that* was a treat.

When we returned to the bedroom, he looked around, frowning.

"Our clothes are downstairs," I reminded him.

"That's right."

I led him back to the living room, and only when I saw his clothes lying all around the place and my silk robe in a pile next to the kitchen counter did the events of the evening sink in.

Wow, that had escalated quickly. I grinned. Lately, I was all for that.

I felt Rob behind me. He hooked an arm around my waist. Oh, how I loved feeling that muscular arm around me, keeping me hostage against an equally muscular chest.

"Get dressed," he murmured in my ear.

"What?"

"We're going to my house."

"Why?"

"That was the plan before you seduced me, remember?"

I turned around. "*I* seduced *you*?"

"Did you or did you not open the door wearing a robe?"

"Why were you knocking at my door in the first place?"

"Details."

I pushed him away playfully. "I can't decide what to wear."

"I'll help you decide. Try clothes on in front of me."

I glanced at him speculatively. "Why?"

"How else should I make up my mind?"

"Why do I feel like we might not leave after all?"

"You don't trust me much, huh?"

"Considering you attacked me because I was wearing a robe?"

"Attacked you? That's what we're calling it?"

He braced his palms on either side of me on the counter. I couldn't get away from him if I wanted to… not that I did.

Instead, I used the one weapon I had: wiggling against him.

His eyes darkened almost instantly. I just loved this, especially when he flattened himself against me. His cock pressed against my belly. Wow. He was semi-hard, and I was certain it wouldn't take much for him to have a full hard-on.

Licking my lips, I squeezed his ass.

"Woman, you want to test me?"

"Damn, thought I already was. Mental note: must improve my seduction skills."

Rob chuckled, leaning forward and biting my neck lightly. I shrieked, getting away from him.

"So let me get this straight," he said. "You feeling up my ass is seduction, but me kissing you in your robe is an attack?"

"Hmmm… you're right. That was a little judgy of me. I'll consider upgrading that to seduction too."

He smacked my ass lightly.

"Hey, that's no way to earn that upgrade."

Amusement played on his lips. Next thing I knew, he sat on the couch, pulling me in his lap. Yeah, right on his erection.

"This is more like it." Without taking his eyes off me, he held up the black lace lingerie. "Put this on. Then get dressed."

I wiggled my eyebrows, laughing. Rob slipped

his free hand in my robe, palming my breast. Pushing down my robe, he kissed the other breast, teasing my nipple with his tongue.

I tugged at his hair greedily, wanting more of whatever he planned to do. I didn't even need to know. I was on board with everything. Except with the fact that he stopped kissing and touching the very next second.

I pouted. "What are you doing?"

"Put them on," he said. "Or we'll never eat."

"Fine, I'll be ready in a few minutes."

Gathering the dress too, I headed upstairs.

"Why don't you change here?" Rob asked.

"My clothes are upstairs."

"I'll come with you."

I waggled a finger. "No, no. You stay here."

Rob grinned from ear to ear. "Still don't trust me?"

"Nah, just don't trust myself right now."

I noticed Rob's grin widen before I raced up the stairs. In my room, I glanced at the sheets once and felt my face explode in a grin.

Alone in my bathroom, I had to make a concerted effort not to grin. How was I supposed to apply lipstick this way? After dabbing some on my lips, I pressed them together, forcing my mouth in a serious expression. Bingo! To my dismay, the second I parted my lips, I discovered I'd transferred half the lipstick to my teeth.

Oh my God, and it was the waterproof type, which meant my teeth needed a vigorous brushing before it would come off. Then I decided I wasn't going to apply lipstick again. I put on a simple black dress and black flats.

Back downstairs, Rob was buttoning up his shirt. Ah, it was slightly crumpled, since I'd tugged at it like a madwoman, but I was surprised his pants were still barely wrinkled. All in all, he had a just-fucked look about him. I loved it.

My purse clinked against the railing, and Rob looked up. His eyes darkened. Mission accomplished. Entering the room, I twirled once, slowly. His eyes were even darker when I faced him again. I picked up his tie from the couch, tying it around his neck.

"It's not a very formal place, my house," he said.

"Hey. I want the tie."

He curled his lips in a smile. I would have thought nothing about it... except it had a dangerous edge to it.

"What?" I asked.

"Imagining how it would look wrapped around your wrists."

Holy shit. The visual caused heat to curl through me. Even my fingers prickled on the fabric of the tie.

"Shall we?" I batted my eyelashes, taking a step back and dangling my purse in front of me.

"Show me what you've got," I teased once we were inside his house. His eyes flashed. Oh, heavens.

"After you."

Rob placed his hands on my shoulders, leading me to the barstool at the kitchen island.

"What are you doing?" I inquired.

"Making sure you have a great time."

"Oohh... I like the sound of that. Are you going to feed me?"

"And show you my... methods."

"I thought you already did that."

He grinned. "That was my secret weapon. Would've been smarter to keep the best for last, but...."

"So what's the rest entail?" I asked eagerly. Rob bent under the island, retrieving a bottle of Malbec. I threw my head back, laughing. "Wine, of course. Did I mention I like you?"

"Not explicitly, but I'll take my cues from earlier," he answered, looking me right in the eyes.

I blushed, patting the granite counter. "I'll have a full glass, please."

"Right away."

He poured wine for both of us, and we clinked glasses.

"Wow, this is amazing," I said after the first sip. I appreciated fine wine, but any would do for me, honestly. I'd gotten used to the cheap stuff in college, and it tasted good enough, so I usually grabbed what was on sale out of habit.

"It's a Malbec from vineyards at a high altitude in Argentina. It's heavier than the usual wine."

I licked my lips, humming a little. "It's just

perfect. Are you trying to get me drunk and take advantage of me? Oh, wait, you already did that."

His eyes glinted with amusement as he retrieved a platter with canapes from the fridge, placing it between us.

"Oh, you're not cooking." I pouted but immediately shoved two in my mouth. They were a mix of smoked salmon and ricotta, as far as I could tell. I might not be a wine connoisseur, but I'd always been a foodie.

"No, I had these delivered," he said in between bites.

"Hmm… don't know how I feel about that."

He cocked a brow. "Why?"

I bought myself time by eating two more canapes, but Rob was looking at me intently.

"You look super sexy cooking. Flexing muscles when you reach for stuff, things like that."

He burst out laughing. I looked at my glass. "What's in this? I've just had two sips and my tongue is already loose."

"Told you it's a little stronger than the usual stuff."

Since I was already on a slippery slope, I could also voice the rest of my thoughts.

"But since you can't delight me with your sexy moves, maybe you can find something different?"

Rounding the corner, he came up behind me. He skimmed his thumbs up the sides of my neck. Heat speared me from the point of contact right down between my thighs. My nipples tightened. I moaned at the unexpected sensation, and Rob stepped closer, bringing his mouth to my ear.

"Or we can just do this," he said.

"Ha! I knew it. You lured me here for more sexy times."

He spun me around the next second, until I was face-to-face with him. His eyes were hard, his mouth set in a firm line. He pressed his thumb on the bow of my upper lip, and I was on fire. It was all I could do not to squirm in my chair.

Next thing I knew, he lifted me up. I hung tight to him with one hand and held my glass precariously in the other.

"Hey, don't make me spill my wine."

"You can just leave the glass there and I'll bring it to you."

I tilted my head back as if I was considering it, then shook it vigorously. "Nah, don't want to be apart from it. Not even if it means I could fondle you with both hands."

"One glass and you're already preferring Malbec over me?"

I wiggled my eyebrows. "What can I say? I'm easily swayed."

He brought me to an armchair. At first, I wondered if we'd both fit on it, but we did. Well... almost. I had to half straddle him, but I wasn't complaining.

"I'll see how I can sway things back in my favor," he murmured.

I took another sip from my glass before

putting it on the small side table next to us.

"I can give you a few tips." I rested my head on his chest, playing my fingers down that gorgeous six-pack.

Then, suddenly, I remembered a detail.

"When are you going for your run?"

"I'll skip it tonight."

"Want to do Pilates with me tomorrow morning? You still haven't said anything about that deal."

"Skye, no way in hell am I doing Pilates. That was just a ruse."

"To get in my pants?"

"To spend time with you… and yes, get in your pants."

"I appreciate your honesty," I said, just before I burst out laughing. Rob chuckled.

We just sat there, entwined, except for the few minutes in which he went to the kitchen, bringing the bottle and his glass back with him.

"You're great at this. I haven't been so relaxed in a long while," I said after a bit. It wasn't the wine, it was him, just him. "Almost forgot about that stupid text."

Rob groaned. "Almost isn't good enough."

"Well, honestly, I just remembered because I was thinking hard about why I was pissed off in the first place."

"How long did you date him?"

"About two months."

"So not a long-term thing."

"No, honestly... my last long-term relationship was in college. Afterward, it was mostly dating, not relationships, you know?"

"Was that something you wanted or just the way things worked out?"

"Both, I guess. There was rarely a guy who stuck around for too long or didn't try to pull one over me. Once, I discovered that a coworker who was flirting with me had a long-term girlfriend."

"Shit."

"Yeah... that felt just like that. Like I was shit."

"You're an amazing woman, Skye. Don't let anyone's actions make you think otherwise."

God, his words were so kind and sincere.

"Thank you. Anyway, all in all, I actually embraced the single life. I like it. Did that sound weird?"

He laughed, kissing my neck. "No, just honest. And I understand where you're coming from. Haven't had a long-term relationship in years either."

I was happy we were having this conversation, that we were both so relaxed about sharing everything.

"What time is it? I should probably go home," I murmured.

"No you don't. I told you I didn't get enough of you today, and I meant it." He drew his thumb over my lips, watching me intently. "Do you have to be at the store tomorrow?"

"No. Tess and I are trying this new thing

where we take off the entire weekend and are leaving our sales associates in charge."

"Good. Then we can stay up late and be up to no good."

"That's right."

Chapter Fifteen
Rob

Next morning, I woke up to a light headache. Red wines contained a lot of tannin, which could result in headaches. Skye was sleeping peacefully next to me on the king-sized bed.

I realized why I'd woken up when my phone rang. Grabbing it from the nightstand, I darted out of the room before it woke her up.

Anne was calling.

"Morning, brother."

"Hey!"

"Oh, you sound as if you just woke up."

"I did."

"Sleeping in? That's a first for you." She was right. I was usually up early even on weekends.

"I'm up now. Or will be, after some coffee."

"Lindsay and I want to stop by with breakfast. If that works for you."

"Sure. Just give me twenty minutes to be decent."

"Okay."

When I returned to the bedroom, Skye was up too, yawning.

"My sister and niece are coming over," I said.

"Oh, wow. Okay." Bolting to a sitting position, she looked at herself, then around. "I slept in your T-shirt."

"You did. Looks good on you."

She stumbled out of bed. I took her hand, steadying her. "Mmm... not a fan of that wine anymore. My head weighs a ton."

"We should've drunk some water last night as well, but I was too distracted."

"Oh, really? Why was that?"

"I had a gorgeous woman on top of me."

She held up a finger, grinning. "Half of me. The other half was super comfy on that armchair."

Glancing around the room, she nodded at the heap of clothes next to the bed. "There are my things. I'll be out right away."

When she picked up her clothes, she lost her balance a little. I gripped her waist from behind. She spun around, smiling, pressing her dress to her chest. She was sexy as hell, but that wasn't the only reason I couldn't stop touching her. Now that I had her here, I wanted to keep her in place.

"You have to let me go if you want me to put some clothes on."

"Maybe I don't want that."

"That'll give your sister and niece something to see, that's for sure."

Reluctantly, I dropped my hands. "Come back."

"Hmm?"

"Have breakfast with me, Anne, and

Lindsay."

"Wow, I'd love to. I do need twenty minutes to freshen up though."

"Don't let those twenty minutes turn into forty again."

"Why, will you come bang down my door, then bang me?" Skye batted her eyelashes.

"Fuck yes, I will."

"Okay, okay. I'm hurrying."

***

Fifty minutes later, Skye still hadn't joined us. Okay, so being punctual wasn't her forte. I filed that in my memory and would plan accordingly in the future.

"Uncle Rob, you have the *best* house," Lindsay exclaimed. After asking me to show her how to make sunny side-ups, which she then immediately downed, she went swimming in the blow-up kids pool I'd put in the backyard when I'd arrived. My sister's negotiation skills had always been sharp, but I appreciated her even more now. Getting Lindsay out of the water hadn't been an easy task.

"You had to put up a pool, huh?" Anne teased as we went out to the table in the backyard.

"You can come here any time you want," I reminded her. Just then, I noticed Skye through a window.

Anne pointed a finger at me. "Wait a second. That look." She glanced from me to Skye's house, then back to me. "Oh, Rob. You're involved with her, aren't you?"

"Yes."

Her shoulders slumped. "Why did I ever think you'd behave?"

"I always feel five years old when you scold me."

She patted my cheek before tugging at it. "This isn't scolding. Just me expressing surprise, that's all."

When Anne wasn't looking, I texted Skye.

Rob: Want to hurry? Save me from my sister?

Skye: Why do you need saving?

Rob: Just come over.

Skye: Sure. But I'll find out what's going on before deciding if I'm on your side or hers.

I laughed, putting my phone back in the pocket of my jeans.

"What?" my sister asked.

"Skye is coming over."

Anne blinked in surprise. Wait, what was that glint in her eyes? It didn't look like scolding anymore.

Before I could ask anything though, I heard Skye's back door open.

She sauntered toward us with a big smile. Her hair was pulled to one side, held in place with some sort of clip. She was wearing a casual white dress with a tie under her breasts.

"Hi, Anne. Hi, Lindsay."

"Glad you could join us," Anne said. "We were just about to make some coffee. How about you?"

"I never say no to coffee."

Anne winked at Skye.

"I'll take care of that. Anything else, my ladies?"

Skye batted her eyelashes at me. "If there are any of those delicious canapes left over, I'll have those too."

Anne's eyes bulged. I realized on the spot what threw her off: the familiarity between me and Skye. It wasn't something she was used to when it came to me. Hell, I wasn't used to it either, but damn if I didn't like it. I could practically see questions popping into Anne's mind.

Lindsay insisted on pressing the button on the coffee machine. I kept looking her way, ready to jump in if she was in danger of burning herself, but she wasn't clumsy at all.

"You're great at this."

"I do it for Mommy every morning," she announced proudly. "And I make a hot chocolate for me."

"This one doesn't have that function."

She jutted out her lower lip. I could imagine her downgrading this from being "the best house."

I brought the coffee outside, Lindsay the canapes.

"Leftovers, as requested."

Skye rubbed her stomach, doing a ridiculous little dance in her seat. "I love how your leftovers are more delicious than 99 percent of the food I eat."

She batted her eyelashes at me, and I just couldn't resist. I bent, kissing the side of her neck, squeezing her waist. Skye stood ramrod straight for a few seconds before relaxing into my touch.

We hadn't discussed how public our relationship should be, but as I stood up, I was pleased with the deep blush on her cheeks, and her smile.

Anne was looking at us with an amused glance. Let her figure it out... and then explain it to me too, because this was new to me.

We all sat at the table, devouring the canapes. Just as we finished, Anne's phone rang. I knew who it was without her saying anything, because my sister went from smiling to frowning in the span of a few seconds. Her shoulders slumped, and her hand hovered in the air for a bit before she turned to Lindsay.

"Honey, Dad is calling."

Lindsay squealed, immediately leaping to her feet and grabbing the phone.

She pressed it to her ear tightly. "Hi, Daddy."

That was all we heard, because she went inside the house with the phone. My eyes were trained on Anne, who was shrinking into herself with every passing second. Damn, I wanted to throttle that moron for messing with my sister.

"Anne, Rob tells me you're the CEO of Dumont Gourmet," Skye said. "I've been reading about the company. You're doing a fabulous job. And thanks for the generous donations you make for the galas each year."

"My pleasure."

"You should join us sometime. Not to sing my own praises, but they're fabulous."

"I might just come this year. My... ex wasn't a fan of charity events." Her eyes clouded again. She shook her head. "Anyway, I read that you own a lingerie business."

"That's right. Any tips, from one CEO to another?"

Anne immediately straightened up, her expression sharp and focused.

"Oh, where to begin. Any area in particular you're looking at?"

"Work-life balance?"

Anne waved her hand. "Yeah, big tip. Don't read any articles on this. They fill your head with nonsense and make you feel guilty for giving your business the best you've got. Of course some times are more demanding than others. I think the trick is... create a life you want, so you don't look forward to escaping from it, you know? Take a time-out when you need it, don't just schedule breaks."

For the next few minutes, Anne explained how she took impromptu breaks even with her crazy schedule. Skye amazed me. Somehow, she'd known exactly how to take Anne's mind off things, at least until Lindsay returned with her phone.

"Daddy wants to talk to you," she said quietly.

Anne grabbed the phone and went into the house. Lindsay climbed onto the chair she'd just vacated.

"What's up?" I asked.

"Daddy said he doesn't have time to visit next weekend. Or the one after that."

A vein thumped in my temple. If I opened my mouth, I was liable to go on a name-calling spree. I gripped the armrests of my chair tightly. Skye put one hand on my leg, squeezing a bit, then just held her hand there. It was comforting. To my surprise, the anger faded, at least enough for me to be civil in front of Lindsay.

"Work sometimes gets in the way, Lindsay," I said.

"But I was going to show Dad my new dolls and everything."

"You have new dolls? Can you show them to me?" Skye jumped in, trying to help lighten the mood.

"I only have one here. I'll get it." She slid down her chair, retrieving her doll from the play corner she'd declared as hers. Upon returning, she handed the doll to Skye.

"This is really beautiful," Skye exclaimed.

"The others are just as pretty."

"I live next door, so just tell your uncle to call me when you're here. I'd love to meet all of your dolls."

Lindsay smiled from ear to ear. "Okay."

Skye winked at me while she continued to chat with Lindsay.

I just watched her, fascinated. She truly was

saving the day, erasing the pain Lindsay's asshole of a father caused.

"Oh, by the way, your uncle bought something for you yesterday," Skye said.

I'd completely forgotten about the necklace. I went into the house, not too close to Anne so she wouldn't think I was eavesdropping. I didn't need to, anyway. Her body language gave it all away. She was hunched at the island, whispering. I knew she was hurting; Walter had done a number on her.

Gritting my teeth, I checked the pocket of my suit jacket, which was still in the living room, then returned outside with the box.

Lindsay opened it up carefully, pulling at the bow, then taking off the lid.

"Wow," she whispered, eyes wide, mouth open. "Is it magic?"

"I think it is," Skye said. "Want me to put it around your neck?"

Lindsay nodded eagerly.

Anne returned then, glancing at her daughter's new pendant. "Someone's got a present."

"Yes, I have a magic talisman now. And Skye says I can bring *all* my dolls and show them to her."

Anne laughed, glancing at Skye. "Oh, Skye. You have no idea what you've just gotten yourself into. But we have to go now. We're meeting Dawn and her mom, remember?"

Lindsay nodded, looking a bit regretfully at Skye.

I was studying my sister closely, and as I

walked her and Lindsay to the car, I pulled her to one side.

"Do I have to beat someone up?" I wasn't even joking.

She patted my shoulder. "No, just the usual. Making excuses for having no time for Lindsay. Not that much of a difference, really. She barely saw him when we were married anyway."

"Anne...."

"Don't."

"You don't even know what I was going to say."

"Offer to *talk* with the dickhead, which is code for breaking his jaw, giving him a black eye?"

"Possibly."

"See? I know you. There's nothing you can do. Except spoil us, like today. And ask Skye over too. She's fab."

I agreed 100 percent.

"Have fun in France."

"We will," she said. They were leaving tomorrow. Still frustrated at my sister's situation, I wanted to talk with her more, but Anne got in her car and drove away before I could say anything else.

I walked out to Skye, who was sitting, enjoying the sun. I kissed the side of her neck.

"You were amazing with Lindsay and especially Anne. How did you know just what to say?"

She shrugged. "Instinct, I guess? It's important to be reminded what you're great at in those moments when you doubt yourself and every decision you've ever made."

She cast her gaze down. Was she talking from experience? Who'd made her doubt herself? I wanted to make sure it never happened again.

"Did that happen to you?" I asked calmly. She straightened, opening her eyes.

"Dad left when we were little, so… yes."

"Shit."

"Mom went through a rough time, especially because she was a homemaker. But she regained her confidence bit by bit after starting her job as a teacher and realizing she was really good at it."

"Did she remarry?"

"Yeah, a few years ago. Mick is a great guy."

"Do you have any contact with your dad?"

"He did pay some child support, but since the company he'd worked for had gone bankrupt and he was unemployed, that didn't amount to much. We never saw him again though. But that was a long time ago. We moved here from Boston. He remained there."

"Your mom moved here on her own with four kids? That was brave."

Skye chuckled. "Yeah, Mom's tough like that. She also was looking after our cousin Hunter too, so technically five kids. We were all crammed in this tiny apartment. Tess and I shared a bedroom, the boys another one, and Mom slept on a pullout couch in the living room. We used to pretend the fire escape was our domain, gave the neighbors hell traipsing all around it."

"How did your mom cope with the divorce?"

"I don't think she did, honestly. The first few weeks after Dad left, she cried for hours every day. Things got a bit better after we moved to New York. I think the change in scenery helped. But there were still these moments when I could tell Mom was just gone, disappearing into her grief again. She'd stare into space, and her eyes were glassy. Tess and I learned to read those signs, and we'd quietly go with the boys to another room, to give her some space. Or... we plied her with ice cream. We adapted depending on the supplies in the freezer. But I think that time wasn't all bad, you know? We grew very close together, and it made us appreciate every little thing we had." With a grin, she added, "Cole and Ryker invented their own games that made no sense to me and Tess, but we pretended to go along with it. Anyway, I do have lots of good memories from those years."

I liked that she saw the positive side in everything. She was a dreamer but a fighter too.

Smiling, she sank lower in the chair, closing her eyes again. "This is such a gorgeous day."

"Do you have plans right now?" I asked.

She opened an eye. "I should get on with my Pilates. Have anything else in mind?"

"A few things."

She opened the other eye too, smiling. "I'm all ears. Oh, before I forget, there's a show on Broadway I want to see. I'm going with Tess and probably our almost-sister-in-law. I'm going to buy tickets on Monday. Interested?"

Pulling out her phone, she showed me the synopsis. It was an obscure one I hadn't heard about, which explained why there were still tickets available.

I kissed her forehead, then sat in the chair next to her. "Restaurant Days is coming up, so I'll barely see you for the next two weeks."

It was a fourteen-day-long festival where restaurants in New York showcased special menus to attract new clientele.

"Oh? You need to be there personally?"

"With my deadbeat of an ex-in-law quitting, it'll be good for me to be seen, give interviews, just generally be in the restaurants and greet critics."

"Makes sense."

"I'll probably sleep in Manhattan at a hotel."

"Boooo. So I won't see you run anymore?"

"It's gonna be tough to make it work."

She pouted, rising from her seat and grabbing her empty cup of coffee. "I need more of this."

"Me too. Let's go inside."

"So, what exactly did you have in mind for today?" she asked in between yawns while the coffee machine filled our cups.

I wiggled my eyebrows. "We could both go on a run. The adrenaline will wake us up."

"Pffft… that's a firm no."

"I have another proposition."

"Unfortunately, you missed your chance to impress me."

I stepped right in front of her, so close that her breasts pressed against me. I had her trapped.

"Doesn't seem like that to me."

"You just caught me by surprise."

"And that blush is because you're surprised, or because you can't wait?"

"Depends on the proposition."

"I skipped my routine last night; you skip yours now."

Skye laughed. Again. "It's all or nothing with you, huh?"

"Damn right it is."

"If you think you can make it worth my while…," she teased.

"We have a deal."

I hadn't known Skye for long, but one thing was clear: with her, I wasn't in control of myself. I wanted her in my bed. Last night we'd just slept there, but now, I wanted to sink inside her.

Laughing, she clasped her arms around my middle. First on the agenda, I was going to worship her body. We went up the stairs, straight to the master bedroom. I immediately reached for the hem of her dress, but she pushed me away. My biggest priority right now was to have her naked. She looked up at me, eyes wide and playful, clearly with other thoughts on her mind. She walked over and sat at the edge of the bed, her hand on my belt.

"I like where this is going," I said. I liked watching her take charge.

She took her time undoing my belt, tugging

down my pants. I took off my shirt, watching her face as she smiled, tracing a finger down my chest, slowing as she continued farther down. I was already hard, my erection just in front of her. She moved her finger up the length of it, right to the tip.

Lowering her mouth to my cock, she took it all in, wrapping her hand at the base. I rocked back and forth, gritting my jaw so hard that my teeth were grinding. The urge to claim her escalated instantly.

I drew my fingers up her neck to the back of her head, moving my hips. I was going to explode, and I wanted to be buried deep inside her when that happened.

"Lie on the bed," I said.

She didn't, ignoring my request as she just licked around the tip, her eyes playful.

"Skye. Bed. Now." I was losing control and needed her obedience.

Pouting, she leaned back on her elbows, watching me hungrily. Then she sat back up, taking off her dress. I couldn't decide what was sexier, Skye in that white lace, semitransparent bra and panties or Skye naked.

Instinct took over. I barely remembered that we needed protection.

"I have condoms in my bathroom. I'll get them. Stay here."

"Not going anywhere."

I was excited at the prospect of spending the whole weekend with her, happy she and Tess were delegating both days to their sales associates. I was usually happy with keeping everything casual and not defining the parameters of a relationship. But now, I wanted more with Skye, and I wanted to shed my old ways. They felt like a suit I'd outgrown.

Chapter Sixteen
Rob

On Monday, I kick-started Restaurant Days with a board meeting. Frowning, I glanced around the table. I'd lost my train of thought. *Again.* Everyone in the boardroom was giving me strange looks, because this was very unlike me. I didn't lose focus, didn't forget what I was talking about *while* talking. I was known for my sharpness and shrewdness. I had to stop rehashing the weekend in my mind, incredible as it had been. Skye was occupying my every thought. Usually, I had no problems leaving my personal life at the door before stepping into the office. But things were changing—I had to pull myself together before I made an ass out of myself in front of everyone. I didn't want to lose credibility in front of the team. Once again, I'd gathered management as well as chefs and sous-chefs to discuss the week and our goals for the event.

"I'll be making the rounds at the different restaurants in New York these two weeks," I said. "My schedule will be sent to all of you so you can keep track of me. Keep an eye on the ones where I'm not, make sure everything runs smoothly—that means that the critics are pleased, but more importantly, that customers are happy. Got it?"

Quite frankly, I didn't care much about critics. They'd always find something to criticize, but customers were our bread and butter. When they thought about their *favorite* restaurant where they were guaranteed delicious food and a great time, I wanted them to visualize one of *ours*. Restaurant Days always took place at the end of July. It was a staple in the city's life, and I wanted everyone to remember that we were the best.

"Do you want the chefs to stay behind the scenes or also mingle with the customers?" Tatiana asked. She was the chef of our largest restaurant and had been with the company for as long as I had. She'd even been in LA for a year but then came back here, declaring she was too much of a New Yorker to be able to withstand the LA scene. She'd also been the one to blow the whistle on Walter when she'd caught him banging another chef.

"Play it by ear. Tell the staff to feel out the mood."

"Got it."

"Okay, that's a wrap, everyone," I declared.

There was a screeching sound as everyone pushed their chairs back. I arranged a dislodged cuff link as everyone filtered out.

Well, I'd saved that well. Sure enough, my brain had already switched to replaying the weekend. I chuckled at myself. I was addicted to Skye.

"What's got you so chirpy today?" Tatiana asked. I hadn't realized she'd lingered.

"Mind your own business." I was only semi-serious.

"I will, as soon as you tell me what's got you so upbeat."

I glared at her.

"Who is she?"

"Who said it's a woman?" I asked, utterly perplexed.

"Call it sixth sense, intuition, whatever." She shifted her weight from one foot to the other, her smile fading. "How is Anne?"

That was the real reason she'd stayed back.

"Moving on."

"Sometimes I wonder if I did the right thing."

"You did," I assured her.

"But she's avoiding me... I think. She's my friend, and I just don't know how to reach out to her after all that's happened."

"Tatiana, give her a bit of time. She doesn't blame you."

"She avoids me."

"She's in France now. I'm sure she'll have moved on even more once she and Lindsay get back."

They'd gone to high school together, and their friendship went way back. I was sure my sister was grateful to Tatiana, but I could also understand why she wouldn't want her close right now. I believed the *don't kill the messenger* saying, but I didn't think it was that black and white. Tatiana was a reminder of everything that went down, and that was something

Anne didn't need right now.

"Okay, well… whenever she's ready, or if she needs anything, I'm here for her."

"I'll let her know."

"Thanks. Oh, and don't think I forgot about your mystery woman. I'll get it out of you eventually."

"Tatiana! Work. Now." I couldn't help but smile though, and it was all Skye's fault.

"I'm going. I'm going."

I surveyed my agenda for the next two weeks, thankful to my assistant for making reservations at a hotel for me in Manhattan. My days started at six o' clock, and from previous experience I knew they'd last until past midnight.

I didn't like that I wasn't going to see much of Skye for the next two weeks. I wanted her to know that I was constantly thinking about her. Would she relax on her own, without me there?

We'd had a fantastic time together, and I didn't want her to forget it. I just had to make sure I was front and center in her mind for the following weeks.

***

Skye

On Monday, I was at the store one hour before our opening time, preparing for the week.

I was in the back, working on a backlog of tasks until Tess called me up front.

"We just got this." She held up an envelope as I approached the counter.

"Open it up." I drummed my fingers against my thighs, giddy with excitement.

Tess did just that. "We got tickets to the Broadway play tonight! Did you order them?"

"No, I'd meant to, but…. *Oh my God.* I think Rob sent them."

Tess looked up, and we both had widespread grins. "Holy shit, I'm his fan already."

"You and me both, sis."

I couldn't help myself and took the tickets from her hand, surveying them, then turning them over, as if expecting to find a few words from Rob scribbled there or something.

I immediately reached for my phone, calling Rob. He didn't pick up though. I sent him a message instead.

Skye: WE GOT THE TICKETS. THANK YOU 😊

I wasn't just giddy now, I was honestly euphoric. He'd sent us three tickets, as I'd told him that I was going with Tess and Heather—but unfortunately, our future sister-in-law couldn't join us anymore. I was already wondering who else from the family would like to come with us.

In the afternoon, we switched spots, and Tess worked in the back while I tended to customers. Jane joined us too—she was closing this evening, since Tess and I were going to the show. Usually I didn't keep my phone on me when I was in the front, but today, I chose to forget that rule. I kept the phone in the back pocket of my jeans, just in case Rob wrote back.

He didn't though, until Tess and I headed out to Broadway.

I loved the city this time of year. Everyone was in vacation mode, and it showed. The streets were crowded, and everyone looked more relaxed, especially in the evening.

Rob: This is the first break I got. Enjoy the play. Sorry I can't be there.

Skye: The first break??? Holy shit, that's intense.

Rob: And I'm still looking at another five solid hours.

Skye: Maybe I can use some of your... methods... to help you unwind tonight?

Rob: I'm staying at the hotel.

Awww, I'd forgotten about that completely.

Tess glanced at me as we stood in line. No, *inspected* me was a more appropriate word.

"What?" I asked.

"Trying to figure out what's got you in a twist."

Oh well, might as well admit it. The family knew how deep I was into him. "Won't see Rob for two weeks. He's staying in Manhattan during the festival."

"He's got a place here too?"

"No, a hotel."

My sister narrowed her eyes, glancing at me intently. "Okay, let's do this."

"Tess…." I knew what was coming, but I couldn't stop it. I was going to be on the receiving end of one of her *detective actions*.

"You miss him. That's so cute." She wiggled her eyebrows. "You could crash his hotel room. Just saying. I'm sure he won't mind."

"I don't want to cramp his style." Also, I wasn't sure we were at that point. What if I was butting in and he needed his space?

I mulled this over as we walked toward the venue. Halfway there, Cole called Tess.

"Hey, we're heading there now," she said. "What do you mean you're coming too? You don't like plays."

Tess blinked at me. I shrugged. We'd told him this afternoon that we had plans for the evening and a spare ticket.

"Mmm, sure, we'll wait for you in front." Pocketing her phone, she glanced at me. "What's up with Cole?"

"No clue, but we'll find out soon enough."

As we waited in front of the venue, Cole joined us. We still had twenty minutes until the play started, so we headed to a street vendor and indulged in our guilty pleasure, hot dogs. I ordered mine with extra ketchup and mustard. Cole was suspiciously silent as we headed back outside, standing as we devoured our food.

"What do you think?" Tess asked me in a

conspiratorial tone. "Cole wants advice? Consolation?"

I surveyed my brother, trying to get a feel for the situation. There was something different about him.

"Maybe I just want to enjoy an evening with my sisters," he said playfully, mustard dripping down his chin.

Tess whirled a finger at him. "You would've just offered to join us for drinks afterward. Instead you're willing to suffer through a play."

"Okay, maybe you're right," Cole admitted. I handed him a napkin, indicating his chin, and he wiped himself clean.

Tess clapped her hands, nearly dropping her hot dog.

I giggled at my sister's enthusiasm, then asked Cole, "How can we help?"

"I don't recognize myself."

Tess and I glanced at one another in awe.

"Meaning?"

"There's this woman I met recently…." He shook his head.

"What's the trouble?" I pressed.

"I keep asking her out. She turns me down. My womanizer reputation isn't doing me any favors," he said.

This was so different to Cole's MO, all cocky swagger and an extra dose of confidence, that I was thrown off.

"Ouch. Honestly, I'm not sure how to fix

that."

Cole glared at me, finished up the last of his hot dog, then said, "You're no help."

Tess held up a finger. "Let's think about this from another perspective. If I were in her shoes, and some guy with a shady reputation asked me out, I'd be reluctant too. *But*, if he proved he really did just want me... maybe I'd give it a shot."

"Prove how?" Cole asked as I grabbed our trash and threw it into a nearby can.

"You know, by not being flirty with everyone in sight, things like that."

"Tell us about her," I encouraged. "Maybe then we can give you more tips on how to *charm* her."

I was teasing him about his nickname, the Charmer, to egg him on, but also just to make him smile.

It worked. Cole straightened up, wiggling his eyebrows.

"Hey, I've still got game," he said with a grin. "Just need to learn the rules of this one first."

"Damn, I never thought I'd see the day when you'd be willing to change your rules for anyone." Then again, this time with Rob had made me think that maybe I could have a normal relationship. The man was just so amazing that it was impossible not to get carried away. I found myself smiling just because I was thinking about him.

"Please don't tell Ryker. He'll give me so much shit." Cole looked at me pointedly.

"Can't. The no-secret policy runs so deep in

me, it's practically part of my DNA."

Tess laughed. "Besides, we do like it when Ryker gives you shit." She nudged his shoulder, saying, "Are we terrible or what?"

"Yes, yes you are," Cole exclaimed as we approached the theater entrance. "Come on, let's go in and find our seats."

Tess and I each took one of his arms, flanking him as we headed inside. We loved plays and musicals.

At the end of the show, the audience hollered for an encore, which would probably be another twenty minutes or so. I looked at my siblings, and they appeared ready to go. "Let's ditch it."

Tess took one look at Cole and nodded. Making our way out was not easy, climbing over everyone as we tried to scoot out, which attracted a lot of attention. A few swore at us, and I honestly couldn't blame them. It was dark when we stepped outside, but the sheer number of people milling up and down Broadway had increased. Manhattan was even more alive in the evenings during summer.

"You're making me feel really special," Cole said. "I know how much you girls like to watch these things until the end."

"We won't kick you while you're down," Tess teased. "We've already tormented you enough."

"Much appreciated. Anyone up for cotton candy?" Cole said, pointing to a street vendor with a mobile cart under one of the streetlights. He must have just pulled up, because we hadn't seen him there before.

The smell of sugar was thick in the air. My stomach rumbled despite being full, and I found myself nodding right away. There was a line already, and while we waited, I took out my phone, texting Rob, wondering if he was still working. I just couldn't stop thinking about him.

I only looked up when I realized my siblings were suspiciously silent, and I found them watching me intently.

"What?" I asked.

Tess grinned from ear to ear, nudging our brother. "See? That's what a woman who can't take her mind off her guy looks like. So caught up in texting him, she forgets the world."

"I'm taking notes," Cole said with mock seriousness, and the three of us burst out laughing. What could I say? My sister was 100 percent spot on.

Chapter Seventeen
Skye

Rob: How was the play?

I read his message just as I slid under my covers.

Skye: It was amazing. Thank you for the tickets. Cole joined us too. You're so thoughtful.

Rob: Did it for selfish reasons.

Skye: Oh?

Rob: Wanted to make sure you don't forget me these two weeks.

Wow. My heart rate sped up so quickly that I almost hyperventilated. I called him, because it was easier than just typing back and forth.

"You're difficult to forget," I said. There weren't more than ten minutes this entire evening that I didn't have Rob on my mind. The play didn't even capture my full attention, which told me how wrapped up I was in this man.

"And why is that?"

"I can't tell, exactly." And that was the truth. Besides, we were not at that stage in a relationship where I would tell him even if I could.

"Then I haven't done the job right, impressed you enough." Rob's voice was deliciously sensual.

"Hmmm... I feel like the kind thing to do is to tell you that you more than impressed me...."

"Good, but there's so much more I've planned."

"Are you wooing me, kind sir?"

"How can you tell?" he asked.

"You have that alpha thing going on."

He chuckled in a way that made my body tingle. "You're right. Did you relax at least?"

"Definitely. One of the reasons I like to watch plays is that they require my full concentration and then block out any other thoughts." Except those of Rob, it seemed. "How was your day?"

"Still not over. I'm on a break, which is just about to end."

"Wow. I'll leave you, then. Don't work too hard."

"Skye, I'm glad you called."

I squirmed in my bed, my body feeling almost a physical ache at his voice.

"Have fun for the rest of the evening."

"You too. Dream about me. Good night."

Oh yeah... I was definitely going to dream about him.

I fell asleep with Rob on my mind and woke up the same way. How was this sexy man hijacking my thoughts all the time? That was a feat no one before him had succeeded in doing.

"You've got an important meeting ahead," I told myself in the mirror while I smeared body oil with an orange aroma on my legs. I had a system for almost everything. Relaxing lavender body oil before going to bed and invigorating orange oil before going out of the house in the morning. "You need to focus. Don't let anyone hijack your thoughts again."

I didn't go directly to the store. I was meeting our website designer downtown to discuss some budget changes. Since we updated products routinely and ran sales on older merchandise, she had to make changes on the go all the time, and the costs were adding up.

I loved handling this, and so did Tess. Every day was a new day, nothing mundane about retail. She always said whenever we needed to break some news to our business partners, "You do it, you're more efficient. When the dragon side of you shows, no one dares contradict you."

Our website designer, Maisie, was waiting for me in our go-to coffee shop in Bryant Park, sitting outside on the comfy couches. If given the choice, I always preferred a spot in the sun as opposed to inside.

"Morning, Skye," Maisie greeted. "Already ordered your favorite."

"Thanks, Maisie, you didn't have to. How are you, good?"

"Fine, things are okay. Let's get straight to business, okay?" Maisie smiled, but she was less bubbly than usual. She seemed a little pale too.

"I like your efficiency."

I got out my laptop, opening the budget spreadsheet. "Okay, so I know Tess and I wanted each sale to have a different layout on the website, but making those changes costs so much. Can we just get a template we can use for every sale?"

"Theoretically, yes... but it's all going to look the same."

"Big retailers do that too, so I think consumers are used to it. And we really want to cut costs."

"Okay." She sighed, writing a few notes on her iPad. Something was definitely off. I kept my voice firm, but I wasn't inconsiderate or mean, so I didn't think her mood was just because of our conversation. No, something was wrong before I got here.

"Maisie, are you okay? You seem a little out of sorts."

"Oh, it's that obvious?" Biting her lip, she added, "I've just broken up with my boyfriend."

I winced. "Awww, girl. I'm so sorry. Do you want to talk about it?"

"Hell no. Don't have time to talk. Or even breathe."

"But you won't say no to an ice caramel Frappuccino with extra topping, will you? I'm buying."

Maisie laughed, seeming to loosen up a bit. "Sure. I'd rather have that than this coffee. Thanks, Skye."

We ended up ordering a sugary drink each.

Despite having a million things to do, I just didn't have it in me to leave her alone.

We parted ways one hour later, and I rushed to the store. When I arrived, Tess was busy with two customers and mouthed to me, "Go to the back."

I nodded. Wait… what was that twinkle in my sister's eyes? Hmmm… she was up to something, I was sure of it, but I headed to the back anyway.

Holy shit, there was a mountain of merchandise to be sorted. Jane wasn't coming until the evening, so I rolled up my proverbial sleeves and got to work. Truthfully, no matter how dull the task, there was this sense of accomplishment that no one could take from me. It was something Tess and I had built together; it was ours, only ours. We'd already survived an investor ditching us and a business partner trying to scam us before that. I'd almost thrown in the towel any number of times, but Mom had given me some tough love.

She'd been very supportive of the business from the start. "Your business can't wake up one morning and decide it doesn't love you anymore" had been her mantra since Dad left. My Mom was the strongest woman I knew, raising us on her own. I wished she'd slow down a bit now, considering she was in her seventies. She could retire but chose not to, most likely because Mick was still working. His job as a concert organizer took him all around the country.

When I paused for a few minutes to rest, I discovered I had a message from Rob.

Rob: How is the feisty lady today?
Skye: In a frenzy.
Rob: I can try to drop by the store for a quick dinner if you have time. It's the only free evening I have.

And he was choosing to spend it with me? I had butterflies in my stomach.

Skye: YES, YES, YES.
Rob: I like your enthusiasm.
Skye: :-)

To my astonishment, I was twice as fast with the next few boxes. Channeling butterflies into nervous energy? Maybe. I grinned, placing a palm on my stomach. I couldn't believe I was so full of fuzzy feelings. I was going to see him today!

When I felt as if my arms were about to fall off, I joined Tess in the front of the store. She was changing the bra on the mannequin next to the counter.

"Can we finish sorting out the merchandise later? We only have two boxes left."

"Sure." Tess was all smiles. And that fishy look in her eyes I'd spotted in the morning was still there.

"What?" I asked.

"Nothing."

I pointed at her. "That's not a *nothing* face. You can't fool me."

"Fine, it's not nothing, but that doesn't mean you need to know about it."

I jerked my head back. "Hey, you came up with the no-secrets policy."

And I lived by it. So did Tess... at least, I'd been under that impression.

She shrugged, smoothing the silky robe on the mannequin before refastening the belt, even though she'd just done that and it had looked perfect. *Aha!* She was avoiding my eyes too.

"Let's grab something to eat. I'm starving," I said, deciding to drop the subject. I needed a new angle, and I couldn't come up with it if I was hungry. This was going to be super late lunch for us.

"Sure, I'll get us something. Tacos, pizza? Or want to try a burrito from that new food truck?"

"Yeah, let's try that and give the guy some business."

Before we ventured into entrepreneurship, I'd been a creature of habit: always ordered from my favorite restaurants, went shopping at my usual stores. Afterward, I opened myself up to new experiences.

"I want extra cilantro with a side of cilantro," I said.

Tess shuddered. It was one of the few things we disagreed on. She insisted it tasted like soap. I claimed it was the best herb.

"Oh my God, this is to die for," I exclaimed twenty minutes later as we were both devouring burritos.

"I know, right? We need to take this to a

working lunch." My family would love this.

"I was just thinking about that."

"Was there a line?" I asked, keeping my fingers crossed for a yes. The guy really deserved to sell out.

"Unfortunately, no, but it's still early in his business. He's super nice. And hot, and single."

I laughed. "How did you find that out in the time it took you to order?"

"Well, I only needed two seconds to figure out the hot part. He just gives off a nice vibe, and I told him his girlfriend would get a discount at our store. He said he wasn't seeing anyone."

"Damn, you're efficient."

"I know, right?" She did a small pirouette, laughing. "Who knows, maybe he and I will click."

"Oh, Tess."

She had a dreamy smile on her face.

The other thing we didn't see eye to eye on? *Love.*

Even though Tess had taken Dad's leaving harder, she still believed in love... more than I did, at any rate. She had dreams of big weddings and huge families, and I tried to keep my expectations low.

"Sooo... since you're in such a great mood, want to tell me why you're so secretive?"

I was betting on the fact that our delicious lunch would loosen her tongue.

She rolled her eyes. "It's nothing. I'm just observing some interesting changes about you."

I tried not to look too pleased that my bet had

been so spot on.

"And what's the verdict?"

She shook her head. "None yet. Still in observation phase."

"I see. Well, you can add to your pool of data that Rob will stop by with dinner tonight."

"Oh, duly noted."

The rest of the afternoon just flew by, and it had been one of our best days yet. Damn, I was sure my good mood was having a magic effect on my clients, because I managed to upsell a lot more than usual.

At six o'clock, my phone beeped with an incoming message.

Rob: Can't make it after all. Got a last-minute meeting. I'll make it up to you, I promise.

Oh no. My stomach bottomed out. I'd been looking forward to our dinner *so* much. I swear, even my heart seemed a little heavier. I couldn't believe I was so disheartened.

All of my past relationships had ended in disappointment, but I tried to channel Tess's optimism. Besides, this was different. Rob seemed to legitimately care. He wanted to see me again, but he was just having a tough week. I needed to get out of this melancholy.

Pasting a smile on my face, I turned to my sister.

"Looks like Rob can't make it after all."

"Oh no." Pouting, she placed both hands on my face and pressed her forehead to mine. "What do you say to another serving of burrito?"

"I'm in."

***

On Friday, I officially had Rob withdrawals, which was why I had the crazy thought of surprising him tonight. He'd told me which restaurant he was at, so after closing the store, I stopped by Ladurée to grab some macarons and then headed to Tribeca. The closer I got, the giddier I felt.

This whole week he'd been texting me, sending me pics of dishes, the crowds—his week had been crazy, yet he was thoughtful enough to text me.

The restaurant was so packed that I could barely make out anything, let alone spot Rob... or find a table. It took a lot of eyelash batting and begging to convince the guy at the entrance to let me in even though I didn't have a reservation.

After some more eyelash batting, they showed me to a tiny bar table against the wall that only had space to seat one person.

Wow, this place was amazing. Even though it was packed and the noise level was beyond loud, I loved it. It had a high ceiling, with warm lighting coming from modern light installations and cozy red brick window arches. It was a contemporary look decorating a very old interior—nice. At the very back was the kitchen, which was open for everyone to see.

You could even sit at the counter there and watch the chefs in action. To my surprise, Rob was one of the chefs. He hadn't told me that *he'd* be cooking. He was explaining something to one of the cooks, but of course I couldn't hear anything from where I was seated.

I left the Ladurée bag of sweets on my seat and made my way through the crowd. The closer I got, the heavier the air was with delicious aromas.

I just watched Rob, committing every detail to my memory. Damn, he was even sexier cooking in front of a large crowd than at home. He had a white apron on embroidered with the name of the restaurant, Dumont's. Charisma poured off him as he explained the easiest way to prepare a shrimp salad.

"The secret ingredient to every salad tasting more delicious is… parmesan," he said. I realized he had a small mic clipped to his collar. Everyone laughed. But I was with him on that; even though it was a simple ingredient, parmesan was the best—if only it didn't have a million calories.

He noticed me, and at once, his smile changed. I couldn't tell how, but it matched that predatory glance in his gaze, making me squirm as heat coursed through me. Not even the three rows of people between us were enough buffer for his smolder. He whispered to a member of staff standing nearby before starting with the next course.

Two minutes later, one of the servers approached me.

"Ms. Winchester, Rob asked for you to come

with me."

"Oh, thank you. I have a bag I left on my seat."

"We'll bring it to you." He smiled as he prompted me forward. "This way, please."

"Oh, well, okay, that's great."

I was led to a fantastic table on the right side of the kitchen, where I had an amazing view of Rob.

"How is this table even available?" I asked in amazement.

She winked at me. "We always keep two great tables open just in case a notorious critic or a business partner decides to stop by spontaneously. Would you like to eat something?"

"Yes, what do you recommend?"

"We have a tasting menu this week. You can order individual courses or the entire menu, and then you'll get smaller portions of everything, like small plates."

"Oh, that sounds perfect. I'll take the whole thing."

Indulging in delicious food while watching this delicious man? Yes, please.

When Rob trained his gaze on me, I winked at him. It was a good thing he'd gotten me this swanky table, because this would probably take another few hours. I felt so VIP, especially when the server returned with my Ladurée bag and a bottle of Dom Perignon, pouring me a full glass.

"On the house."

The menu was absolutely delicious. I wasn't

even sure what some of the items were, but the flavors just blended perfectly in my mouth. I was watching Rob more than what I was eating anyway.

Every time he glanced over, he had a protective look, sultry maybe—I wasn't sure, but I felt special to him, like I never had with anyone else before.

This was so unlike me, just showing up here without a plan. I usually liked to know everything ten steps in advance. I didn't consider myself impulsive or spontaneous… but I just liked doing this because it was for Rob.

When one of his other chefs took over the main demonstration, Rob texted me.

Rob: Why didn't you tell me you were coming?

Skye: Decided just before I came over.

Rob: Stay until the end.

Skye: That's what I intend.

Rob: It's gonna take a few more hours, but I'll make it worth the wait.

Skye: I'm counting on it.

He looked up from his phone, and I could swear his gaze darkened. Even from this distance, I felt there was something feral in it. I averted my gaze after a few seconds, feeling flushed and turned on.

His alpha vibes were potent even from a distance. On second thought… Dom Perignon might have contributed to my susceptibility. The servers had been refilling my glass, so I wasn't totally sure how much I'd drunk. I took another sip, hoping to cool off from Rob's attention. It worked... right until I looked up again and Rob trapped my gaze in his once more. It was full of delicious promises. I'd shown up here to surprise him, but I had a suspicion that I was the one about to be surprised tonight.

Chapter Eighteen
Rob

I loved seeing Skye in the crowd.

It hadn't been part of the plan for me to be a front man tonight, but one of the chefs had a cold, so I stepped in.

After midnight, the crowd thinned... but not enough for me to just throw Skye over my shoulder and get the hell out of here. I had to make do with glimpses of her and quick text messages.

"We have one more dish to walk the crowd through," my sous-chef said. I nodded, getting back to work. I felt just as comfortable in a suit as in a chef's uniform. I liked mixing things up. This was a welcome change from numbers, spreadsheets, meetings, setting goals, and bossing everyone into doing their jobs.

Here it was just me, the ingredients, and the kitchen utensils. The simplicity and repetitive nature of it relaxed me. The added task of explaining each step to the audience wasn't a problem... except that now I couldn't look at this counter and not imagine all the ways I could have Skye on it. I'd trail my mouth all over her delicious little body.

Later!

I shook my head, trying to dispel the shockingly clear and vivid image.

Once the last dish was over, the patrons left in droves, as did the critics. As usual, only our business partners stayed until the end, or those who hoped to do business with us.

I knew their game. They hoped to sway me into buying more product by offering larger discounts. If you were good, everyone wanted a piece of you or your success. That was okay with me, because it was when they didn't come calling that you had to worry.

They were going to leave disappointed. Two things had led to Dumont Foods growing by leaps and bounds since I took over.

One: I was a tough negotiator.

Two: I liked setting goals and was relentless in my pursuit of them.

The second I joined the crowd, a supplier approached me.

"Robert. Good to see you back."

"Happy to be in New York again."

"Think we can talk about a discount offer I've got for your restaurants over a few drinks?"

"You know my policy. No negotiations happen outside meeting rooms," I said coolly, leveling him with a stare. *Come on, you gave it a shot. Now go.*

When he finally left, the place was empty except for Skye and me. The staff had gone—they'd already cleaned while I was preparing the last dish. I crooked a finger at Skye. She shook her head, mirroring my gesture with a sassy smile. I walked right to her table.

"Hello, stranger," she murmured.

Instead of greeting her, I just captured her mouth, not holding back anything, tugging at her lower lip. I forced my hands to stay firmly on her waist, or I risked cinching her dress up and making a spectacle of us both. I was starved for her, and when the lights switched off, I dug my fingers in her waist, pulling her to the edge of her seat, parting her thighs and stepping between them. I could feel my self-control slip away, so I reluctantly stopped the kiss.

Eyes still closed, Skye hummed low in her throat. She blinked them open, smiling.

"I didn't know you'd also be cooking."

"A staff member was sick, so I took over, but I do that sometimes anyway. I like it. On occasion I'll even go in the restaurants and work side by side with the team. I like feeling the pulse of the restaurant—also helps me gauge if the team is happy, if the customers are satisfied."

"That's very smart. I bet it's relaxing for you too. At least, you looked relaxed from where I was watching."

"It is."

I liked that she understood me so well—how I ticked, what was important to me, that she wasn't looking down on the work in the kitchen the way some of my peers did.

"So... I remember you promising to make it

worth the wait," she said playfully.

"I keep my word, Skye."

"Before I forget, these are for you."

She held up a bag from Ladurée.

"Buying from the competition?" I teased.

She blushed. "Oh… I didn't think about that. Umm… they're not really competition though."

"I'm joking, Skye. I like their macarons."

I liked even more that she'd done this tonight. She'd come here for me.

"Good to know. This place is incredible. I can't believe I haven't been here before. And such a smart idea, to have part of the kitchen visible to the public."

"Want a tour?" I asked.

"Sure."

"I'll just get rid of the apron first."

I took it off, placing it in the pile with the rest of the soiled linens. Underneath I wore my white broadcloth dress shirt and grabbed my suit jacket, which was hanging inside a special cupboard I'd designed. Stuffing my tie in my suit jacket, I took Skye's hand and led her through the kitchen islands. I pointed out the various workstations the chefs maintained, mentioning their responsibilities and why the counter space was arranged as it was, in straight lines. It all was situated to improve the flow of food in a timely manner so when the dinner was completed, it was warm and ready for its customer.

"As a kid, I came here a lot. I didn't go home after school, just hung around here."

"Helping out?"

"When I was old enough, yeah. As a kid, I just liked being in the middle of it all, even though I was mostly a pain in the ass." We chuckled at my comment.

"So your parents were hands-on like you as well?"

"Yes. Besides, back then, the offices were in this building too, on the upper level. We just keep one here now; the rest are in the new headquarters. We can go upstairs after the tour."

Skye skimmed one hand along the stone counters, smiling.

"You're the third generation of Dumonts doing this, right?" she asked.

"Yes. Grandpa started as a chef before opening a restaurant. Worked right until he couldn't keep up with his sous-chefs. Says arthritis doesn't belong in the kitchen."

"Seems like he had a bit of humor," Skye said, hopping on one of the counters.

"Has. Still very much alive. He's ninety-three."

"Holy shit," she exclaimed. "Those are some awesome genes."

I chuckled. "He says one teaspoon of butter a day keeps the doctor away."

"Is he in New York?"

"Nah, he's originally from France, and he went back there after retiring. My parents are also there."

"You're half French?" she asked. "I mean… duh. Your last name is Dumont."

"A quarter."

"Do you speak it?"

"A bit."

"Say something to me." Her eyes were full of excitement.

"*Tu m'as tellement manqué*. Means I've missed you so much."

"Your sexiness score just skyrocketed."

"I didn't know it needed improvement."

"Ha! It certainly didn't. On a scale from one to ten, it used to be on fifteen."

"And now?"

She frowned, drumming her fingers over her cheek. "Hmm… not sure. Somewhere between twenty and twenty-five."

I laughed, leaning against the counter. Skye pointed to a leather-bound notebook we'd framed on that wall. "What's that?"

"A notebook with the original recipes. We still cook some of them, but they're modified. We want to show homage to our history but keep up with the times."

"Smart. I bet your family is really proud of you."

"I think they are. I hope so."

She studied me for a beat before saying, "That's very important for you, isn't it?"

I couldn't tell how she'd guessed that, but I nodded.

"Yes. It's not even the money driving me—or not *just* the money. I want to create something long-lasting… you know, for future generations."

That thought had popped in my mind unexpectedly. I'd never thought about the future generation except for Lindsay… until now.

"Keep the legacy going on and growing," she finished.

"Yes, exactly."

I liked that she wanted to know more about my family, that she was curious and cared. Most of all, I liked that she understood what drove me.

"Want to see the office?" I asked.

"Sure."

Taking her hand, I led her up a narrow spiral staircase and then opened the door to my office. The windows were red brick arches, as they were downstairs, but that was the only similarity. A leather couch and office chair and a huge mahogany desk took up the entire space. I was rarely here, but it had every comfort I wanted.

"Oh, Rob, I love this place. It's so… alluring." She went straight to the desk. "Oh, I like this so much."

I walked up behind her, pushing her hair to one side, kissing her upper back, drawing my fingers up her arms. I touched my lips to her skin, then my tongue. Goose bumps rose on her arms. I smiled against her back. Her reaction to me was just so damn intoxicating.

"Rob…," she whispered.

I moved my mouth to her shoulder, pushing the strap of her dress to one side before applying the same treatment to her other shoulder. Gripping one of her hips, I pulled her into me, pressing my cock against her ass. She gasped when she felt my hard-on.

"I want you so fucking much," I said. She reached back, tugging at my pants, as if she wanted to yank them off. I couldn't wait to oblige her. I kissed up her neck to her ear. "Je pense toujours à toi."

"What does it mean?"

"I always think about you."

"I'm all yours tonight." Her tone was sassy, but I wanted to make one thing clear. Turning her around, I looked straight into her eyes.

"Skye, you and me... we're exclusive."

Her eyes widened. I needed to know that she was in agreement.

"I'm not sharing you. Not your body or any part of you."

Her eyes flashed. I drew my thumb over her lower lip, pressing at one corner before capturing her mouth. She kissed me back hard.

I spoke against her lips.

"Just you and me, understood?" My words were almost a growl, but she nodded. "I'll fuck you right here on this desk, Skye. Every time I'm here, I'll think about you naked on it, begging for my cock."

Skye let out a sound between a whimper and a moan. She wanted this just as much as I did. I lifted her ass on the desk so we were at the same level before kissing her hard and deep again.

She was working my belt, undoing the zipper of my pants. I liked that she took what she wanted.

I stepped back, looking her up and down. I wanted to explore her inch by inch... I just had to decide where to start.

She pouted, making a come-here motion with her finger. My sassy spitfire.

"Patience," I murmured.

She pouted even more. I hitched her dress up her thighs, then past her ass.

I skimmed two fingers between her legs, drawing them along the hem of her panties. She squirmed at my touch, holding her breath. I teased her, moving my fingers to touch the elastic seam under her belly before dipping inside her panties. Skye kissed my jaw down to my Adam's apple.

I groaned at how wet she was already and felt her smile against my neck. I drew small circles around her clit, feeling her become even more turned on. I didn't want her to come like this though. I wanted her naked, pressed against me, having as much skin-on-skin contact as possible. I stopped touching her and stepped back. Skye hopped down from the desk, pushing my jacket over my shoulders, discarding it on the chair. My shirt went next. She slowed down when she reached for the belt again, kissing my chest as she undid the buckle. She went lower, teasing my nipples. I gripped a handful of her hair, watching her intently. When she was low enough that her chin pressed under my navel, she looked up at me. My erection pulsed against her throat. I lifted her back up before pushing down my pants. She then yanked down my boxers, lowering herself on her haunches as I stepped out of them. She licked once along my cock, from the base all the way to the tip.

"Fuuuuck."

I was naked, but she was still wearing all her clothes. I rectified that the next second, yanking her dress over her head. I nearly came just seeing her lingerie. She wore a black bra and panties that were almost see-through.

"You've been wearing this the whole evening."

"Yup."

"Good thing I didn't know. Take them off, Skye."

She ran her hands seductively over her breasts to undo the clasp between them. I grabbed a condom from my wallet, sliding it on. I swallowed hard, watching Skye intently. She lowered her panties down her legs with exquisite slowness.

While she was bent, I went behind her and ran a finger over her spine. She gasped, wobbling in surprise. Gripping her hips, I steadied her. When she rose, I pressed her against me. We were both naked, and the contact was just driving me insane. My cock was trapped between us. Pressing down the middle of her back, I bent her over the desk, kissing her body, pausing every few inches to take in her reactions. I parted her thighs, drawing my fingers between them. I skimmed my fingers up and down along her entrance until goose bumps broke out on her ass. Then I touched her clit with light strokes, watching her writhe against the desk—her fingers pressed against the hard wood.

"Ah." Her moan was laced with frustration at not being able to hold on to something. Pulling back, I searched the pocket of my jacket for my tie, handing it to her.

"Do whatever you want with this," I said in her ear.

I wouldn't be able to be in this room again and not think about this moment: Skye naked, bent over my desk, hanging on to my tie. Bending over her to kiss the back of her neck, I pushed my cock between her thighs, rubbing the length of it along her entrance. I was teasing and tempting her but not penetrating. The tremor in her body intensified in anticipation. She was hot and wet, and I couldn't wait to be inside her.

"Let's move to the couch," I murmured. "I want you to be comfortable."

She pushed herself off the desk, turning around to face me. I kissed her the next second. I needed her mouth. I needed all of her.

Walking her backward, I led her to the couch. She tumbled onto it, laughing, pulling me on top of her. I propped my arms at her sides, holding myself up so I didn't crush her.

She laughed, looking around. She'd dropped the tie halfway to the couch, but she didn't need it now. She could scratch her nails into the couch any way she wanted... *or me.*

"Mr. Dumont, you're being bad. Defiling your office like this."

Pushing myself back on my knees, I drew my hands down her inner thighs, from her apex to her knees, then to her ankles. Lifting them up, I propped one on my shoulder, the other on the backrest. I liked seeing her like this, ready for anything I wanted to do.

I kneaded her ass cheeks, pulling her closer to my cock. I slid in the tip, watching her shutter her eyes, her nostrils flare.

"Rob...."

Tilting forward, I drove inside her inch by inch, trying to breathe through the pleasure. It was impossible. When I was inside her to the hilt, her inner muscles clenched tight around me.

"Fuck," I whispered. "Fuck, fuck, fuck."

She lowered her foot from the backrest, propping it on the couch, moving her hips upward, meeting the rhythm of my thrusts. I lowered her other leg too, leaning over her, drawing the tip of my nose over her chest and neck, just wanting more of her. I kissed her long and deep, and somehow, the pleasure intensified. She pulsed tighter around me; I moved faster, stroked deeper, my balls thrusting forward with each movement, connecting with her ass. I wanted to reach between us to touch her clit, but my balance would be too precarious if I did that. Instead, I pulled out of her, changing our position. I was on my knees and helped her on hers too, turning her so her back was to me.

"Hold the backrest like this," I instructed.

The second she gripped it, I slid inside her again, unable to hold back any longer. She moaned, and I was right there with her.

It felt even more intense than before. I brought my hand in front of her, teasing her navel before lowering it slowly down her pubic bone in a straight line to her clit.

The second I touched her soft flesh, I felt all her muscles contract. Pleasure reverberated through her, ensnaring me too. I increased my rhythm, growing more desperate. My muscles burned in protest, but I was relentless. I wanted to give her every drop of pleasure possible, bring her to a high she hadn't known before.

She exploded only a few seconds later, coming so hard, squeezing me so tight, that I had no choice but to surrender to my own climax. I lost any sense of space, and my balance. Gripping the backrest with one hand and Skye's hip with the other, I held tight until we both slowed down. Skye was trembling a little as I leaned over her. I kissed her back before we both collapsed on the couch, squeezing on one side to both fit.

"Je suis fou de toi."

"Translation?" she murmured.

"I'm crazy about you."

She wiggled her ass, laughing softly. We were both silent for a few minutes, and then Skye headed to the chair where she'd dropped her bag.

"Woman, why do you have so much energy?" I asked.

She looked over her shoulder, smiling saucily. "Why don't you find out? I can give you some tips for helping me get rid of it."

I laughed, watching her return with wet wipes. We cleaned up quickly.

"I think we both deserve a macaron for our effort," Skye said playfully.

"I see. So you brought them for me, but now you want me to share?"

She held up one finger. "I never said they were only for you."

She brought the Ladurée package, taking out four macarons, two with pistachio, two with caramel. She gave me two, keeping the others for herself.

"Why are you smiling?" she asked.

"Eating macarons naked in my office in the dead of the night is a first for me."

Skye grinned, fighting a yawn.

"Want to spend the night at the hotel with me?"

She yawned again before pointing at me. "Promise you'll let me sleep."

I gazed straight at her. "I don't make empty promises."

"Damn, so you're possessive and potentially a sleep thief, and you think I'm still going with you?"

"Yes. Can't wait to show you more sides of that possessive bastard. Might involve staying up all night."

Skye laughed, stealing one of my macarons too. "What can I say? You sure know how to win me over."

Chapter Nineteen
Skye

We ended up not going to sleep at all. I had no idea how that happened. One minute we were under the covers, talking about our lives and families, and next thing I knew, the sun was coming up.

"Wow, this is gorgeous. I haven't seen a sunrise in years," I murmured.

We didn't even leave the bed, just turned on one side, watching through the enormous window of the hotel room. The cream-colored drapes were pulled all the way to the sides, so we had a great view of the sky and Central Park.

Rob was behind me, one arm around my waist. He drew the tip of his nose up and down my arm slowly.

"Hey, don't miss the sunrise," I teased.

"I'm just making the most of it." He went on to kiss my shoulder and arm. Warm, fuzzy sensations skittered along my skin. I didn't remember the last time I felt so content and just... happy.

"Should we order breakfast?" Rob asked, now moving dangerously close to my nipple. I shivered.

"Are they open this early?"

"Room service is available twenty-four

hours."

How could he talk and turn me on at the same time? That shouldn't be possible.

"Sure, why not?"

Instead of ordering anything, he pushed me on my back, baring my breasts to him, and continued his ministrations. First, he drew the tip of his nose around my breasts, and then sucked on my nipples. I pulled at the sheets, licking my lips.

"Did you mean me when you said breakfast?" I teased.

Rob looked up, grinning. "That too. But I think you're still a little sensitive from last night."

I grinned back. "I am, but don't let that deter you. You can move waaay farther down if you want to."

Rob threw his head back, laughing, but he did just that.

Our breakfast arrived while we showered. It was all laid out on the table when we got out of the bathroom, wearing the hotel robes.

"Yummm," I exclaimed as we sat down at the round table. We'd ordered eggs benedict, fried bacon, charred tomatoes, and some sort of red lentil puree. Everything was delicious. Afterward, I just leaned back in my chair, watching Rob get dressed. He only caught on as he was buttoning his shirt.

"Enjoying the show?" he asked.

"Oh, yeah. You get almost full points."

"Almost?" he looked stunned.

"Yeah... next time, you should move even slower. Then I can absorb every detail better."

He barked out a laugh. "I can't believe you're giving me pointers."

I shrugged one shoulder, yawning.

"Your turn," Rob said. His voice was deliciously low and thick. "Go very, very slow."

Ah, I'd walked right into that, hmm? Rob sat at the edge of the bed, and I felt his gaze on me as I headed to the dresser, where I'd put my clothes last night.

I put on my bra, avoiding eye contact at any cost or I might end up bursting into flames. And then I just tugged the dress over me, putting yesterday's panties in my purse.

"What are you doing?" Rob asked.

"I don't have spare panties, so it's commando for me today."

"No way are you going out on the street like that."

That bossy mouth. I loved it so much. Except when he was being unreasonable. I mean, it was hot, but....

He rose from the bed, walking straight to me. Holy hell, he looked even hotter than usual when he was on a mission like this.

"Skye. Panties. On." He emphasized every word.

I rolled my shoulders back, looking him straight in the eyes. "Rob. You don't get to boss me into this."

"What if the wind blows or something?"

"The dress is long enough. No one will see a thing."

"I'm going to go crazy knowing you're completely bare under that dress."

"That's your problem," I teased.

He grinned devilishly. "Want me to make it yours?"

"What?"

Before I realized what he was up to, he slid one hand under my dress, drawing his fingers up my inner thigh, farther and farther up, until he *almost* touched me intimately. He didn't though. Just teased me until I couldn't take it anymore. Swatting his hand away, I rolled my shoulders again, pulling myself together. He cocked a brow. I flashed him a sassy smile, proud that I'd successfully resisted his charm. Okay, so judging by how turned on I was, I'd been only semi-successful, but no need for him to know that.

"When do you have to be at the restaurant?" I asked.

"Should've been there ten minutes ago."

"You're joking."

"Not at all. It's an intense week."

"Let's hurry, then."

"Nah, I can be another hour or so late. Let's just take a short walk before I have to head over there."

"Mr. Dumont... I'm a bad influence on you."

He kissed my forehead, then skimmed his

nose down my temple. "I want a bit more time with you. I'm glad we didn't waste time sleeping."

I laughed. "I'm glad too, but I think we're going to both pay for it today."

"No regrets here." He straightened up, looking me in the eyes, the unspoken question hanging between us: *You?*

"No regrets here either," I reassured him. "But we should go if you don't want to be overly late."

"I don't really care. I'm the boss. I'm allowed a cheat day."

I narrowed my eyes. "How often do you take cheat days?"

"This is the first one."

I all but melted. I suddenly felt so jittery that I barely kept from breaking out in a happy dance. I wasn't ruling out the possibility of that still happening as we walked out of the room arm in arm. The elevator was empty, and I only saw staff members milling about the lobby.

New York on Saturday morning at six o'clock was surreal. Aside from garbage trucks and occasional cabs, there wasn't much traffic.

"I don't think I've ever seen the city empty like this," I said.

"I've seen it a couple of times during Restaurant Days."

"I'll take you to the restaurant and then head to the store," I said. "I've still got some time."

He shook his head. "I'm not going to the

Tribeca restaurant today but one outside Manhattan. It's in the opposite direction."

I pouted as Rob instructed the doorman to flag two cabs for us. Chuckling, he brought a hand to my face, resting his thumb right against my mouth.

"I take this as a sign that you're sad we don't get to share a cab."

I nodded, pouting in an even more exaggerated manner. I rarely behaved so childishly, and mostly with my siblings, but I couldn't seem to help myself. What was this man doing to me? And when he pinned me with those smoldering green eyes, smiling until dimples appeared in his cheeks, I forgot all about pouting. I was too busy trying not to swoon right here.

"What are you doing tonight?" he asked. Wow. He already wanted to make plans?

"I don't know. I think I'm just going to close the store and then probably crash."

He drew his thumb from the center of my mouth to one corner.

"We'll see about that."

My heart was beating fast. "Oh?"

"You'll see." He winked, opening the door of the first cab. I slid onto the back seat.

"Give me a hint."

He leaned in, bringing his mouth to my ear.

"I just can't get enough of you."

He straightened up, then reached down to my ear again and whispered, "And when you get to your store, cover your ass—that's mine." Then he stood up and closed the door.

That man. I had to laugh.

My palms were sweating a little as I told the cabbie the address, then pressed my nose to the window when the car lurched forward, watching Rob get into the second cab.

I tried to analyze the situation, but this was so new for me, so different from any experience I'd had with men, that I just had no basis for comparison. So, I just relaxed against the back seat, unable to hold back a smile. Suddenly, I wished it were evening so badly that I just wanted to fast-forward the day—another first for me.

I arrived before Tess at the store. Since we still had two hours until opening time, I checked our online orders before answering some customer questions.

"You're wearing the same clothes as yesterday," Tess said the second she stepped inside the store, pointing at me.

"I know. I'm doing the walk of shame, right? Except I feel absolutely zero shame."

She laughed. "You're happy. Just saying, but it's a good look on you."

"Thanks, sis."

"Any particular reason?"

"Rob and I agreed yesterday that we're exclusive."

"Oh, that's lovely."

"And I'm just... I feel like I'm going to burst

with all this joy. Is that weird?"

We'd also talked this morning about not using condoms anymore. I'd been on the pill for years but didn't share it with him before, out of instinct, I guess. Now that we were exclusive, I was ready for the next step.

Tess grinned. "Not at all, sis. Just enjoy this moment, bask in your happiness."

I nodded, my usual cautious nature somehow forgotten. Rob had awoken something in me I hadn't been aware of before, and I was powerless to fight it. In fact, I didn't want to, and that really was a first for me. I was grinning from ear to ear as we opened the door to customers.

In the afternoon, Mom stopped by with Ryker's fiancée, Heather. Her dark brown hair was pulled into a high ponytail, and she was wearing gorgeous silver earrings in the shape of butterflies.

"Hey, why didn't you tell us you were coming?" I asked, kissing each of their cheeks.

"We were just in the neighborhood," Heather said. "We looked at some wedding decorations."

"Oooh, show me," Tess said. My sister was a little sad that she didn't have time to involve herself in the wedding planning in the same way she'd done for Josie and Hunter, but it was impossible to make time for it with how busy we were. They were getting married in December, so the theme was winter wonderland. It was going to be epic, I was sure of it.

Heather pulled out her phone, showing Tess

several types of twinkle lights for the bride and groom table. They looked identical to me, but the two of them immediately started discussing the pros and cons of each.

"I think my wedding planner is going to have a heart attack if I ask for more changes," Heather murmured.

"Hey, it's your big day," Tess said. "Don't let her intimidate you."

Mom pulled me to one side. "Do you want me to help with anything?"

"No, you can just relax, okay?"

"I can't. I get anxious if I don't do anything."

That was true. Mom was one of those people who just couldn't sit down and do nothing, even for a few minutes.

"Oh, by the way, I have an announcement to make," Mom went on.

Tess and Heather looked at her immediately.

"I've decided to finally have laser surgery on my eyes. It's so damn hard to read that small print, even with glasses. And the prescriptions they're giving me for new lenses are so thick they're just awful. Anyway, I'm just done with them. I'm going to do it in three weeks. I'll be good as new by the time school starts," Mom said.

"Good for you," I replied. She'd wanted to do it for years. "Do you need us to help you with anything?"

"No, Mick is going to be with me that day. It's just an outpatient surgery, and the recovery time is minimal. I'll be fine."

"But you'll let us know if something comes up?" Tess pressed.

Mom nodded, and my sister and I exchanged a glance. We'd just have to spam Mick with messages, because Mom wasn't exactly in a sharing mood when she was sick.

When we were kids, she once didn't even tell us she was in the hospital for gallbladder surgery just so *we* wouldn't worry. She'd asked a neighbor to watch us and told us she was at a conference. We gave her an earful once we caught on, but it didn't accomplish much. Mom had her own way of handling things, but as far as I was concerned, she'd been the best role model I could have asked for.

"Josie said her brothers and sister are in town the weekend after my laser appointment, and I invited everyone for lunch on Saturday."

"You think you'll be up for it?" I asked. "Maybe you'll need time to recover."

Mom waved her hand. "I'll be just fine, but I will need some help with preparations, because Mick will already be gone for setup of one of his concerts."

"Sure. We'll help. I can't wait to see everyone," I said. I loved to catch up with our family, and Josie's siblings were always a lot of fun. They were scattered around the country, moving around for work, and we typically only ever got together for holidays or weddings. Her brothers, Ian and Dylan, gave Ryker and Cole a run for their money on practically everything. And Isabelle, Josie's sister, was a girl after my own heart. Josie kept saying she wished they'd all move to New York, and I couldn't agree more.

After Mom and Heather left, Tess and I immediately decided to organize a girls' evening out while Isabelle was in town.

"Come to think of it, we haven't had one in a while," Tess said. "Hey, I have an idea," she continued. "Why don't you and I do that tonight? And you can spill the beans about the walk of non-shame and your sexy CEO."

I wiggled my eyebrows. "Why not? I just have to warn you that my sexy CEO looked as if he had nefarious plans in mind for us tonight."

Tess opened her mouth, then closed it again. "Was about to ask what you meant by nefarious plans, but I think that would be too much information."

I nodded excitedly. "Far too much."

The no-secrets policy did not include sexy details, and I liked it that way... because there *was* such a thing as oversharing.

We messaged Heather and Josie, but neither of them had time to stop by the store tonight, so Tess and I decided to just have fun by ourselves. At nine o'clock, we turned the sign on the door to Closed and made ourselves comfortable on the couch in front, with pizza cartons set between the two of us.

"Okay, I eat, you talk," Tess instructed. I

laughed, but that seemed like a fair deal. I told her about my impromptu visit to his restaurant yesterday and our night together. My mouth was dry by the time I finished talking. I took a swig of soda, then devoured my pizza. Tess was watching me with a smile.

"You're totally into him," she concluded.

"I am."

"It's the first time I've really seen you this way."

"I've never felt like this before," I admitted. I loved talking about these things with my sister.

Tess clapped her hands, shimmying on the couch. "Yes! You go, girl."

"Can I ask you something? How do you do it... always get so excited? You never hold anything back."

Tess munched on her last bit of pizza, finishing it before replying. "I am afraid of things too, you know. I just don't show it." She swallowed and continued, "I want to find someone, but I'm also afraid that it could all go wrong. I still remember that horrid feeling of Dad leaving, of not being wanted."

Her words were like a punch to my stomach. I nearly doubled over from the force of it. I remembered that feeling in vivid detail. Most times, I just did my best to forget it.

"We all do, I suppose," I muttered. Did my past affect my dating life? Was I fearful of someone leaving me? Well, it wasn't like it hadn't already happened, and yes, it bothered me—but this time, with Rob, it was different. I just knew it was.

Tess shook her head, straightening up. "I didn't want to ruin our mood. Especially since—" She tilted her head to the right, peering over my shoulder. "—I think your sexy chef is outside the store."

I turned so fast that I heard my neck snap. Holy shit, he really was there. I mean, he'd told me that he might crash my evening plans, but he hadn't texted or anything, so I'd sort of assumed he got caught up at one of the restaurants.

I went to the door, and Tess followed me.

When I opened it, Rob glanced between the two of us.

"You didn't tell me you were coming," I said.

"Figured I'd find you here." His confident nonchalance gave me chills, good ones.

Tess placed both hands on my shoulders from behind. "Hey, keep doing what you're doing. Sis here is smiling more than usual, so I'm a big fan of yours."

I blushed, feeling my face getting hotter, and even the tips of my ears.

"Good to know," Rob said. "Ready to go?"

"Oh, yeah." I nodded, looking around. "Just let me get my purse."

In a few minutes, Tess and I turned off all the lights and locked up the place. Rob waited for me patiently by the door. Hmm... I was trying to guess what he had in mind for the evening, but he had a great poker face. Except for that smoldering gaze. Holy hell, I'd only been in his presence for a few minutes, but I was already simmering. I hoped Tess didn't notice I was perspiring.

"Tess, do you want to share a cab?" Rob asked once the three of us were outside the store. "We can drop you off at home."

My sister shook her head. "No, no, no. I have a firm rule about never being a third wheel. And you've been throwing sis here hot looks since she opened the door, so...."

I groaned. "Tess...."

"What? I just call it like I see it."

Rob's eyes had a knowing glint of sorts. There was no mistaking his intentions.

So much for Tess not noticing. I blushed even more violently.

"Do sleep a little though," she teased. My sister kissed my cheek, then Rob's before sashaying down in the direction of the main street.

"Very observant," Rob muttered.

I cocked a brow, placing my hand on my hip. "Orrr... you're very obvious."

"That too." A small smile played on his lips, which then morphed into a grin. He pulled me flush against him unexpectedly, and I pointed at his face.

"You have a plan," I said.

"How can you tell?"

"I don't know. You just give off that vibe."

"So you're both observant." Taking my hand, he kissed the back of it, rubbing his thumb in small circles on it. "I have a proposition."

"Uhhh... so I was wrong. Not a plan."

"Yet."

"Let's hear it."

"Two options: Either I take you home and pamper you for a bit, then head back to the city. I have an early morning tomorrow again. Or... we drop by your house, you pack a suitcase for the next week, and come back to the hotel with me."

I blinked, sucking in a breath. "Oh, wow."

"I told you I want more of you, Skye." He cupped my face with both hands, looking at me intently. "I understand that it might make things complicated for you, or you might just prefer to sleep at home, but I'd really like it for you to consider it. Next week will be even more intensive, and I will literally not have time to see you at all otherwise. After Restaurant Days wrap up, everything will be back to normal."

I frowned, feigning that I had to think very hard about it, then held up a finger. "I've considered it. And the answer is a resounding yes."

I only briefly managed to see the relief in his eyes before he pulled me flush against him and kissed me hot and heavy, right there for all Soho to see. He kept one hand firmly at the small of my back. Yeah, I lost the battle and gave in to swooning. I was going to spend every night this week with him!

His gaze was determined and, well... sizzling when he pulled back.

"God, I was hoping you'd say that."

"What would you have done if I said no?" I asked.

"Used some tricks to change your mind."

"I knew it. You're a tyrant just pretending to play nice now and again."

"I fight for what I want, Skye. And I want you with me. All the time."

Oh, this man. I wasn't even done swooning, and here he was doing it again.

"Let's go, then, because I take a long-ass time to pack. I can't wait to wear panties again."

He jerked his head back. "You're still commando?"

"Yes, sir."

"You own a lingerie store. And what did I tell you when I put you in that cab?"

"Yeah, like I was going to let you boss me into anything. Besides, I never wear panties without washing them first."

"Holy shit, woman. You're going to drive me crazy."

"No, no. I plan to do that only after we reach the hotel. Hey, we're going to get a bit of sleep now and then, right?"

His expression morphed into a full-on grin. "I can't make any promises."

Chapter Twenty
Rob

Few things were able to anger me past the point of reason. At the very top of that list was my shitty ex-brother-in-law. I'd meant to keep my promise to Anne, I really had. Until he had the audacity to show up at headquarters the day after Restaurant Days were over. He asked for me to help him with a new business, to put in a good word for him with the banks so he could get the loans he needed.

He'd chosen the worst possible moment to approach me. Anne and Lindsay had just returned from France, and Lindsay had mentioned that he'd forgotten to call again.

"Let me get this straight. You hauled ass without notice, divorced my sister, and now you want my help?"

"Yeah."

"You're out of your mind."

Why did I let him in the building in the first damn place? Why didn't I just kick him out on the street from the start? He'd hurt Anne, and I wanted to hurt him. He just went on with his life, the arrogant prick, while my sister was a ghost of herself.

Fucker.

Lindsay! I couldn't forget about Lindsay. She'd have the most to lose if I connected my fist to his jaw.

"Get out," I said.

"What?"

"Get out. Before I forcibly remove you." I yelled louder to make sure he heard me this time.

"I was the CEO of this company. You can't just ignore that."

"Yes I can. And I will."

"There's plenty I can say or do to hurt the image of this company."

I smirked. "Go ahead. Think any bank will approve you for a loan after that? I have them all in my pocket."

"Are you threatening me?"

"Yes."

"You bastard. I'm not the first person to divorce his wife. Anne got boring as fuck, so I looked elsewhere for fun."

I didn't even realize when I lunged over to him. Anger pushed out any thought. Instinct prevailed. I punched him square in the stomach, relishing the way he curled forward from the impact, letting out a strangled cry.

"That's for hurting Anne and Lindsay," I said, pushing him back. He nearly crashed into the door. "Let me make one thing clear. I forbid you to hurt or disappoint my niece. It's too late to take back all the hurt you caused Anne, but you *will* call Lindsay on a regular basis. Spend time with her. Or else."

"Or else what?" he challenged.

"The name Dumont means something in this city. The whole country. Piss me off, and you'll see just how much power it has."

"You don't intimidate me." Though he sounded damn intimidated.

"Call her. Man up and be responsible." I was at the edge of reason again. "Now get out."

He opened his mouth, closed it again. I was standing straight, feet wide apart, hands in my pockets, balled into fists. Something in my body language must have made it clear that I was out of patience, because he left my office immediately.

I was restless for the rest of the day. Even I could tell I wasn't just being difficult at work, as usual—no, I was being a jackass. When my assistant burst into tears because I barked at her to hurry up with a report, I knew it was time to give up on this day.

Outside, I sat on a bench in Tompkins Square Park under the shade of elms. Damn it, I was still restless. I had no idea how to cool down. Sitting here wasn't helping either. No, I wanted something else.

I needed Skye.

That thought just slammed into me all on its own. Taking out my phone, I hesitated with my thumbs above the screen. I wasn't used to needing anyone. When shit happened, I dealt with it on my own or ignored it until it wasn't an issue any longer.

But this last week, I'd had her with me every evening at the hotel, and it had been glorious, no matter if we were talking, if I was sinking inside her, or just falling asleep curled into each other, which happened on two nights the second we slid into bed because we'd both been exhausted. I craved her nearness.

I finally made the call.

"Hey," she said, sounding happy to hear from me, but I detected unease in her voice too.

"What are you doing?"

"Trying not to pull my hair out."

I laughed. "That good, huh?"

"We had a zillion cancellations today, and I just figured out it was because our payment system crashed. It's just not keeping up with demand. You?"

"In Tompkins Square Park."

A pause followed before she said, "Damn, so your day is worse."

"How can you tell?"

"Hanging out in parks without a reason? Not your style."

"You've got me all figured out, huh?" Surprisingly, I liked the thought of that. And just like that, she was cheering me up.

"Well, no, but everything you do has a purpose."

"I suppose you're right. Can I persuade you to hang out with me?"

Say yes. I was breathing easier just at the prospect of spending the evening with her. It was just six o'clock, but maybe she could leave the store earlier.

"Depends, what do you have in mind?"

"Nothing, but I'm open to suggestions."

"Have you ever been to Ancient Aire Baths? I haven't been in a while, and we have a sales assistant here tonight. She can close without me."

"No, but I know them." They were practically across from the restaurant in Tribeca.

"Well, you're in for a treat. I love them. Meet me there in half an hour?"

"I think I'll need forty. I'm in the East Village."

"Okay. Unless you want to do something over there instead?"

"And miss out on the opportunity of seeing you naked?"

Skye laughed. "You don't know how these thermal bath things work, do you? We wear bathing suits."

"I'm sure we can sneak some naked time somewhere."

"Oh my God! Promise you won't."

"Won't what?"

"Tempt me."

I smiled for the first time since my encounter with the jackass. "Can't lie to you, Skye. See you in forty minutes."

I arrived earlier than anticipated. Skye was already on the white steps, waving at me. Just seeing her did things to me I couldn't explain.

"Hey, broody guy. Let's go inside."

Instead of answering, I pulled her to me. We were in full view of Tribeca, so I limited myself to a simple press of my lips against hers. For now.

Inside at the reception desk, I was given onetime-use shorts. Skye had brought a bikini from the store. We both received flip-flops and towels.

"I know my way to the changing rooms," Skye told the receptionist. Taking my hand, she led me down a few corridors, right to a series of changing rooms. We'd been given the same one.

Stepping inside, Skye hung her bag on one of the hooks, her dress on the other. Watching her take off her clothes was a special kind of torture. She seemed oblivious to my pain as she kicked off her underwear, putting on a simple black bikini. Her ass and breasts looked too fucking delicious. Groaning, I gripped her ass, sliding my fingers inside her bikini.

"No funny business." She swatted my hand away playfully.

I drew her to me the next second, kissing her wet and deep, digging my fingers in her ass, rubbing against her. It was so easy to get wrapped up in her taste, her scent. I only came to my senses when I pushed her against the metal wall and buried my mouth in her neck.

"You haven't changed," she murmured.

Pulling back, I wiggled my eyebrows. "Want to help me?"

Laughing, she shook her head. "I'll wait for you outside, or we're never going to make it in the water. Come on, hurry up."

I didn't want to let her out, but changing with her in here was too risky. I was already hard and having trouble behaving myself. I could already imagine bending her over, one leg up on the bench, sinking inside her. After she left, I took off my clothes, putting on the shorts. They were a little more fitted than what I'd wear, so I waited two whole minutes for my hard-on to subside before joining her.

She took my hand, leading me out of the changing rooms and down a corridor that opened to a huge hall that did the name *ancient baths* justice: high ceilings sustained by columns and brick walls. There were multiple pools of various sizes. All light fixtures resembled candles or torches.

"That's my favorite one," Skye said, pointing to one of the larger pools. "It has saltwater, and it's warm."

I was pleased that the place wasn't too full. We had one corner of the pool all to ourselves. Skye floated for a bit. I swam a few lengths, but I tired quickly from the warm water and the steam, so I stretched my arms on either side of a corner. Skye joined me, looking at me intently.

"Want to talk about what drove you to *hang out* in a park?"

"Anne's ex showed up at the restaurant, asking me to vouch for him with the bank."

"Does he have a black eye?"

"No, but he got a punch to the stomach. He

tried to blackmail me. The idiot."

"How?"

"By implying he can say shit about us in interviews. So I blackmailed him back. Said that if he doesn't own up to being Lindsay's dad, he's gonna have a problem getting a foot in the door at any bank."

Her eyes bulged, but then a smile edged at the corners of her mouth. "I like how you think."

I laughed, tugging her closer by the shoulders. "Really?"

"Yeah. I like that you care so much about Anne and Lindsay's happiness and that you fight for it. But I thought he was calling her?"

"He promptly forgot they existed while they were in France."

Skye grimaced, drumming her fingers up my arms. "I'm sorry. I think it's great that you're insisting he call. A divorce does leave marks, you know?"

Suddenly, she seemed smaller, vulnerable. I put my hands on her waist, pulling her closer, wanting to make it go away but knowing I couldn't.

"Do you want to tell me about it?" I asked.

She shrugged but nodded. "It's just that... sometimes, even when I'm happy, I can't shake off the fear that I can lose it at any moment. We were all affected in our own way by the divorce. Tess the most. She thought I didn't notice, but I did. I just didn't know how to comfort her."

"Fucking hell, you're amazing. You were hurting, but that didn't stop you from wanting to care for those around you."

She shrugged, like it was no big deal, but it sure as hell was. Even tonight, despite having her own issues at the store, she'd put them on the back burner to focus on me. I wanted to return that every way I could. Make her see how important she was becoming to me.

"But I think it's going to be different for Lindsay," she said, and something in her tone told me she didn't want to talk about herself anymore. "She's got you too, and she's still seeing her dad."

"I just hate that he's hurting them both. I was hoping that the time in France would do them all good." That Walter would come to his senses and at least be a civil asshole and call his daughter. "It was Anne's and my happy place as kids."

"You spent a lot of time there?"

"Just a few weeks in the summer. Two with the grandparents, two with our parents. We looked forward to it the whole year. We practiced speaking the language, ate local produce, made new friends. Our family had a house in a village about two hours from Paris. Now they've moved to the south of France."

"Who speaks French in your family?"

"My grandfather and my father are fluent, whereas Anne and I do okay. We used to speak French with each other when we didn't want Mom or our grandmother to understand. It drove them nuts. They tried learning the language but said it's impossible."

"I agree. We had to choose between Spanish and French at school, and I went for Spanish. Not that I'm any good at that either."

"France has always been my happy place. I want that for Lindsay too."

I wanted to show Skye everything that was important to me, just share everything with her. I kissed her cheek up to the shell of her ear.

"*J'ai besoin du toi.* I need you. I just need you," I said in both French and English because I wanted her to understand how much she meant to me.

"I love the sound of that," she whispered. I understood her fear; I just wanted to prove to her that there was no need for that with me.

"Tell me more about your vacations in France," she urged.

"It was like a time-out from our routine. We were outdoors all the time. Anne spent all day long in this huge swing, reading."

"Hey, I like swings."

"I noticed. Why is yours indoors?"

"It almost got blown away in a storm when I had it outside. I'd love a sturdier one in the backyard but just haven't found one yet."

I made a mental note about that.

"You know… my house actually reminds me a bit of the one in France. Just the coloring. I figured that out after I moved in."

Skye looked at me with a huge grin. "Awww, that's sweet."

"This hot water has a weird effect on me."

She laughed, wiggling her body against mine. "Why, because it's making you reveal all sorts of things? I kind of like it."

"I bet you do."

She splayed her fingers on my neck, bringing her mouth to mine. She licked my lower lip with the tip of her tongue before slipping it in my mouth. I groaned, kissing her back just as wickedly.

Pulling back, she looked at me playfully. "Lay your head back on the edge."

"Bossy?"

She pressed my shoulders down. I sank lower in the water, leaning my head back. Feeling her mouth moving down my neck was driving me insane.

"Skye, we're not alone in the pool."

"I'm just kissing you. And besides, the steam is pretty thick. We look blurred to anyone who's paying attention."

She was teasing me with small, chaste kisses, but they were completely messing with my senses.

"We're moving into another tub in a few minutes anyway," she said.

"No, I like what you're doing."

"Weren't you complaining just a minute ago?"

"Not complaining. Warning."

She was kissing my right shoulder now. I wrapped an arm around her waist, pressing her against me.

"Hey, you're interrupting my exploration."

"I want to feel you against me."

"Hmm... that works too."

I didn't get her to myself for too long, because they informed us that our red wine bath was ready.

We walked to an adjacent room. It was very small, containing a stone basin. There were grapes and candles on the edges. We sat inside, and when we turned on the faucet, a red-colored water came out of it.

"That's actual wine?" I asked, perplexed. "What a waste."

"No, silly. It's wine without alcohol in it. That would dry our skin."

"Still a waste of perfectly good grapes."

She rolled her eyes. "It has antioxidants. It's good for us."

Waste or not, I had to admit this whole evening was relaxing, and when the staff brought a platter with cheese and grapes, I learned something new about Skye: she loved cheese.

"This is my favorite thing to do to relax," Skye said.

"You come here often?"

"I used to do it all the time before, but not since opening the store."

"You've been here with another guy?" I asked. The question popped out all of a sudden, but then an image of Skye with someone else shaped up in my mind, in that corner of the pool, kissing him like she kissed me, and I was seeing red. *No, just no.*

"Think I'd waste this experience on random guys? Nah, I mostly came here with Tess." She looked straight at me, pointing to my eyes. "What's that? Possessive streak rearing up again?"

"Can't help it. I can't stand the thought of you with another man."

"So stop thinking it," she said playfully, climbing in my lap, lacing her hands behind my neck.

"Easier said than done. Want to take my mind off it?"

"Gladly."

She pressed her mouth to mine, wiping every thought except one: if I couldn't entertain the thought of Skye with another man in the past, I sure as hell wouldn't let that happen in the future.

Chapter Twenty-One
Skye

The day after Mom's surgery, Tess and I had planned to stop by to see her in the evening. Mick had told us yesterday that the procedure had gone well, but it didn't make sense to visit her because she was medicated and would probably sleep the rest of the day. Today they'd gone back to the doctor for a checkup, so when Mick called us at eleven o'clock, I grabbed Tess so we could talk with him together.

"Let's go in the back room," I said.

Jane was here today, so we had more flexibility than usual.

We closed the door to the office, putting the call on speakerphone.

"Hey, Mick. We're both here. How did it go?" I asked.

"There's signs of an infection," Mick said. Every muscle in my upper body stiffened. A weight pressed on my chest. I couldn't inhale deeply, but I drew in small, conscious breaths.

"What does that mean?" Tess asked.

"Her eyesight is blurred for now."

"Is she in pain?" I asked.

"No, not at all."

"That's not so bad, then," I said.

"Well, no, but the doctor ordered for her to stay in for the next two weeks. She needs to wear blackout glasses to keep her eyes safe from light. She's not even worried about the recovery, just pissed about all the things she can't do because she won't be able to see."

I couldn't help but laugh, because it was a testament to just how well Mick knew Mom.

"Mick, does something else worry you?" Tess asked. "You sound on edge."

"Yeah... I'm supposed to be on the road this next month. Already asked my boss for time off, but he said no."

Tess and I exchanged a glance, coming to the same conclusion.

"The gang's large enough that we can work this out amongst us, Mick. Don't worry."

"Yeah, but I don't love the idea of being away when she's like this."

"We'll take good care of her," Tess assured him. "We're going to drop by in a few hours." Then she paused and corrected herself. "Actually, wait... Skye, we could drop by now, right? Jane can take care of the store on her own for a while."

I nodded in agreement.

"Okay, we'll be there in about forty minutes. Want us to bring something to eat?"

"We're good for today. I'd stopped by and picked up some carryout stuff for us on the way home."

"Did you talk to the whole gang already?" I asked.

"No, I called you girls first."

"Thank you, Mick. Okay, we'll tell everyone else," Tess said.

We spread the news efficiently, so by the time we jumped on the train to head to Mom's, we'd already informed the rest of the family.

Despite Mick's assurances that they didn't need food, we bought some delicious pralines. Whenever Mom was on edge, they always helped calm her.

The second we entered their apartment, it became clear the pralines weren't going to cut it. Mom's eyesight wasn't just blurry—she couldn't even move around the house by herself.

"Holy shit," Tess exclaimed.

"Mick, have you been taking a page out of Mom's book? Where you don't tell us the extent of the situation at hand so we don't worry?" I threw my hands up in the air. We needed to know everything in order to figure out what to do. Mom was going to need round-the-clock care for a few days at least.

Mick looked between the two of us hopelessly. Tess glared at me. Shit, poor Mick didn't need my venting.

"Sorry," I said. He was just doing his best, after all.

Tess and I sat with Mom in her room while Mick heated up lunch for everyone.

"How are you feeling?" Tess asked her.

"Very pissed. I was supposed to be on my feet by now, not bumping into my own damn walls."

"Just give it some time, Mom. What did the doctor say?" Tess asked.

"They have me on some pills, antibiotics I guess, and a ton of eye drops, and we're supposed to go in for checkups every third day. They said it should pass in about two weeks."

"See, it's not even that long," I added, trying to appease her. It didn't really work though. Her mood further darkened during lunch, when she needed help with every spoonful.

It was mid-August now, and school was starting in two weeks, so Mom had plenty of work to do before term began. Tess and I had assumed that watching Mom would mean visiting her after work, shopping for her, and so on, but it was obviously going to be more involved.

After we finished eating, while Mick helped Mom back to bed, Tess and I went into the room they'd converted into a reading room. It was cozy and comfy, with leather armchairs, floor-to-ceiling bookshelves, and an enviable bar. The perfect getaway for a drink and a good book.

Tess and I sat opposite each other, calling Cole, Hunter, and Ryker for a conference.

"We can take shifts spending time with her," Hunter suggested.

"Yeah. We're flexible, working for ourselves and all that," Cole answered.

"I can schedule my face-to-face meetings all

in the morning and stay with Mom in the afternoon," Ryker said immediately, but I knew that wasn't really smart. The fund he worked at on Wall Street wasn't going to appreciate him working remotely.

"Mom needs a lot of distraction," Cole said. "I vote we reveal all the shit we did that we kept from her."

Ryker laughed. "We want her to get better, not give her a heart attack, bro. Though we probably can select a few harmless events."

"Boys, why don't we keep things as they are? Mom is convinced we were on our best behavior when we moved to New York. Let's not mess with that. Anyway, Tess and I should take turns sleeping here," I said.

"Yeah, I think Mom will feel better with one of us here at night," Tess added.

"Wait, Josie says she can also spend the night there." I could hear my cousin-in-law's voice in the background as Hunter spoke.

"And Heather says that she's flexible on the days she doesn't have interviews," Ryker added. Heather was a journalist, and when she wasn't doing field work, she usually worked from home. Her daughter Avery was seven years old and in school until midafternoon, so I knew Heather could stop by before lunch only. It warmed me all over that Josie and Heather wanted to help. My cousin and my brother had found good women. I was happy for them.

"Does everyone have their calendars on

hand?" I asked.

After a chorus of "yes" and "wait a second," we all had the app open. The call took well over an hour, but we had a schedule at the end of it. Heather and Josie were going to take morning shifts, Hunter and Cole the afternoon ones, and we all convinced Ryker that there was no need for him to take time off.

Tess and I were spending the evenings and nights here. Even though Josie offered to sleep over, Tess and I figured Mom would prefer one of her daughters to help her shower and so on.

"Damn, we're so productive when we put our minds to it," Tess said on a smile.

I grinned. "True."

We tiptoed out of the room and then out of the apartment, because based on how quiet it now was, it was obvious both Mom and Mick had fallen asleep. Even though it was early in the day, we didn't want to wake them up after the busy morning they'd had.

***

Rob

Something was off with Skye. She'd texted me that she wanted to talk to me. That was a few hours ago. I called her as soon as I saw the message, but it went to voice mail. I assumed her phone's battery was dead. As a result, I just wanted to get this day over with and head to Soho. I was certain I'd find her at the store.

But before that, I needed to finalize this meeting. I was at our restaurant in the West Village. It had the lowest rating in our customer satisfaction survey.

"We're going to up our game and take every complaint seriously." I was speaking to the entire staff of this restaurant.

Lionel, the manager, just stared at the ground. I had enough authority that they did what I asked even though they may not agree.

"Among the most frequent complaints are long waiting times as well as unfriendly responses when they ask about their order."

"You should hear how some of these people talk to us," one of the servers said.

"Customer is king." As always, I kept my voice calm but cold. "I've instructed my assistant to send me online reviews weekly."

Lionel's eyebrows shot up. Most business owners in my position would consider this micromanaging, but years of observing my grandfather and parents and how they ran the show taught me one or two things.

"Unless anyone wants to add anything else, you can return to your tasks."

The second I dismissed the team, I left and ordered an Uber, heading straight to Soho. It had been a fucking long week, and I just wanted to take my woman out to dinner or back home and spend time with her. Skye and I had had dinner with Anne and Lindsay every evening for the past week, but tonight I wanted her all to myself.

Soho was buzzing with people, even more than usual. A few big stores were running sales, which seemed to be the reason for the extra foot traffic. Once I reached Tess and Skye's store, it was obvious why Skye hadn't picked up. They were overrun with customers. They still had ten minutes until closing time, so I sat in a chair at the ice cream shop.

Just watching her had a calming effect on me. As the minutes ticked by, I grew impatient. I wasn't satisfied with simply watching her anymore. Even after nine o'clock came around and the store emptied out, Skye and Tess didn't show signs of slowing down and closing for the night. I headed inside.

"I'll be right with you," Skye said automatically. She had her back to me, not realizing I wasn't a customer.

"I know."

She whirled around, eyes wide. "Hi! What are you doing here?"

"Came to see you. I got your text."

"Crap, did you call? My phone was out of battery, and the afternoon was so crazy that I didn't even have time to charge it. I don't know why there were so many people here."

"I passed Zara and H&M just now, and they had huge sales."

"Oh, that explains it."

I walked straight to her just as Tess came from the back.

"Rob, hi! Come to rescue my sister from herself?"

"That's right."

Tess smiled. "I thoroughly approve. She's been in a frenzy the whole afternoon."

Skye stared at her. "So have you."

"Yeah, but I have no plans tonight, whereas you have this fine specimen waiting for you. All I'm saying is… take advantage of the situation. I'm going to leave you two and will look over the online orders we have yet to check from home. Can you close up?"

"Sure."

Tess retrieved a small bag from under the counter, slinging it over her shoulder. She sent an air kiss toward us before leaving the building.

"When's the last time you took a break?" I asked Skye when it was just the two of us.

Skye bit her lip. "Ummm, lunch?"

"Okay, that's it. Let's go."

"You're going to boss me into leaving?"

"Damn right I am."

She laughed, putting a hand on her hip. "Bribing me might work better. Just don't tell my brothers. They think I'm incorruptible."

I stepped right into her personal space, capturing her mouth. Fuck, how she surrendered to me, instantly parting her lips. I coaxed her tongue, lowering my hands under her ass, pressing her against me. I was barely holding back from sliding my hands under her T-shirt. All I wanted to do was touch, kiss, and explore my woman.

"Mmm… that works too," she murmured when I pulled back. "I still have to sort these out though." She grabbed a fistful of straps from the shelf next to us.

"Put those down or I swear I'm throwing you over my shoulder and getting you out of here."

Skye's eyes widened. "My God, you're not even joking."

"Not one bit. You need to relax. Let me take care of you, Skye."

"Mmm… I might need some more convincing. Mind kissing me again?"

"As long as you agree to leave afterward."

"We've gone from bossing to negotiating. Progress."

"Nah, I just know how to convince you."

"That you do."

I leaned in again, but she put a finger against my lips, shaking her head.

"Let's go to the back. Then you don't have to keep yourself in check." She glanced down at my hands. They were firmly on her waist.

"Don't tempt me, Skye."

She smiled saucily, leading me to the back. I placed both hands on her shoulders and realized they were hunched with tension. I pressed my fingers into her flesh, from the clavicle up the curve of her neck.

"You're tense," I said. "More than usual, I mean."

Sighing, she turned around.

"What's wrong?"

"I forgot to tell you about Mom. Her procedure didn't go as seamlessly as we hoped. She got an infection, and her eyesight is super blurry so she's bumping into things."

"Well, shit."

"Yeah, I know."

"At least she's not in pain."

"That's what I think too. It's inconvenient, but once it passes, she'll be just fine. But for the next two weeks, she's going to need extra care and attention. She's always down when she's sick."

She was so sensitive to other people's well-being. I hadn't met anyone like her in my whole life.

"Mick is leaving the city for work tomorrow. Tess and I will take turns spending the night at Mom's house for the next week, maybe longer if needed."

My face fell. Skye's smile dimmed when she noticed my expression, and I immediately schooled my features, wanting to reassure her. True, I'd been hoping for more time with her, but I was adaptable.

"Which nights?" I asked.

"I'll be there tomorrow night, and Tess the evening after that."

"So tonight, I get you all to myself."

She nodded, still eying me warily. "Oh, by the way, I bought something for Lindsay. Don't let me forget to give it to you. I went by Tris's shop, and she had a bracelet that goes well with that pendant."

"I'm sure she'll love it."

With everything going on, she still had made

time to stop and buy something for Lindsay? That touched me for reasons I couldn't explain. I skimmed my hands over her body, barely restraining the urge to yank off her clothes.

"Lie back," I said.

"Bossing me some more?"

"Lie. Back."

She did as I said, watching me intently. I pressed my fingers in her calves, moving up quickly to her inner thighs.

"I see. So you're feeling me up under the guise of a massage. Clever."

"I'm not pretending at all."

"I did bring you back here with hopes for more hot kisses, but so far nothing," she teased.

This woman was going to be the death of me. I pulled her back to me the next second. Her ass pressed against my thigh, but I wanted her on me. I scooped her up, placing her in my lap, legs bent at the side. Cupping the back of her head, I brought her closer, swiping my tongue over her lower lip. She shuddered, clenching her hands on the collar of my shirt.

She wanted a kiss? She was going to get a whole lot more than that, because I planned to make the most of this evening and any other she was mine.

I had no idea when I'd gone from my casual, laid-back ways to wanting to maximize every moment I spent with her, but I liked the change. It felt so normal, so right, and I wanted to make sure we were on the same page.

I fully intended to pause the kiss and broach the subject, but when Skye bit my tongue lightly, popping open a button of my shirt, she completely diverted my attention.

"So, Mr. Sexy and Bossy Man, plan to make good on that promise or what?" she whispered.

"Fuck yes."

Chapter Twenty-Two
Skye

"Hon, you don't have to hover over me every minute you're here," Mom said.

I held my hands up in defense. "No hovering."

Mom lifted a brow. She might have blurry eyesight, but that didn't take away from her feistiness. Okay, so I might have been hovering. I'd arrived at the apartment about an hour ago and had so far brought her water twice, changed the bedsheets, arranged her towels, and fluffed her pillows.

"I hope I'm gonna be better by Saturday. I want to at least be able to entertain my guests properly."

"Oh, that's right." I'd totally forgotten Josie's brothers and sister were coming to visit. "If you want to cancel, let me know."

"Nonsense. I'm getting stir-crazy already."

I didn't think her eyesight would necessarily be better by Saturday, since it was only two days away, but I knew for a fact that with the house full, she'd forget all about it.

I was just about to ask her if she wanted me to close the curtains when the doorbell rang.

"Are you expecting someone?" I asked.

"No."

"Okay, I'll go and see who it is."

I opened the door to find a delivery guy there with a huge box from Dumont Foods. I hadn't ordered it, but I was convinced Rob did. He'd called me while I was on my way here, asking if we needed anything, if we had any food.

"Just let me find my wallet," I said.

"There's nothing to pay, miss."

I tipped him generously, carrying the box to the kitchen before heading to Mom's room.

"We just got dinner delivered," I announced.

"I heard. Something from Dumont's, right?"

Well, well. Seemed like Mom's hearing had gotten sharper lately.

"Yes. I know the owner—"

"The hot man you're dating."

My jaw dropped. "How do you...? You haven't even met him."

"Well, no, but Tess described him in *a lot* of detail."

Laughing, I shot Rob a message.

Skye: We just got the food. THANK YOU SO MUCH.

Rob: Anytime. Want me to schedule daily deliveries for the next two weeks?

Oh, wow.

Skye: That would be a huge help. Thank you.

Rob: You're welcome.

I laughed, pressing my palm on my belly, but there was no taming that giddy sensation coiling through me. And after all, why should I?

"So tell me about him," Mom said.

Ha! That was all the encouragement I needed. I went on a five-minute monologue about Rob while helping Mom to the dining table.

"You sound so happy," she said once we sat down.

"I know, right? I am happy."

We ate salads with chicken, lettuce, feta cheese, and baked potatoes. The perfect blend of healthy and delicious comfort food.

"So, how serious are you two?"

"We're just having a great time together," I replied slowly, which didn't exactly answer her question. The truth was, I had no idea. I was happy knowing we were exclusive, but I hoped with every fiber of my being that it might end up being more.

Usually, I didn't even let myself think too far ahead in the future. Being here in Mom's apartment, I couldn't pretend I didn't know why: the fear of the man I loved just up and leaving me was lodged deep inside me.

This was the first time hope was stronger than fear. Rob had changed me.

After going to bed, I tossed and turned most of the night. The couch in the reading room was a pullout designed for guests to sleep on, but it was very uncomfortable. That wasn't why I was awake at two o'clock though. I had Rob on my mind. I squeezed one of the fluffy decorative pillows to my chest, sighing. I'd never been one to harbor romantic ideas… but now I was. There was no denying it. Just thinking about Rob made me fiddle my toes against one another and smile for no reason at all.

The next morning, I woke up with a surprising bout of energy despite only having slept a few hours. And still thinking about Rob, which was why I texted him first thing.

Skye: My neck is stiff.

Rob: I can help with that.

Skye: I know. That's why I'm telling you. So you can prepare accordingly.

Rob: Duly noted.

Cole was spending the day with Mom, taking her to the doc for her checkup too, and Tess was staying with her this evening. At least, that was the original plan.

But Tess was caught in a meeting with our distribution partner until late. At six o'clock, she texted me.

Tess: Can you head over to Mom's? One of the guys was an hour late to the meeting, so this will take forever. Cole has a dinner meeting he can't cancel. I'll come afterward.

Skye: Just go home and I'll spend the night there.

Jane was closing the store, so we had that covered, but I had to cancel my dinner plans with Rob. I wasn't upset with Tess, but I really wanted to see him, and I began to feel pouty.

Skye: I won't be able to make it tonight. Tess is caught up in a meeting, so I'm heading to Mom's.

Rob: See you tomorrow?

Skye: Not sure when. There is a gathering at Mom's house—all my siblings will be here, and those of my cousin-in-law.

Rob: Oh, right! You told me that. I forgot.

☹

My stomach rolled. We hadn't made plans for tomorrow, because Josie's family was in town and I wasn't sure how long the gathering at Mom's house was going to take.

God, I hoped he wasn't going to get annoyed with all of this and decide I was too much trouble. I shook my head, chastising myself. That was no way to think, but I couldn't help myself, not after my horrid experience with Dean.

He called as I was about to descend to the subway station, so I stopped next to a waffle shop instead to take the call. The smell was weakening my knees, and my resolve not to snack before dinner. Why, oh why did Soho have temptations at every corner?

I pressed the phone to my ear, turning my back to the waffles.

"Hi," I said.

"Hey. Here's a thought. Would you like company? You and your mom?"

I nearly swallowed my tongue. "Wait, what?"

"I can have dinner with the two of you. If you think that's going to be okay with her."

For a second, I couldn't answer. Giddiness bubbled up my throat, prompting a very large and silly grin on my face and an army of butterflies in my stomach.

"She'd like that." I was trying to sound casual, but I was fairly certain he could tell I was grinning, because my voice changed a bit.

Holy shit! He wanted to meet Mom.

"When are you going to be there?" he asked.

"In about forty minutes. I was just about to hop on the subway."

"Okay. I'll need a bit longer."

Holy shit, giddy didn't even begin to describe my feelings. As the conversation finished, I smiled even as a passerby bumped into me. The appropriate response to that in New York was to snap back, or at least glare, but right now, I was in my own bubble.

Once I arrived at Mom's place, I barely had time to tell her that Rob would be joining us when the doorbell rang.

"He's here early," Mom said.

"It seems so."

"Don't keep him waiting dear," she urged.

"I'm going, I'm going."

I was smiling from ear to ear as I opened the door. Rob was standing there with a bag of takeout.

I almost jumped him before remembering we were at Mom's place.

"Come in," I said, stepping back.

He gave me an amused glance but walked in.

I led him straight to the living room. Mom was sitting at the dining table. Her eyesight had cleared enough so she could eat on her own, but she did need guidance through the apartment or she risked bumping into things.

"Rob Dumont, ma'am. Nice to meet you."

"Likewise. I'm Amelia," Mom said.

"I hope I wasn't out of line, inviting myself over."

"Nonsense. I've heard so much about you."

"Really?" He looked at me with a smile.

"From both of my daughters," Mom clarified.

Rob chuckled. My cheeks heated up.

Having him at dinner had the unexpected effect of actually relaxing Mom. I hadn't seen her in such a good mood since before the surgery.

Rob was telling her his grandfather's credo about butter, which, of course, Mom immediately approved of.

"Your grandfather sounds like a very sensible man."

"I'll let him know you said that."

"So how come you moved next to Skye?" Mom asked.

"Well, I was looking for a place close to my sister and niece. It was hard to see them traveling back and forth from the city; it takes a lot of scheduling. Now they just spontaneously drop by for breakfast or dinner whenever they feel like it."

I hadn't told Mom that, and I could tell by the

slight jerk in her head, the way she gripped her glass tightly, that neither had Tess. She smiled warmly. Yeah, he'd just completely charmed her.

At eight o'clock, she said she'd rather I helped her back to her room.

"But it's early, Mom," I said.

"I've discovered audiobooks," Mom explained, but I knew she also wanted to give Rob and me some privacy.

Once she was inside her room, I went back to the living room. Rob was standing next to the couch, watching me intently. The air between us just crackled with tension, intensifying with every step I took.

"Do you want some wine?" I asked when I was just a few inches away.

"Whatever you want. But first, this." He slid a hand along the side of my head, wrapping his fingers in my hair. His mouth was desperate on mine, sucking my lower lip, biting my tongue lightly.

I wrapped both hands in his shirt, tugging at it.

No, I can't undress him in Mom's living room.

But instinct always won when I was with him. It went even beyond that, a need so deep, I couldn't explain it.

Letting go of his shirt, I drew my hands up slowly over his chest. I only became aware that we were moving when we fell on the couch: Rob on his back, me on top of him. This couch was even smaller than the one in the study. I had no idea how we fit on it. A glance backward revealed that Rob's ankles were hanging over the armrest.

Laughing, I hid my face in the crook of his neck. His hands wandered from the sides of my breasts down to my waist, and even farther down to my thighs. He stopped on my ass, fondling it. Big surprise.

"What do you think you're doing, Mr. Dumont?"

"What does it feel like?" He wiggled his eyebrows.

"You're being inappropriate."

"Skye, this isn't inappropriate," he warned. "And you know that." He ran his fingers over the crack of my ass, then under one cheek, resting it on my thigh. Sliding his thumb between us, he skimmed the edge of the front of my panties.

Even through a layer of clothes, a heat so intense curled through me that my nipples instantly turned hard. Licking my lips, I slid to one side so I half straddled him, but he placed me back on top.

"That's exactly where I want you," he said.

I placed one hand on top of the other, and my chin on that, looking him straight in the eye.

"You're extra demanding tonight," I teased.

"Sweetness, I want to have my fill of you. Who knows when I'll see you next time."

I bit my lip, trying to ignore that irrational fear clawing up my throat again, but I didn't know how.

***

Rob

"True, the next few weeks are going to be pretty busy," she said.

"I imagine."

"I... I don't know how much free time I'll have."

Her voice suddenly became small and vulnerable. Frowning, I slid my hand under her chin, raising her head.

"What do you mean?"

She sat up, fiddling with her thumbs before rising from the couch altogether. Grabbing plates from the table, she brought them to the small nook adjacent to the kitchen. What was going on? She was in a state I hadn't experienced before, and I wanted to get her out of it.

"It's just that...." She wasn't looking me in the eye. I walked to the kitchen until I stood right in front of her. Still, she looked down.

"Skye, talk to me."

"I know this is not exactly fun or sexy. If you've changed your mind about us...."

"Let me get this straight. You think that I'm just gonna bail?"

She fiddled with her thumbs some more. "I'm not saying that. I'm just saying I've been dumped before when shit hit the fan—"

I cupped the back of her head with one hand, cutting her off. I didn't want her to finish that sentence, even remember a time that made her feel worthless.

"Skye, I told you that you're mine. I meant it. I want you to count on me, to call me, to know I'm here for you. I like being with you whenever, however possible. What we have goes beyond sex. For me, at least. Tell me you feel it too."

Unease gripped me like a rope, tight around my whole body, especially my throat. I'd laid myself bare in a way I never had. When she nodded, I felt as if I could suddenly breathe in deeper. She put both hands on my chest, not as if she wanted to avoid looking at me but more as if she was searching for the right words.

"I love you," she murmured. "I'm not sure how it happened."

"It happened because we fit," I replied easily. "Skye, I've been in love with you for a while now."

The corners of her mouth lifted up slowly, as if she was registering my words in slow-motion. They surprised the heck out of me too. I didn't even have to think it over. It was just true.

I moved my fingers to her temples before tracing a line downward to her jaw. I couldn't stop looking at her. She was so fucking beautiful and real.

I rested my thumb on her lips. She pushed the tip of her tongue against it, teasing me.

"Rob, we can't do this here," she whispered, clearly still rational. But I wasn't. I wanted to show her how completely she owned me, the only way I knew.

"Where do you sleep?" I asked.

"There's a couch in the study."

"Show me. Now."

Her breath was labored, her pupils dilated. I slid my hands down to her hips, pushing myself against her, capturing her mouth at the same time. I was so damn hard already. She whimpered against my mouth, deepening the kiss before taking a step back. She turned around, taking my hand, leading me toward a door I hadn't paid attention to next to the entrance. Past it was a small room with floor-to-ceiling shelves and an armchair with a small lamp. Skye turned it on. On the other side was a couch, pulled out into a bed, with a mattress on it.

"We have to be silent," she murmured as I walked her backward. When we reached the makeshift bed, she pulled her dress over her head before sitting down.

"I'll keep you silent, Skye. This is just for you."

I wanted to remind her that I worshiped her in every way there was, make her feel that deep in her bones, in every cell of her body. I trailed my fingers down her stomach, into her panties. I didn't even have the patience to take them off. I didn't want to wait. She was so fucking wet that I nearly burst in my pants. I teased the sides of her entrance, going down slowly, then back up. I captured her mouth as a moan escaped her lips, tangling our tongues. Every moan vibrated through my body. When I started circling her clit, I could feel every single shock wave radiating through her, pushing me further to the edge.

Tease and please.

I followed this rhythm, teasing around her clit, touching it just long enough to provide a brief release before ramping up the anticipation, until she tugged at my shirt with so much force that she pulled it out of my belt.

"Please, please, please." Her words were low and pleading, and I couldn't deny her a climax any longer.

Covering her mouth, I rubbed two fingers from her entrance up to her clit, and she exploded beautifully, pressing her legs together, trapping my hand there. Her hands went to my shoulders, pulling me closer. I held her until the aftershocks subsided but kissed her even longer than that. There was something so intimate about kissing her when she was like this, ravished and content... and belonging completely to me. Just like I belonged to her.

"*Je suis à toi*, Skye. I'm yours."

"Oh, Mr. Frenchman, you really can't make me swoon right now," she whispered, curling even closer to me. "I can barely breathe as it is."

Sometime later, Skye showed me to a tiny bathroom where we freshened up one after the other because we didn't both fit at the same time.

"This couch is uncomfortable as fuck," I said when we were back on it.

She giggled. "I know. My neck's still stiff from last night."

Chuckling, I checked the mattress. "This is

easy to take off. Let's put it on the floor and sleep there."

She just blinked at me. "You're staying?"

"You haven't been paying attention. I'm not leaving tonight."

Skye grinned, but then it dimmed to a reluctant smile. "I'm trying to imagine my mom's reaction in the morning."

"Think she has anything against sleepovers?" I asked.

"Naked sleepovers, you mean?"

"She doesn't have to know they were naked." I wiggled my eyebrows before kissing her on the forehead. "I'll sneak out in the morning."

"You don't have to do that. We're not teenagers."

"No, but your face turned red just at the thought of your mom knowing I spent the night here."

She grinned, helping me move the mattress to the floor. She gave me the pillow she'd used as a sound muffler and took a decorative one for herself before tossing it aside and snuggling up to me.

I was sleeping on a floor, on a dreadful mattress, but I couldn't remember being this carefree and happy before. I barely recognized myself.

"You're right, it is more comfortable here. Especially because I can use your arm as a pillow. In fact, I can use your whole body for that."

"You sure adapt fast." The next second, I pulled her under me, parting her thighs, pressing my semi against her belly. She gasped, eyes wide. "Let's see what happens when *I* use *you* as a pillow."

Chapter Twenty-Three
Skye

I woke up early the next morning and heard noise from the living room. *Holy shit, is Mom moving on her own?* I jumped from the mattress, only then registering that it was empty. I pouted. I hadn't even heard him leave.

Opening the small bag I'd brought, I dressed in a yellow skirt and a white shirt with spaghetti straps.

To my surprise, it wasn't Mom who was moving through the living room but Rob. I grinned from ear to ear when we made eye contact. I knew we'd agreed he'd sneak out, but he hadn't, and I was glad for that.

Wait a second.... I vividly remembered the suit he'd worn yesterday: dark navy shirt and gray pants. Now he was wearing jeans and a khaki shirt.

"You're wearing different clothes."

He winked. "I know. I woke up early and went home to change. I can say that I just came back this morning."

"And it's not even a lie. You're a genius."

I tiptoed toward him, spying avocado toast on the counter behind him.

LAYLA HAGEN

"What are you doing?"

"Breakfast. But if you have other suggestions, I'm all ears."

I grabbed a quick bite of bread to get rid of morning breath. Then I wrapped my arms around his neck and gave him a hell of a smooch.

"I'll prepare breakfast every morning if this is what I get in return."

"Yes, please."

"Any other wishes?"

"Hmmm… I have a whole list, but are you sure I should voice them? You can't unhear them."

He threw his head back, laughing. "I'll take my chances."

I bit his Adam's apple lightly, moving my hands down his chest. It didn't even matter that the pesky shirt covered it. I knew exactly what was underneath.

"This was on your list?" he teased. "Great minds think alike. It's on mine too."

"I'm just so happy you're here. I'll go check on Mom, but if she hasn't called me, I guess she's still asleep."

"Let her rest."

"That's the plan, but the whole gang arrives in about two hours, so she can't sleep for much longer. You remember that there's a big family gathering today, right?"

"Yeah, I do."

And he didn't even flinch. Still, I decided to double-check. "And you feel like taking on everyone at the same time? You're probably going to be a hot topic."

"Counting on it."

"Okay."

I tiptoed to Mom's room, but she was sound asleep. Closing the door carefully, I returned to the living room. I took a moment to just watch him, feeling as at ease in the tiny nook as he was in the kitchen of his own house or the sleek and professional ones at his restaurants.

"I know you're watching me," he said playfully.

"Anything against it?"

"Not if you come closer."

"Demanding this early in the morning already?" I teased, but the second he looked up, trapping my gaze in his, my legs carried me toward him almost on their own accord. When I was just two feet away from him, he reached for me. He drew the tip of his nose up my neck, biting me lightly.

"Wait until a girl's had her coffee before unleashing all your charm, will ya?"

"Can't do that, or you'll be fully awake and worrying already."

"Attacking me while I'm half asleep. Interesting strategy."

He pinched my ass. I pinched him right back. "Here you go with the attacking again."

"What else would you call this?"

"Seducing you with breakfast."

***

Rob

Luckily, Skye's family arrived in batches, but even so, remembering everyone's names was challenging. Tess arrived first, followed by her brothers.

"Ryker," Skye said. "My brother."

"And I'm Cole. Also a brother."

Cole shook my hand forcefully. I did the same in return.

"Cole, you can let go now," Skye said. "No need to make this uncomfortable."

Cole cocked a brow. "Just testing the strength of his grip. You know what they say."

"No, I don't," Skye said sarcastically.

Cole let go, waving a hand at her. "Doesn't matter. He passed the test."

"My fiancée, Heather," Ryker said, "and our daughter, Avery."

"Nice to meet you, Heather. Avery."

Skye immediately pulled Avery into a hug. This woman was just adorable.

Her cousin Hunter and his wife, Josie, joined us a while later. There was still a group of three to arrive, but Amelia decreed we should eat already. Surrounded by her family, she was visibly more relaxed than last night. After talking to Amelia yesterday, it was clear Skye had inherited her empathy and steely strength from her.

"Okay, I think we should familiarize Rob with the gang a bit," Cole said.

"I know a lot already from Skye," I assured him.

"Such as?" Cole asked.

"Such as you two always being in competition over... everything," Skye answered.

Cole pointed at her. "That is gross misinformation. I *win* at everything."

"Yeah... especially at bragging," Ryker said seriously. Everyone at the table burst out laughing.

"Don't overwhelm him with stories from the first lunch," the woman named Josie said. Turning to me, she added, "First time I met the gang, I couldn't even remember their names. So I nicknamed everyone."

"Smart." I understood the impulse. "What were the nicknames?"

She pointed to Tess, Cole, and Ryker. "Hurricane, Charmer, Flirt. And Skye got Dragon, though that's Ryker's work, not mine."

I turned to Skye.

"Dragon, huh?" I teased.

"You haven't seen that in action yet?" Cole asked. "Yikes, poor guy doesn't know what's in store for him."

I'd gotten a glimpse of that when she thought Anne and Lindsay were my wife and kid and when that scumbag of an ex asked her for money. Skye was calm and laid-back right until she went into fight mode.

A while later, another group of three arrived. We were done with lunch and spread out across the living room.

"My siblings," Josie told me. "Isabelle, Ian, and Dylan."

I greeted everyone, trying to remember who was who.

"You two, behave, okay?" Josie told her brothers.

Ian shook his head. "But Cole and Ryker are being more and more well-behaved. It's up to us to balance things out."

Josie pressed her chin to her chest. "You two are hopeless."

Isabelle winked at Josie. "Between the two of us, we'll manage to keep them in check. Is there any food left?"

"Of course. Come on, you must be starving," Skye said.

As she led them to the table, Tess approached me.

"You're holding up well," she commented.

"This is a fun group."

"We can also go stir-crazy from time to time. Don't let that overwhelm you."

I chuckled. "Don't worry. I won't."

"By the way, I forgot to tell you. I'm the number-one informant when it comes to my sister. If there's anything you want to know, you can ask me." She said this with a straight face. I, on the other hand, could barely hold back laughter.

"Why not just surprise Skye?"

Tess waved her hand dismissively. "Surprises are overrated in my opinion. They can go so wrong if one doesn't do their homework."

"I'll keep that in mind."

"Good. Now, excuse me, I'm going to catch up with the newly arrived," Tess said.

I liked Tess very much, her vibrancy and zest for life. She was in a great mood, but then again, so was Skye. Being surrounded by family just made her happy. I liked her fierceness and strength, but at the same time, I wanted to keep her safe from everything too.

Skye captivated all my instincts and thoughts in ways I hadn't allowed anyone to do before. I thought that would make me vulnerable, but I was changing my mind fast.

***

Skye

I absolutely loved having everyone here. I hadn't seen Ian, Dylan, and Isabelle in ages and wanted to catch up with them. Theoretically, we could all keep in touch over social media, but there was nothing quite like gathering in person. I couldn't really tell a person's mood through a screen, even if we spoke with the camera on, which I did with Isabelle. Things were different face-to-face.

Isabelle was bubbly as ever. She'd recently colored her hair a vibrant red. Ian and Dylan looked very similar to me—they took after their dad and had dirty-blond hair and green eyes.

Rob was taking everything in stride, and I was quite proud of him for that. Currently, he was with Mom, who appeared to be talking his ear off. I was torn between rescuing him and focusing on Cole, who wasn't his usual vibrant and funny self.

"Cole, what's up with you? By the way, we're still waiting on an update," I said, looking pointedly at him.

"Yeah, that's right," Tess added. "You didn't say anything after our theater visit."

Cole's demeanor changed.

"Wait a second, you're glaring," Tess said.

I nodded in agreement. "That's definitely a glare."

"What are you talking about? What did I miss?" Ryker asked.

"Oh, shit," Skye exclaimed. "We weren't supposed to say anything in front of Ryker."

"No, that's not why he's glaring." Tess was looking at Cole intently. "At least... not the only reason."

Cole shook his head, jutting his hands in his pocket. "She finally agreed to go out with me... and then I discovered she was dishonest about a lot of things."

I winced. "Oh, you have shit luck, brother."

Ryker looked stunned. "Wait a second... what

do you mean, finally agreed to go out with you? You actually had to work to get a woman? Why didn't I know about it?"

"Because I didn't want you giving me shit." Turning to Rob, Cole added, "My family has an uncanny memory for stuff that goes wrong but can somehow never remember my successes."

"That's not true," Tess said. "It's just easier to tease you with mishaps."

"I'm a changed man now. In love with my woman, happy to tie the knot," Ryker said slowly.

"Still doesn't mean you won't give me shit," Cole said.

Ryker shrugged, but his serious expression had been a farce, because it morphed into a devilish grin. "True, but... I'll give you a few days before I start."

"How generous of you. Anyway, bachelor for life, right here."

"Cole, you have one disappointment and you throw in the towel?" Tess asked.

"Yup. I choose my battles," Cole said.

Tess sighed. "Well, I don't. I just asked out a guy I really liked, and he turned me down. Said I'm not his type."

"You didn't tell me that. When?" I asked.

Tess shrugged. "Anyway, you don't see me swearing off love."

Cole rolled his eyes. "I think lightning striking twice is more likely than you swearing off love."

Tess smiled coyly, but I knew she was just

brushing everything off way too easily. Yes, she was always hopeful and optimistic, but she didn't deal well with rejection. I mean, who did?

I couldn't exactly drag her away from the group now though, but I planned to treat her to macarons and cappuccinos back at the store and get the details.

"By the way, are there any wedding changes we should know about?" Tess asked Ryker.

"No, I think my future wife is finally happy with our arrangements," he answered. "And so is Avery." He nodded at Avery, who was watching *Moana* on a tablet.

I smiled at the affection in my brother's voice. I was beyond excited that he was so happy. Heather had been a single mom when he'd met her, and he loved both her and Avery to bits.

"We have great news. I've finalized the adoption process for Avery, so she'll officially be mine in a few days."

"Wow, congratulations brother. I'm so happy for you."

"Thanks. And by the way, I think Mom is giving *the talk* to Rob."

Oh, shit. Mom definitely had her *fierce principal* face on.

"Yeah... looks like he needs to be rescued," I said before heading their way. When I reached them, they abruptly stopped talking.

"What were you talking about?" I asked.

"That's between Rob and me," Mom replied.

I jerked my head back, then turned to Rob, who just nodded.

Well, well. I'd completely misread the situation. Rob wasn't being cornered, he was just charming Mom some more, though I couldn't figure out the fierce expression in this context. But since neither of them was going to share anything, I was going to let it slide... for now.

Chapter Twenty-Four
Skye

We left Mom's place in the afternoon. Tess was spending the night with her, so I had the evening off.

"You look a bit preoccupied," I said once we were on the train, sitting opposite each other. About an hour ago, Rob had started checking his phone every few minutes.

"Things in LA are a bit of a shit-show. The CEO I hired in my place just quit."

"Crap. When, tonight? What are you going to do?"

"Yeah, haven't decided yet. Might need to fly there and put some fires out."

My heart was lodged in my throat. "Oh? For how long?"

"Not sure. It will—" He stopped midsentence as his phone beeped with yet another message. "Sorry, have to check this."

"Sure, go ahead."

I bit my lip, swallowing all the questions I still had. What did *not sure* mean? A few days, a week, a month? It didn't matter. He had to do what was necessary, and he didn't have to consult with me.

This was one of the things I loved about our relationship, that we didn't pressure each other to figure out every detail.

So I resolved to do something else: help him relax for the rest of the afternoon. After all, one could decide better with a clear mind than under stress.

He went back and forth with emails while we were on the train, making two calls as well. I overheard everything, of course, but since I was only privy to his side of the conversation, I didn't get the bigger picture. To give myself something to do, I pulled out a study I'd been wanting to read for a while on my phone. Before long, I was completely lost in it, able to tune out Rob's voice.

"What are you reading?" he asked after a while.

"A study about music and concentration, how it impacts brain waves."

"What's the result?"

"I don't like to talk about the results until I finish the whole thing."

"Wait, you're reading the actual study?"

"Yes. What did you think?"

"I don't know. I usually just read an article summing up the findings."

"I like to know the stuff articles don't include, especially details on how they gather data."

He just stared for a few seconds, blinking. "I thought you did that just for the study about exercising."

"I know, I'm a geek."

"You're a fucking sexy brainiac," he whispered.

My cheeks instantly felt hot. Peeking around, I realized no one was sitting close enough to hear. He opened his mouth, but before he could say anything else, his phone rang, and I dove back into the study.

"All in all, a successful day, I'd say," I announced once we reached his house, playfully shoving my hip into Rob's. He'd slid his phone in the back pocket of his jeans.

"And very informative."

"Meaning?"

"Between your mom and Tess, I've got a pretty good rundown about... everything."

Right. I still had no clue what he and Mom had talked about. And he'd also spoken with Tess?

"Okay, first things first. Why were you and Mom so secretive?"

"No secrets, just exchanging information. She told me a bit about your life in Boston."

"Wow. I'm surprised Mom would even tell you about those times."

"She just told me about you, in general."

"Oh yeah? Find out anything new?"

"Just confirmed a few things. You're a lot like her."

"Thanks." I loved the compliment. And because he seemed to be in sharing mode, I seized my chance. "What did Tess tell you?"

"That if I want to plan a surprise for you, I should consult her first."

I adored my sister to bits!

"And you're going to listen to her."

"Absolutely. But right now, I have other things on my mind."

"Oh?"

He put both hands on my waist and skimmed them up to my breasts, moving his fingers in small circles until I was panting and my chest trembled lightly. He whirled me around, ushering me to his front door.

"We need to go inside for you to put your plan into action?" I teased as he put the key in the lock.

"That's right. We have to be indoors so I can have my fill of you." His voice was raw and hoarse, and it turned me on to no end. He was right behind me. His chest pressed against me; his lips were almost touching my ear. "Ever since I saw you in this little dress, all I could think about was taking it off, drawing my tongue all over you until you beg for more. First, you'll beg, then you'll scream my name."

"You'll have to work for that." I'd meant to tease him again, but my own voice was hoarse. My entire body vibrated, instantly going on high alert.

"I promise I will."

***

Rob

"And how exactly do you plan to keep your promises?" she asked coyly, turning around. What she saw in my eyes made her jerk her head back. A crazy need to completely own her: pleasure, body, soul.

This day had started out great, and then reality just had to break in and turn it all to shit. I'd barely brought things in New York to a balance, and now they'd imploded in LA. It was a damn hamster wheel. I wasn't complaining; I'd taken it on. I was proud to not only carry on my family's legacy but also vastly expand it, but some days were just hard. Period.

Right now, I wanted to lose myself in Skye and forget everything else.

She seemed to realize exactly what I needed, because she pulled that dress up teasingly, revealing her ass and the red lace panties that were covering the upper part of her luscious backside.

"You're going to kill me with all these sexy things you're wearing."

"Would you prefer I don't wear anything?" She batted her eyelashes, turning around and seductively touching her inner thighs until she reached the hem of her panties.

"Want me to go commando all over New York... again?" she teased.

"Fuck no. I couldn't work just thinking about it." Before she could say anything else, I pushed her up my body, over my shoulder, holding her by that delicious ass.

She laughed. "What are you doing?"

"Getting you to a bed." I wasn't patient enough to head upstairs, so I just brought her to the guest bedroom downstairs, putting her on the bed, pressing a knee on the mattress. As she whisked her dress over her head, I lowered myself above her. "No one else gets to see you. Any part of you. Yes, I know I'm possessive as hell, but I can't be any other way with you. It's an instinct. A need."

Parting her legs even wider, I touched between her thighs. She gasped when I pressed the drenched fabric against her sensitive skin. Her panties had bows on the sides, making it all too easy to open them. I pulled at each, then yanked the panties from underneath her.

I ran two fingers from her navel downward, right to her clit. She shuddered, opening up even wider. I changed my position, settling between her legs.

"Rob."

"I want to make you come every way there is."

"Now?"

"Yes. Now. Have anything against it?"

She shook her head. The light coming from the reading lamp was too faint, but I didn't have it in me to move and turn on the overhead lights.

"Take off your bra," I commanded.

She immediately obliged. Her breasts spilled out of it as I lowered my head between her thighs. I drew the tip of my nose on the inside of her right thigh, then applied the same treatment to the left one. Her sounds were completely muffled by the pillow, but her body wasn't lying.

I alternated between pressing the flat of my tongue against her clit and drawing just the tip around in circles as she pulled at the mattress with her hands. But when she attempted to move her legs, I pressed my hands on her ankles, like cuffs. I kept them in place. Not giving her an outlet for the pleasure was only going to make her climax stronger.

When Skye pressed her ass cheeks together, contracting the muscles in them, I knew she was close. I couldn't take it anymore. I unzipped my pants, jamming my hand inside and squeezing my cock tight. It was nothing compared to how it felt when she touched me, but I needed the pressure or I was going to blow.

She exploded the next second, but I was still relentless. I licked and nipped until her sounds subsided and her body stopped shuddering. Then I stood up long enough to take off all my clothes before pleasuring Skye further.

I kissed from above her navel up to her chest. I skimmed the tip of my nose on the soft skin under her nipple. Turning her on one side, I moved my mouth from the side of her breast down to her waist. When I reached her hips, I pushed myself up and just watched her. She was lying in an S-shape, head slightly bent, the pillow under her head. She was shuffling her feet against the mattress, as if she had too much energy to keep still.

I moved behind her, and my cock grazed her ass cheek in the process. *Fuck me.* The contact sent a bolt of energy spiraling through me. Groaning, I pulled back a few inches. She wiggled her ass but missed me. I gripped her hip, keeping her in place while I continued kissing her body from her hip down to her outer thighs.

"Rob...." Her voice was mutinous. I imagined her pouting. Hell, I had no idea where I'd suddenly found all this self-restraint, but I planned to make good use of it while it lasted.

I slipped my hand farther up between her thighs, skimming her slit with my thumb.

She gasped into the pillow. The muffled sound didn't satisfy me. She glanced at me furtively. Her cheeks were flushed. I wanted her to let loose, utterly and completely. I didn't want her to hold anything back. I slid one finger inside her. She clenched her inner muscles so tight that my self-restraint vanished, as if I'd flipped a switch. I turned her to face me. Skye drew her fingers down my chest, curling them against my skin, as if she was so desperate for me that she forgot I wasn't wearing anything for her to tug at.

She looked down between us when I hovered above her and drew my erection against her lower belly, teasing her clit, stopping when the tip was right at her entrance.

Her breath was shaky, and so were her legs. She was holding them up in the air, her hips rolled toward me.

I slid inside her slowly, watching her expression change from anticipating to being overwhelmed by pleasure.

Damn, this felt so exquisite. She was tight and pulsing around me, and when she rolled her hips, taking me even deeper, I buried my face in her neck. A groan tore from me. The scent of her hair and skin were driving me crazy. Resting my full weight on my knees, I moved faster and harder. Pulling my head back, I slid one hand under her ass, pressing her against me, holding her at the angle I wanted her. She cried into the pillow when I touched her G-spot. Her eyes widened in surprise. Her inner muscles squeezed me so tight that my breath was knocked out of me. Pleasure zipped down my spine, shot through my limbs. My muscles tightened.

Skye scratched down my arms and then my back. That was it. She was letting loose, and it was a glorious feeling. I wanted to push her over the edge right now. I changed the angle of my hips, thrusting my pelvis so it rubbed against her clit. She gasped. The pillow dropped to one side, and she clamped her mouth on my arm. She came the next second, arching her back. I felt her heels settle on the back of my thighs, and she grabbed my ass with both hands, pushing me deeper inside her.

I stopped moving, just losing myself in the sensation of her tightening around me, riding out the wave of pleasure. The sounds she was making were delicious. When she dropped her head back on the mattress, her breath was coming out in heavy pants.

There was perspiration at the base of her neck. I drew the tip of my nose on the soft skin between her neck and shoulder before pushing myself up on my knees. Skye's cheeks were flushed, and her body glistened with perspiration. She was still pulsing around my cock, driving me mad.

I hooked my elbows under her knees, lifting her legs up a notch. She stretched her arms wide on the bed, grabbing at the sheets as if needing to brace herself.

"You're so beautiful, Skye. Just perfect. Your skin." I drew my fingers down her ankles. "Your body." I reached her inner thigh and moved up right between them.

"Your pussy." I didn't last long after that. I came so hard that my mind turned blank. Even through the shot of pleasure, I felt my thighs cramping, but I wouldn't stop. Couldn't. I needed to wring out every drop of pleasure. When my legs cramped so hard that I couldn't stand on my knees alone, I fell forward on my palms, thrusting until I could barely move.

Skye touched my face, drawing her hands down my chest, watching me with a wry smile. It took several solid minutes for me to compose myself. Physically, at least. I still wasn't thinking clearly, or at all... nothing more coherent than *Skye. Here. Want. Her.*

If it wasn't for my phone buzzing, I would have stayed with her like that for the rest of the afternoon. After Skye got up from the bed, heading to the bathroom, I grabbed my jeans from the floor and took out my phone. It was Anne. I immediately answered.

"Hey. How's it going?"

"Ummm… it's been rough."

"Want to come by? I have wine, and a rough story too."

"Skye there with you?"

"Yes."

"I'll be there in fifteen minutes."

I was so happy at how close those two had become.

Twenty minutes later, Skye, Lindsay, Anne, and I were all sitting outside.

Before I had the chance to ask my sister what was wrong, Lindsay announced proudly, "I'm going to stay with Dad for two weeks. He's taking me to his new place on Monday."

Anne smiled sadly, and everything clicked into place. Douchebag finally took my threats seriously and was paying some attention to his daughter… but that made things even more difficult for my sister.

"What do you plan to do?" Skye asked Lindsay.

"I don't know. Whatever Daddy wants. I'm going to take all my dolls and show them to him. And my new necklace and bracelet."

Anne nudged her. "Don't forget to thank Skye for the bracelet."

"Thank you," Lindsay said seriously.

"My pleasure."

"So, what was the bad news you had?" Anne asked.

"CEO in LA quit. Now I need to find a new one."

Anne grimaced. "We can't catch a break, can we?"

"Seems not."

"Who are you thinking of making CEO?"

"Denis, Hope, and Alyssa are on top of my list. Or I could hire some fresh blood." Turning to Skye, I asked, "What would you do?"

"Promote from inside. They already know the company, and things will move faster."

"That's what my gut says too," I replied.

Predictably, Lindsay got bored of business talk and asked me to show her how to make grilled cheese sandwiches. Five minutes into the process, she got bored of that too and preferred to play on Anne's tablet. I finished the sandwiches, and when it was time to take them outside, Lindsay said she wanted to stay inside on the couch. Knowing she'd be fine, I went back outside to Skye and Anne.

With Lindsay out of earshot, I focused on Anne.

"How are you holding up?"

"Miserable. I'm happy he's finally paying attention to her, of course. And don't think you're fooling me with that poker face. I know you scared him into it."

"I admit it. I'm not even sorry."

"I'm grateful you did it, honestly, because I can't even bear to talk to him, and I want him to be in her life. But it's the first time I'll be without Lindsay in years, and I already miss her."

I had no idea what to say.

"Let's organize a girls' evening next weekend," Skye suggested.

Anne sat up straighter, finally smiling for real.

"I'd really like that. Just you and me?"

"The group would be a bit larger. My sister, our best friend, our brother's fiancée. Depends who has time, but I think everyone's in need of a girly evening."

"Sold."

I had no idea how Skye could tell exactly what someone needed, but hell if I didn't fall for her even more after this.

"I'm just going to check on what Lindsay's watching and be back in a minute," Anne said before heading inside.

"Why are you looking at me like that?" Skye asked.

"No reason."

Even though we both had challenges with our families and businesses, things between us were falling in place in a way I'd never imagined, but I was looking forward to whatever followed. No matter what, Skye was mine. I'd just realized we were a team, and I liked that so damn much.

Chapter Twenty-Five
Skye

We organized the girls' evening three days later instead of waiting for the weekend. Since it was a weeknight, that decision wasn't taken lightly but more out of necessity.

Tess lacked her usual sparkle, and no amount of macarons brought it back. Isabelle was still in town, but only until tomorrow, and we'd planned to have a girls' evening ever since we knew she was coming to visit. Per her own admission, Anne was already going stir-crazy with Lindsay gone and asked if we couldn't organize the evening right away. I gave in, especially because Mom was severely lacking entertainment, so we were taking the party to her place. Josie was coming as well, but Heather couldn't make it.

Aside from tomorrow being a workday, I had two other reasons that made me look less forward to tonight than usual. For one, I was feeling a little light-headed. And the second reason was that Rob was leaving for LA tomorrow. We'd had other plans for his last evening here (they involved a very sexy nightgown I'd planned to torture him with. He was practically my test subject for new products, and this one was hitting shelves this week).

"I'm torn between letting you go... and chaining you to my bed," Rob said. His gaze was so intense that I didn't doubt he'd pull a caveman move again, toss me over his shoulder and carry me to bed. The best part? I was sort of hoping he would. I was currently on my way out of my house.

Tess and I were both staying at Mom's tonight, because it didn't make sense to travel at night only to wake up early to head into the city to the store.

"You know, this line of thinking isn't helping at all. I'm just as torn. If we both give in to our dark side, we just won't get anywhere."

"Fuck, Skye, I just don't want to let you go." He pushed me against the door, drawing the tip of his nose up and down my neck. The skin on my arms and legs turned to goose bumps.

I playfully pushed him away.

"See you whenever you're back."

He'd mentioned he was staying one week maximum. I hoped it wouldn't be that long.

"Thanks for inviting Anne too."

"Don't you worry about her. Between all of us, we'll take great care of her."

He touched my cheek, resting his thumb on my lower lip. I swallowed hard, quickly leaving his house before he got dangerous ideas again.

Anne joined me on the train.

"Thanks for adopting me," she said.

"My pleasure."

"You really think everyone is going to be okay with it?"

"The more the merrier, trust me," I assured her.

"And your mom? It's her place, after all."

"Mom's excited to meet you."

"Okay." She looked desperately sad, and I just wanted to lift her mood, but I didn't know her well enough to come up with something that would work.

"I usually read on the train," she said.

"I know, I'm the same."

"I recently discovered audiobooks," Anne said. "Makes everything even easier. I get motion sickness sometimes."

"What's the last thing you listened to? I mean, if you recommend it."

"Nah, the last one was kind of a bore, but I did listen to a very informative one about wealth mindset. I forgot the name of the author. It's called *You're a Genius at Being Wealthy*."

"I like the title."

She showed me the cover on her phone.

"Cool, I'll buy the book. Or you know what? I'll give audio a try too."

"I'll help you set up your account."

I took out my phone and credit card, and by the time we reached our station, I'd popped my audio cherry.

Tess was already at Mom's. Josie and Isabelle

arrived ten minutes after us. After initial introductions were out of the way, we took stock of the food, though since we'd been relying on Rob sending over meals, we didn't have much. And speaking of Rob, he outdid himself that evening. When the delivery arrived, it wasn't the usual dinner for two but a platter filled with half a dozen delicious treats.

"My brother is more thoughtful than I gave him credit for," Anne said.

"Well, well. He definitely knows we'd have stuffed our faces with popcorn otherwise," Tess said.

I didn't reply, just smiled from ear to ear. Hiding in the pantry, I texted him.

Skye: Thanks for dinner.

Rob: Anytime.

Skye: You've just saved me from getting super drunk and dirty-texting you.

Rob: You can always dirty-text me.

Rob: Seriously.

Skye: Why doesn't this surprise me?

Rob: :)

Sitting around the dining room table, we stuffed our face with all the goodies, chatting about everything and nothing in particular. Mom was focusing on Anne. She must have sensed that Anne still felt a bit out of place here, but forty minutes into their conversation, Anne's shoulders weren't as hunched, and she was smiling more.

Mom went to bed about two hours into the

evening.

Tess pouted. "I thought she'd stay up for longer."

"She's just tired," Josie said. "By the way, anyone want to check the drinks supply in the library?"

I threw my head back, laughing. "We must remember to tell Mom you were the one convincing us to break into her supply all the time. How come you don't have a nickname? Should be the Marauder."

Josie grinned, rubbing her palms theatrically. "I love that."

We stormed Mom's liquor supply, which was in the reading room where Tess and I took turns sleeping.

The bottom row of the floor-to-ceiling shelves had doors, and behind two of them was Mom's collection of bourbon and whiskey. She was short on wine: just one lonely bottle of merlot. Then again, Mom didn't drink wine.

"Anyone feel sixteen again?" I whispered.

Tess cocked a brow. "Why are you whispering?"

"I don't know. Instinct. Guilt. Take your pick."

My sister pointed to the bottle of merlot. "That looks like just what we need."

"Get drunk as skunks?" Isabelle double-checked.

"No, we all need something to melt off the

stress in our bones, and this merlot here seems just like what the doctor ordered. Me being the doctor," Josie concluded.

"There's five of us. I'm pretty sure we'll need another bottle," Isabelle said.

Josie pointed her thumb to her sister. "See? That's where I get all the marauder genes. Or influence, whatever you want to call it."

Isabelle nodded proudly.

"Hate to break it to you, but this is the only bottle Mom has," I said.

"We'll make do," Tess said, looking around. "Let's keep the party in here, so we don't wake her up."

The couch was too small for all five of us to sit, but as soon as we pulled out the bed, we were comfy, sitting in a circle of sorts. Tess next to me, Josie next to Isabelle, and Anne between the two groups of sisters. Tess, Anne, and I were splitting the wine bottle. Isabelle and Josie each poured whiskey in their glasses.

Tess pointed at Anne. "So, the way this works is we first get out whatever weighs on our mind and then promptly forget it by being silly. I'll start. So, first, I'm super terrified that Skye and I jumped into this business with both feet too fast and it'll all go belly up."

I grimaced, pulling my sister into a half hug. "Tess, we've been worried about this for about a year. At this point, I just see it as a normal part of life. Time will tell. So far, we're keeping our head above water. What got you extra moody this week? Is it the food truck guy?"

"What? No. I think I just drove myself a little crazy, what with Mom's eyes and our new collection coming in."

I raised my eyebrows.

Tess sighed. "Fine, it does make me wonder exactly why I'm not his type. Is it something in my physical appearance? My personality? Both? I haven't been on a real date in a while, and I miss it."

"Awww, girl. You'll have better luck soon," Isabelle said.

"Anne, want to go next?" Tess asked.

"So, I don't know if Skye told you, but I'm divorced. My ex is a jackass... but I'm still half in love with him," Anne whispered. "I hate him for cheating on me all this time, but I don't know how to stop loving him. My daughter is spending two weeks with him, and I miss her like crazy. I know it's good for her, and I'm happy Walter is finally making her a priority. But I miss my girl." Her voice wobbled.

Josie and Isabelle looked stricken. They came from a happy, whole family, so this probably seemed like an apocalyptic scenario to them. Tess and I were from a broken home, so we had firsthand experience of all this heartache and how it shaped you.

"Anne, it's okay to miss her and even to still have feelings for him," Tess said gently.

"Falling out of love with your ex would be good though," Isabelle said. "Might I suggest therapy. I'm sorry if I'm too forward. I am a therapist, and I know how much it helps."

"Are you taking on new clients?" Anne asked.

"I'm not living in New York...though that might change soon."

Josie grinned at this, winking at her sister conspiratorially. This was news to me, but since neither had said one word until now, it was not the time to ask for details.

"We could do it online," Anne said.

"That's a thought," Isabelle replied. "I've been thinking about that lately."

Anne smiled, taking a sip of wine. "Well, let me know what you decide, maybe I'll give it a try.

"Anyone have good stuff to share? Happy stuff?" Anne went on.

"Well, if Heather was here, we could talk about the wedding," I said.

Tess held up a finger. "But since she's not, we can talk about the bachelorette party. Anne, want to join us for that? I'm sure Heather won't mind."

"Sure. When is it? Is Rob going to the wedding with you?" Anne asked.

"It's at the end of December. I haven't told Rob yet," I admitted. "Do you think he'd like to go?"

"Why don't you ask him?" Anne replied.

I pressed my thumb on my glass, looking down into my drink. "We never make plans beyond one or two weeks, and the wedding is still pretty far away."

"I'll have a word with my brother," Anne said sternly.

"No, no, no. Please don't. We're just taking things as they come. And I like that."

Isabelle held up her glass. "Let's celebrate life and not overthinking happiness. It's simple, and most of the time, we just complicate it with our overthinking."

"Hear, hear," I said.

While planning an array of activities for Heather's bachelorette party, we proceeded to bring out all the nail polish we could find and promptly discovered that it was a terrible idea to paint toes when you were light-headed.

We didn't even have enough wine to get tipsy, but our decision-making power wasn't too sharp. Also, Mom didn't have any nail polish remover. Ah, such was life. Sometimes it gave you lemons, and if you were a Winchester, you turned that into multicolored toes.

It was past two o'clock in the morning by the time we called it a night. Isabelle and Josie left, but Anne stayed with us.

The girls fell asleep almost the minute we stretched on the mattress, but I was staring at the ceiling as bits and pieces of our conversation swam in my mind. Once Rob came back from LA, I was going to ask him to Heather and Ryker's wedding. I *wanted* us there together. My heart rate sped up as I saw us attending all sorts of family events and Ballroom Galas together. I could imagine myself introducing him to donors as my boyfriend.

Holy shit, and I'd thought I didn't have a

romantic bone in my body? I'd just discovered all of them.

Chapter Twenty-Six
Skye

The rest of the week was insane. With new designs coming in, Tess and I didn't know our asses from our elbows most days. When we weren't packing online orders, we were attending to customers in the store. We started our days early, and by the time evening rolled in, we barely had enough energy to go home. At least Mom's eyesight had improved considerably. On Thursday, the doctor gave her the all-clear. The infection was gone. Mom declared she didn't need babysitting anymore.

On Friday, my body began to show signs of overworking. While I was arranging a new display, crouched to put on fluffy slippers on our mannequin, ass in the air, head down, my vision faded at the corners. I leaned against the window display for support, straightening up.

"What's wrong?" Tess asked, instantly at my side, helping me up.

"Just... balance issues. My vision went dark for a bit."

"Did you eat today?"

"Yeah."

"Maybe you didn't have enough water. Go sit down, I'll finish up here."

I did as she said, massaging my temples. I only needed a few minutes to recover, then decided to drink a big glass of water, just to be on the safe side. The last thing Tess and I needed was one of us to be sick. We'd fall so far behind on our to-do list that I shuddered just thinking about it. I felt as good as new after yet another glass of water, and just as I was preparing to get back to work, Rob called.

And just like that, the corners of my mouth lifted in a grin. Ah, I should have him call me more often if this was how my body reacted. My heartbeat accelerated. Oh yeah. There was the dose of energy I needed for the rest of the day.

"Hey, you!" I greeted.

"Hey. How is your day going?"

"Bah! It's a good thing you'll be gone this week."

"Why?"

"I have so much to do that you wouldn't even get laid."

His laugh brightened my spirits; I totally loved this man. "I can always make that a priority."

"Aha!"

"Don't tempt me. I can make that happen even from LA."

God, I missed him. "And how would you do that exactly?" I teased.

"Flying in, surprising you in the night."

Hmmm... that was a thought. Suddenly, the

urge to see him hit me hard. To stroke that chiseled jaw and jump his bones.

"Where are you now?" he asked.

"In the back, stuffing boxes for some online orders. Well, cheating, actually, and just looking in a mirror at my hair."

"Imagine I'm there with you."

His voice was so sensual and rich that I had no problem doing just that. It was as if he was just behind me, whispering in my ear.

"Rob...," I whispered, half admonishing him, half urging him to go on.

"Skye," he answered playfully. How he could pack so much sensuality in one syllable, I had no idea, but he did it in spades. "Imagine I'm kissing the back of your neck."

The hair at the nape of my neck stood on end. Goose bumps formed on my shoulders. I let out a quick breath.

If he was here, he'd raise his gaze, looking at me in the mirror. I could practically see the wolfish glint in his eyes... and shuddered.

"What else?" I asked.

"I'd boss you into taking some time off to relax."

I laughed, because I could imagine him doing just that.

"I miss you," I said. My stomach immediately rolled.

"I miss you too. But it looks like I'll have to be here another week."

"Oh?" I just wanted to cry. My emotions were just going every which way these days.

"The person I'd been hoping to promote doesn't actually want the job. We're sorting through other applicants now."

"Oh, wow."

"Anyway, have to go. Next applicant's here. Just wanted to hear your voice for a bit. I love you."

"I love you too."

I sighed deeply, pressing my palm against my sternum. I felt as if something heavy was suddenly pressing me. I couldn't believe I was so emotional just because he'd come back a few days later than planned. This was very unlike me. Was it just the stress and exhaustion of the week catching up to me?

I had no idea what to make of it but hoped customers wouldn't notice.

Tess did the second I returned to the front though. She gave me a speculative glance while tending to a customer, but the second the woman was out the door, Tess pointed at me, a crease between her eyebrows.

"What's with the mopey face?"

I shrugged. "I don't know. I'm emotional but don't get why."

Tess closed the distance to me, placing her forearms on my shoulders.

"I think we're both tired. You know what helps with that?"

"Ice cream?" I suggested.

Tess laughed. "Great minds think alike. I'll go

get us some. You want your usual?"

"Hmmm, actually no. I'm in the mood for some blueberry and lemon."

"You're exchanging caramel for lemon? Who are you and what have you done to my sister?"

"Hey, I feel like being adventurous today."

"You still have time to change your mind. Just send me a message," she said before leaving the store.

Eating ice cream with my sister was one of the finer pleasures in life. I was already rubbing my stomach while watching Tess cross the road.

We both devoured it like we were competing in a who-eats-faster show. We hadn't turned the sign to Closed, so we were just keeping our fingers crossed that no customers came in.

"Sneaky ice cream tastes even better," I said.

"I agree. How's the lemon?"

I grinned. "Lemon-y. Reminds me of dishwasher soap, but I like it." I yawned, suddenly feeling not only relaxed but also sleepy.

"I'm all over the place today."

"Maybe it's PMS," she said.

"I don't have PMS though." I'd never had mood swings, cravings, pain, extra tiredness, or any symptoms.

In a conspiratorial whisper, she said, "Things change as you get older, just saying."

"Hey, I'm not old. You're old." I pinched her arm. She giggled, pinching me right back. I'd always teased her for being older. When we were teenagers, my favorite tactic to annoy her was to point out imaginary wrinkles. But maybe she was right. Come to think of it, I was a few days late.

"I've always had a regulated cycle since being on the pill," I said out loud.

Tess cocked a brow. "I think you forgot half the sentence. What do you mean?"

"That I'm a few days late."

Tess grimaced. "Damn, I think the stress is really catching up to you. Don't come in on the weekend."

"We'll be swamped." Even though our sales associates were handling most weekends, we had a sale this Saturday and Sunday and needed all hands on deck. "I'll call upon the Winchester forces."

"What if they already have plans?"

"By sheer probability, someone will have time. You have to rest and relax."

"You sound like Rob."

"I knew I liked that man. When's he coming back?"

"Not sure. He said he has to stay a few more days, maybe even a week."

"Damn, so I can't count on him to ambush you into relaxing…." It sounded as if she was about to say "but…." She remained silent instead, but her eyes were a little narrowed as she finished her ice cream. I knew that expression. She was getting… ideas.

I didn't have time to investigate though, because the front door opened and three customers walked in.

The next morning, I did get an inkling of what she'd been up to when I opened the door to a guy delivering food at lunch.

"Hi," I said, feeling a little flustered and a lot tired. I'd slept in right until five minutes ago.

"Hi, ma'am. I have a special delivery."

Even through my sleepy haze, my heart fluttered. Special indeed, because I knew I hadn't ordered anything.

"Thank you so much." I tipped him generously, then took the basket with goodies inside the house. Ah, I didn't even need to see the logo of Dumont's on the napkins to know who'd sent this over.

Clapping my hands, I rose from my heels to my toes before rocking back on my heels.

Hmmm… what to do first? Dig into all of these goodies or call Rob and thank him? It was too soon after waking up for such difficult decisions, so I decided to do both at the same time.

Grabbing my phone and a plate, I put cheese and bread on the latter before sinking into my comfy swing.

I dialed Rob first.

"Hello, charming boyfriend," I greeted.

"Hi. Was just about to text the delivery guy and check on him."

"No need. I can confirm that all the goodies are right in front of my nose. Did you talk to my sister?"

"Hey, you're the one who said using Tess as a source of information is fair play."

"True that." Grinning, I shoved a bit of cheese in my mouth, dangling my legs in the air. "Mmmm... this is delicious."

"Skye, fuck."

Ah, what an atomic combination of words. Stifling a giggle, I moaned again, eating yet another piece of cheese.

"You want to kill me?" His voice was hoarse. My lady parts tingled with heat.

"Nah, just trying to sell you on jumping on a plane."

"I'm of a mind to ditch the rest of my plans anyway."

"Yeah, do that. Come over to the dark side."

He laughed. "Can't, unfortunately."

"Hmm... must improve my phone-moaning skills."

"Please don't."

Pouting, I said, "Tell me about the rest of your day."

"Three interviews at the office, and another two during lunch and dinner, then I'll drop dead in my bed."

"See, if you were in my bed, that would be so much more fun," I teased.

"I know."

We spoke a while longer, right until he had to go into his first meeting, and then I devoured a granola bar and a delicious yogurt with chia seeds and strawberry jam.

I felt more than a little guilty about staying home, but Tess was right. I needed to rest before I went from tired to sick.

Skye: I feel guilty for not being there.

In response Tess sent me a photo. Josie was there, along with Ryker, Hunter, and Cole.

Holy shit!

Tess: We're crazy busy. Josie's with me in the front, the boys are packing up the online orders. Cole insists he's the reason we're swamped. First we teased him that he's actually trying to charm his way out of packing boxes buuuut... customers tend to stay 30 percent longer in the store when he's in the front (and buy more).

Skye: Maybe we should include him in the marketing strategy. "Come on in and our brother might charm you into going on a date with him."

I snickered, yearning to have fun with all of them, but truthfully, I felt exhausted despite sleeping in and drinking coffee, so I went back to bed.

Sunday was just as relaxing. I slept in, and it was marvelous.

On Monday morning, I was still feeling as if I could sleep the whole day but forced myself to go into the city. I wasn't showing any signs of even a cold, so I couldn't justify staying home.

As per my usual routine, I first stopped into Joe's coffee shop. I was so hungry that aside from my to-go order, I also bought a vanilla custard puff. My mouth watered as Joe put it on a plate in front of me. Next to me, a preschooler was looking at me with envy. She received a healthy sandwich. I pushed my unhealthy, extra-sugary treat out of her sight.

Way to go, Skye. Being a bad influence starting at eight o'clock in the morning wasn't my usual MO, but today I felt rebellious.

After the first bite, I grimaced. Something about the cream was off. It wasn't sour or anything, it just tasted different. I didn't like it.

"Everything okay, Skye?" Joe asked.

"I usually love vanilla puffs," I muttered. "My taste buds are all over the place lately."

The lady next to me chuckled. "When I was pregnant with my first one, I couldn't even look at tomatoes, and I love tomatoes."

I froze, looking between Joe and the customer. "I'm not pregnant," I said. My stomach bottomed out at the same time as a knot formed in my throat.

"Oh, it's the only thing that occurred to me. Taste bud change happens a lot during pregnancy." She shrugged, heading back out on the street.

"I'll bring you another one, Skye. Maybe something's not right with this one."

"No, that's okay. Just a sign that I should start my morning with healthy snacks." Grabbing the rest of my order, I left the bakery.

I couldn't get that lady's words out of my head as Tess and I set our breakfast on the counter as usual. My heart was still in my throat. It was impossible to swallow anything. This wasn't possible. I took the pill religiously at the same hour every evening, as the instructions said.

Just to double-check, I got out the container. There were exactly as many pills as there should have been. I hadn't missed any... but I still hadn't gotten my period.

"Skye?" Tess asked. "You okay?"

"I'm still late," I said, biting my lower lip. "And I'm worried that...."

I couldn't bring myself to say it out loud.

Tess straightened up, running a hand through her hair. "Think you might be pregnant?"

Ah, of course Tess would ask me straight up, no punches pulled.

"I can't be though." My voice was strangled. "Just looked at the pill container. All gone. I didn't miss any."

Chapter Twenty-Seven
Skye

Tess bit her lip. "It can still happen, I think. If you take it at different hours."

"I didn't. I have a reminder on my phone."

"Some medicine can also influence its effectiveness."

"Like cold medicine?"

Tess nodded. I sat on the couch, trying to remember if I'd taken anything for a cold recently, but I couldn't. My hands were a little jittery. I grabbed the counter to steady them.

Tess was about to sit next to me, but a customer walked in right then.

I jumped right to my feet, thankful for the distraction.

"Hi! What can we do for you?"

"I loved a bra you had two collections ago. It had something like a stone between the cups."

"The one where the bra straps resembled feathers?" I asked.

"Exactly."

"We don't have it anymore, but we have a similar style. I'll bring it out to you."

I was only distracted while I was talking to the

customer. As soon as I was on my own in the back, searching for merchandise, my thoughts were a blur. And my feelings were all over the place. I couldn't make sense of them. My hands were jittery. Hope and fear were so deeply interlaced that I had no idea where one ended and the other began.

I returned a few minutes later. The customer was waiting in the changing room.

"I have three options for you." I held all of them for her to see.

"Oh, they are beautiful. And just my size."

I winked. "Guessed it right away."

"Whatever you do, don't let me buy all three."

"Can't make any promises."

Twenty minutes later, she left happily with all of them.

As the afternoon rolled around, things became even busier. Tess bought us tacos for a late lunch, which we ate standing.

As soon as we turned the sign to Closed, I dropped on the couch in the back. I had no energy left for packing bags for the online orders. Toeing off my shoes, I lay down.

I closed my eyes, pressing the heels of my palms over my eyelids. The couch caved in as Tess sat at my feet.

"How are you feeling?" she asked.

"Tired."

She massaged my feet and my calves, and it was pure heaven.

"You're my favorite sister," I said.

"I'm your only sister."

"Only in the strictest sense. Josie is family too."

"Are you trying to make me jealous?"

Tess pinched my toe. Shrieking, I pulled my knees to my chest, opening one eye.

"I'll downgrade you from favorite if you keep doing that," I warned.

"Just found out I'm not your only sister. A downgrade can't hurt as much." She brought one hand to her forehead theatrically.

Giggling, I laid my feet back in her lap.

"It's a sign of trust. Don't make me regret it," I warned.

"You're the one changing rules of sisterhood *and* threatening to downgrade me," she pointed out.

"True."

I placed one hand on my belly.

"I want to know," I whispered. "But I think the nearest pharmacy just closed."

Tess nodded. "I, er, bought two pregnancy tests when I got us lunch."

My heart rate accelerated. My palms became sweaty. I hadn't expected this.

I sat up. "Why didn't you tell me?"

"I didn't know if you'd want them, but I bought them just in case."

I sat there, not making any motion, trying to steady my breathing.

Tess pressed her lips together. "Or we can find an open pharmacy and walk over there... give you some time to get used to the idea."

I grinned. She knew me so well.

"It's fine, I'm not a coward."

"It's not about that. It's a huge thing. It's okay to be scared."

I smiled, but it was a little wobbly. My whole body seemed to vibrate on the rhythm of my pulse.

Wordlessly, my sister took two small packages out of her bag. "They're different brands," she said.

I grabbed both, heading straight to the bathroom. I was tremendously happy that I was doing this with my sister and not alone.

I did the tests one after the other, drew up my panties, flushed the toilet, and washed my hands before opening the door.

Tess stood against the wall, hands crossed in front of her. Her eyes widened, glancing at the two sticks I held up. They still had no results, but I couldn't take the anxiety of waiting on my own.

"How many minutes?" Tess said.

"I don't know. Haven't checked the instructions."

"That's the most un-Skye thing you've ever said." My sister laughed, putting her hands on my shoulders. "It's going to be fine either way, sis," Tess said. "I know it will."

Everything hinged on the next few minutes.

We sat in one of the changing rooms, huddled together. I was holding my breath. If it weren't for Tess's periodic elbows to my arm, I would have forgotten to breathe altogether.

"Ah!" I exclaimed when two lines appeared on the first screen. "What does this mean? Two lines."

"Pregnant," Tess said. Her voice was wobbly. I clutched her hand, squeezing her fingers. She squeezed right back, taking the second test from my free hand because I was too shaky. Two lines popped up on that one too, and I felt as if I'd been hit by an ocean wave. The floodgates of emotions flew open.

My skin turned clammy and then was so cold that I began to shiver. I pressed one hand to my chest, which seemed to be expanding by the second. Tess was saying something, but I only heard part of it.

"Say that again."

"Congratulations. I'm so psyched."

She was grinning and hugging me, and in my sister's arms, I discovered that among the overwhelming wave of emotions, I was psyched too. I hugged her back tightly, so grateful for her, immediately resolving that I wouldn't have just one kid. Having a sibling was the best thing.

Wow. Where did that thought come from?

"How do you feel?" she asked.

"Happy? Terrified? Is it possible to feel both?"

"Absolutely. I know what you need. Something delicious. That always makes everything better. Umm... so vanilla puffs are not on the list anymore. Mac and cheese? Wait, that's soft cheese, right? Is that good for the baby? Do you have to give it up? Then I promise I'll give it up with you."

"You love mac and cheese."

"I *live* for it. But for my niece or nephew, I can totally make a sacrifice."

"Tess, I think we're okay with some comfort food."

"Thank God. I'll just head to Henry's and pick up whatever looks good."

"Sounds like a plan."

I smiled as my sister sauntered out of the store. I'd never seen Tess like this. I paced around the store, keeping my hands at the sides of my body, almost afraid of touching my belly. What if I *felt* something? A tiny kick?

I rationally knew that he or she was far too tiny for anything of that sort. I was scared of that yet craving it at the same time with an intensity I'd never craved anything in my life. How was that even possible?

What would Rob say? *Oh God, oh God,* what would he say? We'd never discussed our future. One of the reasons we got along so well, why we had so much fun, was that neither of us was putting pressure on the other in any way. I was content with the way things were, and I was certain that so was he. How would this baby change things? Us?

Dread crept up my belly, ensnaring me. Would he decide this wasn't what he signed up for? I didn't want him to feel pressured in any way, yet at the same time, this changed everything.

Tess returned with three bags of goodies.

"Sis, that's all for us?" I checked.

"I couldn't decide."

"Clearly."

"And I didn't know which ones you'd like, so I wanted to cover all bases."

That was when I realized that my sister was just as terrified as I was. Happy... but also terrified.

We turned off the lights in the front and camped on the couch between the changing rooms. We shoved two ottomans together to form a makeshift coffee table.

Opening the packages, we discovered that vanilla puffs weren't the only things my baby was rejecting. I wasn't a fan of burgers either, but I did adore apple pie.

"Look at you, liking fruity fillings," Tess said appreciatively.

"Maybe I'll finally pick up some healthy eating habits."

"When are you going to tell Rob?" she asked.

"When he's back. Don't want to do it over the phone, you know?"

My stomach turned into a tight knot just *thinking* about it.

"That makes sense."

"I'm afraid," I admitted in a whisper.

Tess shook her head. "No, no. None of that. Let's see. The man calls me to make sure he gets the surprises right. All signs point to him being a catch and an all-around decent human being."

"Yes, but we've been going at our own pace,

you know? We don't even make plans for vacations together or anything."

"That's because neither of you has even planned a vacation yet," she pointed out.

"Tess... you know what I mean."

She gave me a small smile. "I do, but I think that you're both mature enough to deal with the... unexpected."

I hoped so. God, I hoped so. I got heartburn just thinking about the alternative.

Tess stood up straighter, smiling coyly. Uh-oh. She was up to something.

"What?" I asked.

"Can we talk names?"

I threw my head back, laughing. Leave it to my sister to push any ugly thoughts to the back of my mind.

"Please, what did you have in mind?"

"I have this list—"

"Wait, what?"

Tess blushed. Actually blushed.

"You know, when I come across a cool name, I put it on a list. You-you don't do that?" Uncertainty flickered in her eyes.

"Umm... no. But lucky you've been doing that. You'll save my kid from being named Frodo or some other nerdy character."

Tess beamed. "Okay, so I have a top three for boys and top three for girls."

"Wouldn't you rather keep those for your own kids?"

"Eh, who knows if I'll have any? At the rate my dating life is going, I'll be a cat lady."

She shrugged, but I could tell she was just trying to be nonchalant. I hugged the living daylights out of her.

"I can't wait to be an aunt."

"I can see that." Seeing my sister all dreamy filled me with a kind of fuzzy warmth that was completely unfamiliar for me.

"Okay, so I have Beatrix, Francine, Charlotte for girls, and Lionel, Richard, and Jake for boys."

"You have excellent taste," I informed her.

"I know, right?"

"Let's hope Rob agrees with me. Tess... how will I juggle the business and everything?"

"Skye... you worked while studying, then practically had two full-time jobs. You read scientific studies in your spare time just *because*. You can pull off anything."

"This is different." It was a human being, someone tiny and lovable who would need me at all times, and I already envisioned myself running around searching for merchandise or packing boxes with a baby strapped to my chest.

"We'll make it work," she assured me. "Don't worry about the business right now."

I couldn't help it though. We'd worked for so long for this dream, planning every step of the way. I was a planner. I always calculated risks, weighed pros and cons, tried to think four steps ahead for any major decision. When Tess and I had decided to quit our jobs, I made three contingency plans. And now? I was honestly too overwhelmed to even come up with one plan.

"Want to call the rest of the gang and tell them?" Tess asked.

"No, I want to tell Rob first. I should go home. I'm super tired."

"You're sure you'll be okay on your own?" Tess asked. "I can come and sleep on your couch."

"I'll be fine, but thanks."

I wanted some time by myself to just think. Now that the initial shock was over, I was ready to go home and just process everything.

Leaving the store, I walked at a leisurely pace, taking the long route to the train. I could think better while on the move. Usually. Now, I was in a weird state where I had so many thoughts that I couldn't focus on just one of them.

The train was far emptier than usual. The suburban commuters were home long by now, and I found a seat right away. As usual, I pulled up my phone to read, but I couldn't focus. Was that because I had so much on my mind or because I was pregnant?

What other things would change?

My thoughts drifted to Rob again, and then my heart somersaulted. I pressed a palm to my chest, just breathing in deeply. His face popped in my mind, and I tried to visualize how he'd take the news.

On the short way from the station to my house, two cravings took hold of me: frozen yogurt and blueberry pancakes. It took all my willpower not to run to the nearest shop. Why could I not crave just yogurt and blueberries? So much for Tess's theory that I'd finally develop healthy eating habits. Ah, I had some interesting months ahead of me.

Usually, my home was my safe space where I could relax and unwind. Tonight, it had the opposite effect. The second I stepped inside, I became jittery, and breathing was a chore. The walls of the house were closing in on me.

I could do my Pilates—no, wait, was that safe for the baby? I googled it, but far from putting my mind at ease, the list of things forbidden during pregnancy just made my stomach roll. I ate soft cheese two days ago, and that was a big no-no. And I'd had wine during our girls' evening. *Okay… breathe in, breathe out.* It couldn't be that hard, right? Except it kind of was, and the constant effort was making me dizzy.

Clearly, I'd been wrong, and I wasn't ready to be on my own. I didn't want to call Tess though. She'd come right away, and she was also exhausted.

I needed to get out of the house. I changed into comfortable clothes and smiled at the

sleepy street. It was quiet except for the occasional TV sounds filtering out through open windows. The usual outdoor chatter and laughter of kids was nonexistent.

I liked the neighborhood like this and started to understand why Rob liked to run at night. It was peaceful.

The end of August air was hot and humid but refreshing at the same time. The smell of London plane trees was thick around me.

I stepped onto a playground, grinning. Ah, I had the swing all to myself. The stones crunched under my feet. I sat on the swing, leaning forward at once. It was plush and comfy, and I loved it. Nothing like the wooden ones I remembered from back when I was a kid. I mean, they did the job just fine, but my adult ass appreciated whatever padding this one had.

Almost instinctively, I touched my belly. Would I be a good parent?

My most burning desire was to make sure my kid never, ever felt unwanted. That had left scars for a long time. The saddest part was that my siblings and I *had* been wanted at some point. My parents had been married for a long time before my dad left. My throat closed up as I remembered those nights I'd spent wondering how he could suddenly stop wanting to be our dad.

What if Rob felt pressured into... I didn't know, being happy now, and then later on he'd realize he wasn't actually happy? I stopped swinging, just leaning my head on the metal railing, trying to banish this ugly train of thought from my mind. It was not anchored in reality, and I refused to allow myself to be swept into this vortex of negativity.

My throat had other plans. It kept closing up. My eyes were burning.

No, I will not cry for no reason at all.

Damn, I needed a hug. But I still couldn't call

Tess. My brothers were great huggers, but I still couldn't make them come all the way here. I could go to Mom's place and crash there, but I couldn't fess up about my depressing thoughts without upsetting her too, and I refused to do that.

Leaping down from the swing, I shook my head, deciding to get myself the next best thing besides a hug: a treat.

Thankfully, the convenience store was too far away, so my best option was the shawarma truck at the station. That counted as semi-healthy, right? It had chicken, veggies, and cilantro... and delicious mayo and fries, but all in all, a balanced treat, right?

Squaring my shoulders, I marched toward the station, already feeling better just at the thought of the shawarma. The mind was an amazing thing, and I was determined to steer it toward happiness territory. My kid would know it was wanted. Also, I was 100 percent certain it would inherit the Winchester unhealthy eating habits.

Chapter Twenty-Eight
Rob

The trip to LA was a success. Despite Alyssa's initial reluctance, I convinced her to take charge. I needed someone I could trust to handle things here, and someone new just didn't cut it. Why was it that competent people doubted themselves while incompetent ones thought they were the shit?

I returned to New York earlier than anticipated. I landed in the evening, and I hadn't told Skye yet, because she hadn't answered my calls yesterday and the evening before. True, it had been late, but she usually didn't go to bed that early. She texted the next morning saying she'd fallen asleep and to call her whenever I had time. The scenario repeated the following evening.

We kept missing each other, but I was determined to get ahold of her this evening. Initially, I'd planned to surprise her by showing up directly on her doorstep, but I couldn't wait any longer. I called her as soon as I landed.

After two rings, she picked up.

"Hey, finally," I said.

"Good evening, oh all-important business guy."

It was so relieving just to hear her voice, making me realize how much I missed her. This woman had become a part of me.

"Hey, you're the one who went to bed before ten two nights in a row."

"I know, I know. I'm a sleepyhead these days."

"Are you sick?" I hadn't considered that.

"Oh, no. Don't worry. How's LA?" she asked.

"Shit. I can't wait to be back." I decided on the spot to keep to my original plan and surprise her.

"Oh, New York charmed you, huh?"

"Not just New York."

"Hmm... what else could it be? Your gorgeous house?" She paused, then said, "I know. It's the food."

I laughed. Damn, I missed her. "How's your day?" I asked.

"Long. I started a little late because the wait at the doctor was ridiculous—"

"Wait, why did you go to the doctor? You just said you're not sick."

She said nothing.

"Skye?" I prodded. My hands felt icy. Was she keeping something from me? "Why did you go to the doctor?"

"Just blood work."

Thank fuck. "Routine?" I double-checked.

"Not exactly. I... I'm pregnant. Oh, shit. I didn't mean to tell you over the phone. It just slipped. I wanted to tell you face-to-face."

I stopped walking toward the baggage area, clutching the phone. "Pregnant. You're pregnant?"

"Yes."

"Why did you let me go on about New York? When did you find out?"

"Three days ago, but I didn't want to tell you over the phone. I'd planned to wait until you were back."

"Tell me everything."

"Well, I was feeling queasy and my taste changed. Someone made a passing comment about changing tastes while pregnant—"

I chuckled. Only Skye could discover she was pregnant because her taste in food changed.

"Anyway, I did two pregnancy tests, and today I went to the doctor. They actually didn't need the blood work, just a urine test."

"So it's confirmed?"

"Yes."

"Boy or girl?"

She chuckled. "It's way too early to know that, Rob."

"Oh, yeah." My mind was spinning continuously. "Okay, so we can start shopping for the room. Wait, where will the room be? Hell, we'll figure it out. We'll just move in wherever is better." My mind was moving too fast for my words to catch up. I was already making lists of all the things that would have to be discarded or adapted.

Holy shit, I was going to be a father.

A father.

Right up until this moment, I'd never realized how much I wanted to be one. We were going to have a kid. A person who would be part Skye, part me—a unique mashup. Would he or she be a brainiac like Skye or a kitchen addict like me?

"Rob, we have a lot of time until the baby is here, so there is no need to hurry. Also, I don't want you to feel like we have to rush into anything."

I frowned. "Rush? What do you mean?"

"Well, these months have been amazing and fun, but we've never talked about our future."

"I know we haven't spoken about it...." I'd definitely thought about it, envisioned it.

"So I don't want us to think that we have to change everything."

"Skye, everything's changing."

"Of course, I mean, we'll have a baby, so we'll be parents. I just don't want you to think that I'm expecting for our relationship to change too."

I couldn't figure out if she really meant to not put pressure on me or if she didn't envision us together in the future. Was this why she'd wanted to wait to talk to me face-to-face?

"You're right. We should talk about this in person."

"Oh, okay." She sounded surprised.

"I've just landed."

"In New York?"

"No, on the moon," I said in an exasperated tone. "Of course in New York. Sorry, I'm all over the place. Okay, so ummm... see you at the house tonight?"

"Sure."

After talking to Skye, I decided I couldn't wait even that long. I called my sister on the way to Soho.

"Wow, I wasn't expecting you to come back so quickly. If anything, I was expecting you to say you need to prolong it."

"Things are looking better in LA."

"Where exactly are you now?"

"Soho. I need to talk to Skye."

"Awww, baby bro. Missing your girl, huh?"

"Yes. A lot." After a beat, I added, "She's pregnant."

Anne squealed so loudly that my eardrum went numb. I held the phone away from my ear until the sound lessened in intensity.

"OhGodohGodohGod. How far along is she? Will you move in with her? When? Can I help? Do you need advice?"

"Anne, breathe."

"Hey, I'm breathing and talking. Always been a great multitasker."

"I just found out."

"Okay. Wow. Is Skye feeling okay? I'll call and ask her myself, actually. What's the plan?"

"Talking to her first."

"Okay. You didn't mention any baby plans, so I'm guessing it's a surprise."

"Yes... she said that we don't have to rush to change anything in our relationship."

"What is it that you're *not* saying, Rob?" Anne's voice was gentle.

"What if she's the one who doesn't want things to change?"

The driver gave me a pitying look in the rearview mirror. Fantastic. He probably thought I was a wimp.

"Rob...." Anne's tone was even gentler than before. "Your relationship is very new. During the girls' evening we had, Skye was even wondering if inviting you to her brother's wedding in December would be too much. This is an emotional time for both of you. Just take it easy and don't jump to conclusions."

"Any other advice?"

No answer. I was putting two and two together though. Especially since I had an inkling that Skye's fears also had something to do with their dad taking off when she was a kid. And I planned to erase those fears. Every single one of them. She was mine, and I loved her.

"I don't have advice, sorry. I'm just picking up the pieces after the divorce, so if anything, I'm the one who needs advice. Let's focus on something positive. Are you excited?"

"Hell yes."

"What do you want? Boy or girl?"

"I don't know. I think I'd know how to handle a boy better."

"You're good with Lindsay."

"That's why you always give me shit?"

"No, I give you tips for improvement."

Laughing, I realized I could visualize my future with Skye in greater detail than ever before.

Chapter Twenty-Nine
Skye

I was jumpy the entire evening. Me and my big mouth. Why did I let it slip that I was pregnant? And then why did I go and make a mess of things? I'd meant it, I didn't want him to feel pressured. But I couldn't shake off the sensation that I'd hurt him. What if he didn't want to move in together just because of the baby? We hadn't even hinted at that before.

I knew family was important to him. I'd seen how much anguish Anne and Lindsay's situation caused him. The last thing I wanted was for him to jump into this out of a sense of duty only to be unhappy later. That was a recipe for disaster.

"I see you're not making any progress," my sister teased. I'd declared that I wasn't in the mood to face customers today, so I'd relegated myself to back-office tasks. We always had a million of those piling up, so I had enough to keep me occupied for the whole day.

"I'm a bit slow today," I admitted.

Tess leaned against the wall, crossing her arms over her chest. "I think that what you need is to call it a night. We've just closed, anyway."

"You can't boss me into going home," I said.

My sister smiled slyly. "True... but I know someone who can, and he's right in the front of the store."

"Ooooh, Rob's here?" I looked past Tess's shoulder, as if I could somehow see through walls. My entire body reacted to the news.

Straightening up, I ran a hand through my hair. I was sweaty and wearing old jeans and a washed-out boy-band T-shirt. It was my back-office attire. The air in here was stuffy, and the lack of natural light made me feel claustrophobic.

"I don't have anything to change into," I whispered.

"I don't think Rob cares," Tess whispered back.

"I look terrible."

Smiling, Tess headed back toward the front.

"She's all yours. Somehow even more stubborn than usual. Good luck," I heard her say. The corners of my mouth twitched.

"Hey, you're supposed to have my back," I said loudly.

"I do, sister. I do."

My pulse went into overdrive even before Rob stepped inside the room. *Breathe in, breathe out... breathe in... breathe out.*

It was no use. As soon as Rob appeared before me, captivating me as usual with one single glance, I hyperventilated. My entire body was craving his nearness. I wanted to jump right into his arms and run a hand through his thick hair, plant a smooch right on his lips.

He strode toward me, his face stern. I tugged at my T-shirt, as if that could make it less outdated.

"Skye, I'm here. Let's talk. Face-to-face, like you said."

Right, I'd said that. So why was I now completely tongue-twisted?

"I don't know where to begin."

Rob searched my face, silent for a few beats. "Let's talk about moving in. Why did you say you don't want us to rush?"

"I don't want you to feel pressured into anything." I'd said that, right? Searching his expression, I didn't detect surprise, so I must have.

"I'm not."

"But we've never talked about taking that step," I insisted.

Rob came closer, raising one hand to cup my cheek.

"And now we are. If there's another reason, if you don't want this—"

I shook my head frantically. He cupped my other cheek too. "I just don't want you to do anything you might regret later... change your mind about...."

"Wanting you?"

"Yes."

"Skye...."

In a fraction of a second, he lowered one hand down my back, pressing me against him. Damn, this man had skills.

"I love you, and I love our kid, and there is nothing that could ever make me not love you, not want you. Nothing."

It was a good thing he was holding me so tightly, because my legs were a little wobbly. So was my smile.

"Rob—"

"I mean it, every word of it. I want it all with you. Sharing a house, our lives, waking up next to you every morning. Bickering about the best time of the day to work out. Telling you that I've read some stuff online that supports my viewpoint... you shoving every study there is under my nose to prove your point. Hear our kids laugh at our conversations."

"Kids?"

"Yeah, I was thinking more than one."

"Our first one's not even here."

"Yeah, but I always thought it must be lonely... being an only child."

I wiggled my eyebrows, suddenly feeling a little brave. "Don't tell *me* that. I come from a family of four. Five if you include Hunter too, which I do."

Rob paled a little. I laughed, throwing my head back. Clearly he hadn't meant *five* when he'd said more than one.

"We can negotiate that later on." I patted his shoulder, laughing harder when he became even paler.

"How long are you in town?" I asked.

"Haven't made any immediate plans to go back to LA."

"That means I have you all to myself?" I batted my eyelashes.

He smiled wolfishly. "No, *I* will have *you* all to myself."

And just like that, my entire body sizzled. He skimmed his gaze up and down my body. Heavens, how could he have such an effect on me? How could my body respond to a look or mere words?

"Oh yeah? How do you plan to do that?"

"First step, getting you out of here. Right now." He traced his thumb down my jaw and neck, resting it on my shoulder. I burned everywhere he touched.

I shook my head teasingly. The truth was, I was dying to be alone with Rob. *Buuut* a little persuasion from him wouldn't hurt. "No can do."

"What's that I hear about needing to boss you into calling it a night?"

I grinned, shimmying my hips a little. "Like you ever need a reason to boss me around."

"Now I actually do." He brought a hand to my belly. It was the first time he touched it, and I could *swear* something stirred deep inside me. It was irrational, of course, but somehow I thought it felt Rob was here with us.

"Baby, if you're just as stubborn as your mom, God help me."

I was in real danger of swooning here. I had no idea how I was planning to go on with my charade, but I loved seeing Rob in persuasion mode. The man was always hot, but when he was trying to half convince, half seduce me? Make that hot times a million.

Pulling back a little, he frowned at my T-shirt, as if he was just now seeing it properly.

"I'm on back-office duty today," I explained. "That's why I'm wearing these godawful clothes. So I can't be tempted to go in the front."

"I can't wait to take them off you."

"Of course your mind went right there."

"You don't like the clothes, and I love you naked best. It's a win-win."

"Rob…."

"I can get you naked here too, if you insist."

"I don't," I said quickly.

His eyes darkened instantly. He skimmed his hands down the sides of my body, gripping my hips. His fingers pressed into my ass possessively. I couldn't resist and gave in just a little, pushing my pelvis into him. He groaned, gripping me even tighter, bringing his mouth closer to my cheek.

"I want to sink so deep inside you." His words were almost a growl. My whole body ignited.

Just then, I heard footsteps approaching. I instantly moved away.

Tess poked her head in. "Sorry to disturb, but I need to find some merchandise for the display before I leave."

"Um, sure. Can I help?" My cheeks were on fire.

"Nah, I'm good."

It took Tess all of two seconds to find a dark green bra, but then she still hovered.

"Tess?"

She held up a finger. "Just trying to get a feel for how this is going."

"Did you really need merchandise?" I asked, laughing.

"Yes, the display is missing a bra. And I just couldn't take the suspense anymore." She looked from me to Rob, then back to me.

Rob pulled me into him, kissing the side of my head. "I'm negotiating getting her out of here."

"Excellent. Can't wait to tell the family."

"Wait, what?" I asked, perplexed.

Tess grimaced. "Um, well… Ryker and Cole were here in the morning before you came in. I didn't know if you could make it, so I called for help. Anyway, I accidentally brought them up to date."

"How can you do that accidentally?" Rob asked. I bit my lip to keep from laughing.

"I blame that on the no-secrets policy. Just makes me instantly share news with everyone in the family. I'll leave you two now. I'm leaving as soon as I put this bra on the mannequin."

She was grinning from ear to ear as she left.

"I like how you switched from bossing to negotiating," I said.

"Sounds smoother. Now, let's go." His gaze smoldered. "Skye…."

"I'm gone," Tess called from the front. The

sound of the door closing followed.

Rob strode closer until he was right in front of me, eyes hot and determined. His whole body language was just smoking hot. Shoulders slightly hunched forward, his biceps flexed as he bent his arms at the elbow, touching my waist.

***

Rob

I barely kept my hands off her. Now that I knew we were alone, I couldn't stop touching her. This woman was just everything I needed. I'd always thought I was happy with my life the way it used to be, that it was enough. Meeting her changed that. Falling for her changed *me*.

I led her to the couch between changing rooms.

"Here?" Skye whispered.

"Here. That way you'll think about me every time you see it."

That, and I couldn't wait another minute, let alone the time it took to get her home.

I touched her mouth with my fingers. She parted her lips, biting one finger gently. It drove me crazy. Pulling her closer, I captured her mouth, then kissed down her neck. I got rid of her clothes in a few moves, then skimmed my lips from one shoulder to the other before descending to her breasts. They almost spilled out of her half-cup bra. I licked and nipped right along the line where fabric met skin, smiling when she pushed her hips forward into me. Kissing her again, I lowered one hand between us, slowing down as I reached the hem of her panties. Her breath was shaky. I splayed her thighs wider with my knee, lowering my hand even more over her panties, running one finger over the center right between her thighs. She moaned against my mouth. Pulling back, I turned her around, pressing her ass against my cock. I wanted her to feel how hard I was.

"Grip the backrest," I said.

Goose bumps instantly broke out on her skin. I barely kept from bending her over right this instant, tugging her panties to one side, and driving inside her. She did just as I said while I pushed down my pants and boxers, then pulled my shirt over my head. I was desperate for her: to touch, claim, own every part of her.

I undid the clasp of her bra before palming one breast. I slipped the other hand into her panties, circling her clit. I needed to get her wet and ready because I couldn't be gentle tonight. I wanted her on a primal level, more than ever before. With one hand, I pulled at each bow holding her panties together at her hips. They fell to the floor, and we were both completely naked now. Still standing right behind her, I strummed my fingers over her pussy. Moaning, she leaned back against me, trapping my cock between my front and her left ass cheek. I could feel the tension build inside her. Every sharp intake of breath, every moan of hers reverberated through me.

"Rob," she gasped as her whole body curved

forward. I leaned with her, kissing her back, letting my hand drop, giving her a brief reprieve. Gripping at the base of my erection, I positioned myself between her thighs, drawing the tip of my cock from her clit all the way down to her entrance, then teased her again.

"Rob, oh...," she whispered. Her legs were shaking slightly.

I wanted to make her come once just like this, but I barely kept from bursting myself. Tension pumped through me. When she was close to the edge, I straightened up, holding her with one arm against me, teasing her clit with my fingers. She climaxed beautifully, arching her back, resting her head on my shoulder as she cried out. I whirled her around, capturing her mouth before she'd even finished coming. I explored her mouth ferociously, moving us both around the armrest. I lowered myself on the couch, pulling her on top of me. She straddled me, her knees at my sides.

"Now you're at my mercy," she teased.

"That's what I let you think."

I gripped her hips, lowering her onto me slowly, watching her face transform with pleasure. When I was all the way in, I let go of her hips, pushing myself up on an elbow. She undulated her hips in a fast rhythm while I explored her upper body with my hand and mouth. Her skin was so smooth, her scent maddening. The sound of our bodies moving filled the space. I felt more connected to her than ever. There was no feeling more perfect than being entwined like this with her. She belonged to me, and I was going to remind her of that every day. I was going to make her mine every day, bring her pleasure and happiness.

When she threw her head back, crying out my name, I nearly came. She was pulsing tight around me. Lifting her hips a few inches, I pressed one thumb just above her clit, driving inside her from below. I wanted to own every drop of pleasure, and I did. When my sensitive woman came yet again, I succumbed to my own climax too, calling out her name and pushing so deep inside her that my vision blurred. My breath stuttered as every muscle cramped and burned.

She leaned forward until her forehead touched my chest. "You bad, bad man," she chastised.

"Bad?"

"How am I supposed to concentrate on customers when every time I look at this couch, I'll remember this?"

"That's the point, Skye. I want to be on your mind all the time."

Laughing, she kissed my neck, stretching over me. "Mission more than accomplished."

Chapter Thirty

Skye
Three weeks later

"I can't believe I've ordered so much stuff," I said, looking at the pile of things in what was still the guest room but would be the baby's room. I'd moved into Rob's house. God, I loved this place so much. I'd loved it even before I helped sell it to him, but now it was *our* place.

Currently, there were bags and boxes everywhere, containing everything from furniture to toys to clothes (for me), and more clothes (for the baby), and God knew what else. Between the wish lists I made with Mom, Tess, and Lindsay and Anne, I went way overboard.

Couples usually waited until twelve weeks to announce the news, but it was impossible to keep such a secret in my family. And once I'd told them, I couldn't hold back from buying all these pretty things.

Rob hooked an arm around my waist from behind, resting his chin on my shoulder.

"I love you, despite your newly developed

shopaholic tendencies."

I'd have blamed it on the nesting period, except I'd read that only set in during the last two months of pregnancy. I must have had an early case....

"Too late to back out now."

"That's right."

"I think I might have gone overboard."

In response, he just patted my right ass cheek right before pinching it lightly. I turned around. Grinning, I took a mini step back, surveying him.

"What?" he asked.

"Deciding where to pinch you." I drew my fingers down his chest, narrowing my eyes as if I was seriously considering it, even though I knew what my target was all along. When I reached his navel, I moved my hands to the side and down, right to his ass cheeks, giving each a good pinch.

"There," I said casually, as if I was checking if they were still there.

Rob chuckled, but his eyes snapped fire. He splayed his big hand over the side of my face, resting his thumb at the corner of my mouth.

"Come on, beautiful, or you'll go in *hangry* mode before we're even at the restaurant." We were having dinner at Rob's restaurant in Tribeca.

I pouted. "I don't understand why we have to go anywhere. I have the chef right here." Batting my eyelashes, I added, "We can stay in. You'll cook, and I'll be your sous-chef. I can even be your naked sous-chef if you want."

The corners of his mouth twitched. He skimmed one hand at the small of my back, pressing me against him. The air between us charged. His gaze dropped to my lips. I had him, I was sure of it.

Clearing his throat, he shook his head. "Not tonight. Come on, dress up."

He was passing up my naked sous-chef offer? Something wasn't right, but I didn't push any further. Taking my hand, he led me out of the room.

I changed into a light pink summer dress and white flats. Underneath, I wore a pink bra with soft padding. My breasts were tender, so these bras were my go-to these days. I didn't have many side effects from the pregnancy yet. The initial exhaustion had worn off (or I'd become better at managing it), but Tess and I were figuring out a system where I focused more on the online side and generally took over tasks I could do from home. The business wasn't yet at the point where I could just take months off, but the plan was for me to do tasks that didn't require me to go into the city every day, at least for a while, and especially after the baby was here.

We'd figure it out.

Rob was waiting for me downstairs, already dressed to go. I took a second at the top of the stairs just to drink him in. His black jeans were somehow making his butt even sexier than usual—kudos to the designer. And that shirt he had on... yum.

When I joined him, I realized he held up a jacket for me.

"It's not cold," I said.

"But it might get cold later."

I laughed; I just couldn't help myself. "Rob, it's the hottest fall in years. I'm sure I won't need it."

"You never know. I need to take care of you." He touched my belly, kissing my forehead. "Both of you."

And just like that, he won me over. How could I say no?

The restaurant was full when we arrived. *Wait a second.* I spotted Mom, Mick, and Tess at the bar.

"What is—" I started to ask Rob, but my words faded when I noticed that Cole, Ryker, Heather, and Avery were next to them. A few feet away, Josie and Hunter waved at me.

"Oh, the whole family is here?" I asked, mystified. That was when I noticed Anne and Lindsay too. "And your family. Are we celebrating something?"

"We sure are, babe. We didn't get a chance to celebrate this." He touched my belly.

"Oh, okay." Of course, what was I thinking?

Since we'd told everyone already, and we'd met every member of our families at least once in the past few weeks and had celebrated with them individually, I still thought it was a little odd. Just three days ago, we met with my siblings and Hunter to discuss the upcoming gala, and we all toasted to the news. But I loved every opportunity to gather with our families, so I wasn't going to look a gift horse in the mouth.

Rob led us to the back room, where the small tables had been arranged into a long one. It was just our group in here. There were already bags hung around the backs of the chairs, meaning at least part of the group had been inside. They'd just been waiting at the bar for the *wow* effect. I loved all this.

Rob held a chair for me, and I sat down along with everyone else. Servers came in with an assortment of drinks, pouring water, wine, and sparkling wine. After they left, Rob rose to his feet. Grabbing a fork, he gently tapped it against his water glass.

He was going to give a speech?

"Thank you, everyone, for coming here tonight. As you all know, Skye and I have something huge to celebrate. We're happy that in seven months, we'll welcome a baby boy or girl. I know everyone's already making bets on what it's going to be."

"Hear, hear," Cole said.

"Not bets," Ryker corrected. "Just giving our opinion... based on the fifty-fifty odds in our family."

Mom laughed, but the whole table went silent when Rob half turned to me. I shoved my chair back a little so I could look at him properly.

"Skye, I've thought about this moment for a long time, even before we knew you were pregnant. Imagining life with you was easy. But this moment? This took planning. I first thought about taking you away for a weekend, but... I know it will mean more to us if it happens here, in front of both our families."

He took my left hand in his. *Oh my God.* He was holding a ring! A sapphire in a rose gold setting. He was going to propose. My heart swelled.

"Skye, you're everything to me. I love you so—" His voice caught. The emotion in it made my eyes misty. "—so much. Marry me, babe."

He sounded as if he'd wanted to say more but decided not to because his voice was too undependable.

I swallowed the emotion in my throat, rising to my feet. I touched his cheek with one hand, holding out the other one, fingers splayed.

"Yes, I'll marry you. I love you."

I laughed as the ring went on my finger, then touched his face with both hands.

He touched his lips to mine in a gentle kiss. I barely refrained from jumping straight into his arms. The tip of his tongue teased my lower lip, and I smiled against his mouth. He was barely keeping himself from kissing me long and deep and wet.

The upside of being surrounded by our families was that we could share this moment with them. The downside? We had to keep the heat to a decent level.

When he pulled back, amusement danced in his eyes.

"Congratulations," Mom said. She sat right next to me and was the first to hug me.

"Anyone know about this?" Cole asked, looking around at the table.

"No," Tess said, her voice a little uneven. "Wow, talk about surprises."

There was a screeching sound as everyone rose from their chairs, coming over to congratulate us.

Cole and Ryker shook Rob's hand.

"We need to speak later," Cole said.

I stared at my brother. "You already gave him *the talk*."

I'd heard that through the family grapevine.

"There are several *talks*," Cole clarified, eyes on Rob. "You received the initial one."

"Now you'll get the serious one," Ryker added.

Cole patted his shoulder. "Congratulations, you've reached the next level."

I grinned at Rob. "You've got to love these two, right?"

My fiancé shrugged good-naturedly as Hunter, Josie, Tess, and Heather came toward us.

My sister just pulled both of us into a hug, wordlessly.

"Welcome to the married club. It's awesome," Josie said.

Hunter nodded. "I agree."

"Congratulations," Heather said, squeezing me tightly to her. After letting me go, she glanced around at all of us. "Okay, so Ryker and I had an idea. We talked about it since Rob invited us here today, because we had a feeling he might propose. Anyway, it's a bit crazy, and you're more than welcome to say no... but how about a double wedding? Everything's all set for us, but it wouldn't be hard to adapt it with whatever you want."

Rob glanced at me, wiggling his eyebrows. "I'm good with it if you are."

Wow, my mind was spinning. "I love the idea. And I love your setting and everything, but... are you sure you want to share your day with us?"

"Why not? It'll be double the fun," Heather said.

Ryker held up a finger. "But we're getting two bachelor parties."

Heather and I burst out laughing.

"One wedding but two bachelor parties? I like your priorities, brother."

"That actually does sound like a good idea," Heather said. "We can go all crazy during *your* party, Skye, and I can blame it all on you. Say it was your idea."

Rob frowned. Ryker glowered.

"Define crazy," my brother said.

Heather smiled impishly. "I don't know yet, but we have plenty of time to come up with something."

Oh, I loved that she went toe to toe with Ryker at every turn. I just loved this woman.

"I already have a few ideas," I piped up, just to up the ante. "Which I will share with you far from jealous, possessive ears."

Now Rob was glowering even more than Ryker. Ah, I couldn't help myself; I stretched up on

340

my toes and gave him a smooch. He deepened the kiss, tilting my head back a little, taking charge. Talk about holding back! We were absolutely hopeless.

Ryker cleared his throat. Rob pulled back, still looking at me intently.

"You know, I'm all for a crazy party. Mine wasn't," Josie said.

"You wanted us to keep it non-crazy," Tess reminded her.

"Yeah... I have no idea why I did that," Josie said. "But I'll help with preparations."

Hunter half glared, half frowned at us.

"Girls, I think we're getting a little ahead of ourselves," I said.

Hunter smiled. "Thanks for being sensible as always."

"Don't thank me too soon, cousin. There's still plenty of time for me to change my mind."

Chapter Thirty-One
Skye
December

I had no idea pregnancy came with so many perks. My family spoiled me nonstop, as did Rob. I could get used to this. In fact, I already was. I patted my sizable belly, waiting for the DJ to play the song for our first dance. Rob winked, squeezing my hand tighter.

The weddings were taking place at a gorgeous hotel at a lake in upstate New York. The restaurant was elegant, with floor-to-ceiling windows that allowed us a splendid view of the lake and the mountains behind it. A white landscape stretched outside the window. Snow covered the ground, and translucent icicles hung from the A-frame roof. All the trees were snowed in. It was a true winter wonderland.

A crisscross of wooden beams spread across the ceiling, giving the space a rustic feel. I loved it. Heather and I were both wearing white dresses, but they couldn't be more different.

While hers was an A-line princess style, mine was mermaid-shaped, highlighting my belly. We'd both chosen to style our hair in buns. Hers was high and centered, while mine was low and slightly to the left. We were both absolutely stunning.

"I can't believe I've been talked into this,"

Ryker whispered. He was on my other side, holding Heather's hand.

I grinned. We'd taken dance classes to learn a special choreography. It had been challenging as hell, but the result was an impressive dance. Rob smiled as we took our positions on the dance floor.

"You've been suspiciously happy about the dance classes," I whispered.

"It had its perks." His gaze was so shameless that my cheeks warmed up and heat spread through me with a lightning-quick speed.

The second the music began, he brought a hand to my waist. My breath caught, and I became so wrapped up in him that everything around us faded. It was a good thing we'd rehearsed so many times, because I was doing this dance by muscle memory only. I didn't think he'd ever cease to captivate me so completely. On a twirl, I lost my balance a little, but there was a firm arm around me... and a smirk on his face. I pinched his arm lightly, and all the guests laughed. Ah, apparently I was more obvious than I thought.

"Don't laugh at me," I whispered.

"You're adorable," he replied. And that... how could I do anything but melt when he said things like that?

After the first dance was over, we welcomed the rest of the guests onto the dance floor. Theoretically I could sit down, but I had this strange energy that made me want to keep dancing.

"Want to rest?" Rob asked.

"Actually, not at all. I don't know what's gotten into me, but I want to keep dancing."

He frowned, looking at my belly. The second-best part of being pregnant, besides being spoiled around the clock, was watching his protective instincts becoming more and more pronounced. Sometimes to the point of being overprotective, but I secretly enjoyed it.

"The doctor said you should take it easy."

"He meant work, not dancing. I asked twice. You were there."

Except lately he thought he knew better, even more so than my doctor. He held my gaze captive until goose bumps formed on my arms.

"Skye...."

"Rob... I'm going to dance. Anything against that?"

In response, he just pulled me flush against him, holding me so tight and possessively that my breath caught again. Damn, this man was determined to make me swoon before this day was over.

"You're getting feisty already, wife."

"What are you going to do about it?" I batted my eyelashes. "Give me the same treatment as you did the kitchen staff?" Tess had informed me just before the ceremony that Rob had scared the living daylights out of the servers and chefs with his *this-is-how-this-will-go* speech. "You just can't turn off that bossy switch, can you?"

"I'll show you just how *on* it is if you keep at this." His gaze darkened at once. He tilted forward slightly, skimming his lips over my cheek to my ear.

"I love you, Skye," he whispered.

"I love you too." I leaned into him, breathing in his woodsy scent before pulling back, blushing. I kept forgetting we were at our wedding... surrounded by guests.

Looking around, I caught Anne's gaze. She winked at me, and I winked right back. She was slowly getting back into the dating scene. Well, more like she'd encountered a hottie during the bachelorette party and sparks had been flying. Rob had successfully intimidated Anne's ex into getting his shit together, so he was now regularly spending time with Lindsay.

Rob's parents had flown in from France, and they were now cuddling their granddaughter. His grandfather had congratulated us via FaceTime. He said he didn't want to face a trip across the ocean at his age. Rob promised we'd visit him soon.

The man looked eighty, tops, and was as charming as my husband. They even looked a bit alike—the same green eyes and cheeky smile. I kept teasing Rob that now that I knew how he'd look in sixty years' time, I was even more sold on him.

Three dances later, I had to admit, I was spent. This was the downside of pregnancy. I tired fast. That, and the cravings. Oh, the cravings. Weirdly, I didn't have a sweet tooth, but I did want everything I wasn't allowed: cream cheese, sushi, medium-rare steak.

Guess who was watching me like a drill

sergeant, making sure I didn't break any rules? My husband. I loved him even more for it.

Grabbing my glass, I gulped down the ice-cold water before smoothing my hands down my dress. Alone at the table, I couldn't deny it, I was on pins and needles.

Mom sat next to me a few moments later. Could she feel that I needed her?

"How are you, sweetheart?"

I pointed to my smile. "Happy, but also super nervous."

She took one of my hands between hers. My pulse slowed down at once.

"Enjoy your happiness, darling. Don't be afraid of losing it. As long as there is love, respect, and understanding between the two of you, you can overcome everything. Money comes and goes. Health too. Some moments will be hard and trying, but if you just remember the things that made you fall in love in the first place, you'll realize they are still there. They'll give you strength. Choose to love and respect your man, and the rest will work out."

She always knew what to say. I looked around the room at my family—they'd always be there for me. And Rob—I was sure we'd have a strong marriage. I'd never been more certain about anything.

"Thanks, Mom." I was absentmindedly patting my belly and caught her looking at me.

"You know, I was thinking about retiring," she said.

"How come?" I asked suspiciously. Not that

we hadn't hoped this for years, but I still wasn't sure she was serious.

"I don't have as much energy to run the school as before, and with my first grandkid on the way… I'll have plenty to keep me occupied."

The corners of my mouth twitched, but I didn't dare laugh. So this was the secret to getting my mom to slow down a bit: give her a grandchild.

She placed an arm over my shoulder and a hand on my belly.

"Mom, thanks for being there whenever I need you."

"Always." She smiled, glancing at the dance floor. Just then, my husband walked up to Mom, holding out a hand.

"Amelia, a dance?" he asked with a wink.

"I'd love to."

Mick didn't miss a beat and whisked me back on the dance floor one minute later. He took my arm, and amazingly, a sense of calm seeped into me. He always emanated this sense of peace, like he had everything under control.

"Mick, I never told you, but I'm so happy Mom found you, that you're part of our family."

He smiled warmly, kissing my forehead. Mick was a man of few words, but he was never shy to show his feelings.

"What's this I hear about Mom retiring?" I asked as we swayed to the slow rhythm of the song.

"I told her you'd probably need her more, what with the store and the baby, and I practically saw her eyes light up."

We laughed together as if we were accomplices. We were, in a way, but I'd just contributed without knowing.

I looked around, grinning when my gaze crossed Heather's. She and Ryker had been dancing nonstop. She was red in the cheeks, and one strand of her chocolate-brown hair had fallen out of her bun.

When the song was over, she and Ryker stalked over to me, as did Rob.

"How about a trip to the photo booth?" Heather asked.

I nodded in agreement. Ryker had insisted on one, and I didn't see the point at the time, but now I totally did. It was so much fun. Josie had found this photographer that had a setup like a booth where he had all kinds of hats and accessories we could wear. Genius! I put on a mustache and a glittery hat, Rob a police cap.

I tugged at the waistband of his pants, playfully whispering, "A striptease, Mr. Cop?"

His eyes flashed as he slid a hand up my back slowly... suggestively. Holy shit! I was getting a striptease later, I was sure of that. And in case he forgot, I planned to remind him.

When we returned to the main room, I noticed Cole. He was standing at the edge of the dance floor, looking every bit the Charmer he was. He was too handsome for his own good in a tux. He ran a hand through his jet-black hair, wiggling his eyebrows at me.

"Why do you look so pleased with yourself, brother?" I asked him. "Even more pleased than usual, I mean."

He chuckled. "Just congratulating myself on being the last bachelor standing."

"I think you'll find Ian and Dylan disagreeing with you." I smirked, nudging my head in their direction. Josie's siblings had arrived for the wedding yesterday. We'd known Isabelle and Ian were single, but it had been a shock when Dylan had arrived without his plus one.

Josie filled us in that his long-term relationship had blown up in his face just the night before. He looked understandably pissed off with life, but by the hot looks he was getting from at least two gals, I was certain he'd have some fun tonight.

"The most eligible, then," Cole said, as if he was determined to win the argument.

"You certainly are eligible to… fall," I teased.

"No, thanks. Bachelor and proud," he said so seriously that I couldn't help laughing.

As if knowing we were talking about them, Dylan and Ian joined us.

"Gents, you're a hot topic here," I informed them.

"It looked like it," Ian said.

"I was just telling my sister that I'm proud to be a bachelor."

"Me too," Ian said, holding up his glass. Cole

mimicked the motion. Dylan just glowered, but he still clinked his glass to theirs.

"You truly know how to bring people on your team," I said.

"I'm talented like that," Cole agreed.

Tess and Isabelle joined us, fanning their cheeks.

"Oh, man, I need a break. Why did you bring the party to the edge of the dance floor?" Tess asked.

"I was just commending Cole on his talent to bring together yet another bachelor pack."

"What's the female equivalent to that?" Tess asked. "Bachelorette pack?"

Isabelle tilted her head, her fiery red hair falling in gorgeous waves. "Hmm... I don't think there is an equivalent. Single?"

Tess laughed. "No, the single pack sounds depressing. We'll come up with something, but not right now. Tonight is for dancing and having fun."

Cole, Ian, and Dylan returned on the dance floor. The girls and I stayed at the edge, watching them. Mom waved at us from her table. I crooked a finger at her to join us.

"Girls, let's get back to dancing," she said.

"I agree," Tess replied.

"You know, I never thought Ryker would settle down. Gives me hope that Cole might follow in his footsteps too. What do you think?" Mom asked.

Seeing as my brother's goal was to charm a gal just for the weekend, I couldn't see this happening soon. I didn't have the heart to wipe off Mom's hopeful smile, and neither did Tess, so we just grinned, leading Mom onto the dance floor.

As for Cole? He was dancing the shoes off one of Heather's bridesmaids. She watched him as if he was the eighth wonder of the world, and he bestowed his trademark Charmer smile on her. Yep… heartbreaker alert right there.

Epilogue
Rob

"Holy shit, I have to send back half of this stuff," Skye exclaimed. We'd just returned from the ob-gyn, who'd informed us that we were expecting a boy. On previous screenings, the baby had hidden from us, so it had been impossible to tell. Skye had insisted her intuition was telling her we'd have a girl, but now, only one week after the wedding, we finally knew.

Skye had jumped right into organization mode.

"Babe, stop. Breathe in."

She bit her lower lip before smiling. "You're right. I don't know why I'm in such a frenzy."

"Tu es adorable," I whispered.

"Wait, I know what that means. I'm adorable, right?"

I chuckled. "Yes. You're a fast learner." She'd started taking classes recently, wanting to be able to teach our kid a second language.

"To be fair, 'adorable' sounds kind of the same in both languages."

"Skye, this is what we're going to do today. Relax for a bit, then make a list of all the girl items you bought and decide which to send back."

"All of them."

"Maybe our next kid will be a girl."

Skye threw her head back, laughing. "I like your thinking."

Gripping her hips, I led her away from the baby's room.

"Let's go in the backyard. I want to show you something," I said, handing her a jacket and taking one myself. It was cold as hell outside.

"What is it?"

"You'll see."

I had a little surprise for her, and this morning had been the perfect moment to build it. Skye went into the city early, and I'd met her at the ob-gyn. I led her outside to where I'd installed a double swing.

"When did you have that set up?" she asked with a huge smile. "I love it."

"I built it," I said. "With Cole, Ryker, and Hunter, this morning."

Skye whirled around to look at me. "Wow."

I nodded, feeling proud. The wooden poles had been easy enough to find, and the swing itself was made from wood too, covered with pillows.

"Looks a lot like the one I told you about from when I was a kid," I said. I'd sent a picture to Anne, and she'd agreed with me. My sister seemed more cheerful lately. She'd even been on a date, though I thought her good mood had more to do with Walter stepping up to the plate, being a dad to Lindsay.

The thought of him still made a vein in my neck pulse, but that didn't matter in the grand scheme of things.

"I love it," Skye said.

Ever since I'd found out she was pregnant, my view on certain things had shifted. I couldn't pinpoint how exactly, but I suddenly found myself having thoughts I hadn't had before, seeing angles that had been invisible to me before. I liked our space, and I wanted to bring as many good things as possible in it from my childhood.

Most of all, I liked that we shared every single experience. Pushing her hair to one side and pulling at the collar of her jacket, I kissed my favorite place: the patch of skin between her neck and shoulder. I propped one hand at her side, the other on top of her belly.

"You make me so happy."

"Glad to hear that," she whispered.

Finally, I felt her relax in my arms, come off that frenzy she'd worked herself into. But I'd gotten used to this. It was just how Skye ticked. She'd spent her first month of pregnancy mapping out a work plan for the other eight and for the first six months after birth. I'd let her do her thing, because she was more relaxed once she had a plan. She and Tess had hired a few full-time sales associates, so they were planning to take a huge step back from day-to-day operations in the store.

"Je t'aime."

"I love you too."

"I like hugging you like this," I said.

"It's the only way you get to hug me these days without my belly getting in the way."

Laughing, I walked with her to the swing. I sat on it, and Skye rested in my lap.

"I can still keep the indoor swing, right?"

We'd brought it over from her old house. "Sure, babe. I've actually started to like it."

"And to think you fought me about bringing it in here."

"I didn't see the point. Now I do." It was relaxing and a great spot for us to huddle together.

"Ah, keep that in mind."

"What?"

"That I have good ideas too, even if you don't agree with them from the start."

"You don't plan to throw away anything, do you?"

"Weeeell, you did have a good point about maybe having a girl in the future, so why go through all the hassle of sending it back and then ordering it again? Think of all the packaging and shipping costs we're saving. And carbon emissions."

I burst out laughing, moving my hand in circles around her belly. We both stilled when there was a kick from deep within her. I felt it even through her jacket. It got to me every time. *Every single time.*

"See, the baby agrees with my hoarding tendencies."

"We'll see," I said vaguely. Skye leaned back

on me, dangling her feet in the air.

I liked to always move forward at breakneck speed, but these quiet moments with Skye were the best part of every day. Right now they were only semi-quiet, because her phone kept buzzing in her pocket.

"Why is your phone exploding with messages?" I asked.

"The dynamic in the WhatsApp group escalated a little after I told them we're having a boy. Ryker and Cole are competing over who will be the good uncle and who will be the reckless one. Right now, I'm deeming both reckless. On top of that, everyone's teasing Cole about being next in line to break out of the bachelor pack."

"That doesn't seem likely."

"I'm with you, but, eh... I was wrong about Ryker too, so I'm going to withhold my opinion for now. He's up to no good most of the time, but…."

Another kick from deep within followed. I held my breath. So did Skye.

"I think the baby likes the prospect of being up to no good," she whispered.

"I'm all for that."

"I think my brothers will have that covered. You can just be the perfect role model. No pressure." She kissed my cheek.

"I can do that." I was ready. I'd had excellent role models, and I was looking forward to walking in their footsteps. I was determined to give the baby and Skye the very best of me every day.

She half turned to me, smiling and looking even more irresistible to me than before. Tilting her head to one side, I kissed down her neck. I undid the zipper of her jacket a little, slipping my hand inside— enough to make my intentions clear but not to give the neighbors a show.

"What are you doing?"

"I don't have to be a role model yet, do I?"

She laughed as I took her hand. Drawing her to her feet, I led her back to the house. "I agree with that 100 percent."

***

The end
***

Other Books by Layla Hagen

The Bennett Family Series

Book 1: Your Irresistible Love
Book 2: Your Captivating Love
Book 3: Your Forever Love
Book 4: Your Inescapable Love
Book 5: Your Tempting Love
Book 6: Your Alluring Love
Book 7: Your Fierce Love
Book 8: Your One True Love
Book 9: Your Endless Love

The Connor Family Series

Book 1: Anything For You
Book 2: Wild With You
Book 3: Meant For You
Book 4: Only With You
Book 5: Fighting For You
Book 6: Always With You

The Lost Series

Book 1: Lost in Us
Book 2: Found in Us
Book 3: Caught in Us

Standalone

Withering Hope

Made in the USA
Middletown, DE
11 July 2020